THE
maiden's
MENU

recipes for the King's Blooming Roses

K&R
*m*INISTRIES

www.KingsBloomingRose.com

THE MAIDEN'S MENU: Recipes for the King's Blooming Roses
Compiled from Readers of "The King's Blooming Rose Magazine"

KBR MINISTRIES is a ministry designed to encourage young ladies to grow in accordance with Titus Two and Proverbs 31:10-31, in obedience to God and their parents. This cookbook contains recipes submitted by "The King's Blooming Rose Magazine" readers. For more information about KBR Magazine, see page 6, or contact us at:

20767 Z Road | Holton, Kansas 66436
Editor@KingsBloomingRose.com
www.KingsBloomingRose.com

PRINTED in the United States of America

ISBN | 978-1-4675-3916-6

COMPILED by Maggie Bullington

EDITED by Dana Bryant, Sarah Bryant, & Maurya Petrick

BOOK DESIGN | ©Sarah Lee Bryant Photo & Design

CALLIGRAPHY | Sarah Hulslander

PHOTOGRAPHY | Page 279

dedicated

to you as you daily seek to honor
the Lord Jesus Christ in your kitchen

thank you

to readers of "The King's Blooming Rose Magazine"—
thank you for sharing your favorite recipes with
other daughters in this cookbook

to Maggie, editor of the "Cook's Cuisine" column
in KBR Magazine—thank you for your diligence in
compiling recipes, tips, & interviews for this cookbook

About
The King's Blooming Rose
MAGAZINE

*W*ould you like to receive encouragement in your walk with Christ? Would you like to meet other young ladies serving our King? We invite you to join us on our journey to Biblical womanhood!

"The King's Blooming Rose Magazine" is published quarterly to encourage young ladies to grow in accordance with Titus 2 and Proverbs 31, preparing for godly womanhood. KBR's mission is to encourage you as a daughter in femininity, godliness, and homemaking. Readers of all ages contribute to each issue, which feature spiritually-challenging articles, Christian fellowship, delicious recipes, homemaking tips, photography, and much more. Subscribe today and be encouraged in your walk with the Lord!

K R
MINISTRIES

Visit our website for more encouraging resources:

WWW.KINGSBLOOMINGROSE.COM

Favor is deceitful,
and beauty
is vain: but
a woman that
feareth the

LORD,

she shall be
praised.

Proverbs 31:30

on the menu

welcome!

by sarah lee

Welcome to this compilation of recipes from Christian young ladies who love to provide meals for their family! *The Maiden's Menu* contains recipes printed in Volumes 1 through 8 of "The King's Blooming Rose Magazine," and also contains countless new menus from girls across the country. It is our prayer that as you bring nutritious meals and scrumptious treats to your family's table, they will be a joy to all and a wonderful preparatory learning experience for you.

Though food sustains our bodies, Jesus Christ, the Son of God, said that *"man shall not live by bread alone, but by every word that proceedeth out of the mouth of God"* (Matthew 4:4). Just as nourishment enables our active service for the Lord, so does His Word satisfy our soul; in John 6:35, Christ says, *"I am the bread of life: he that cometh to Me shall never hunger; and he that believeth on Me shall never thirst."* Jesus is the only recipe for everlasting fulfillment and life. Because we as humans have broken God's laws (Exodus 20), we each deserve eternal punishment (Romans 3:23). However, Jesus Christ laid down His life to take the justice due to us for our sins; He is the only Way, the Truth, and the Life (John 14:6). The ingredients to the recipe of eternal Life through Jesus are repentance of our sins (Acts 3:19), faith in Jesus Christ as our only way of salvation (John 5:24), and then walking in obedience to His will (Romans 12:1-2). In a sense, God wrote His own ultimate "cookbook" for us to live by—the Holy Scriptures. Thus, God's Word is the Bread of Life (John 6:48) and Honey from the Rock (Psalms 81:16) by which our souls are fed.

In these life-giving Scriptures, we find examples of godly women of character who ministered to others through food. The Proverbs 31 woman especially paints a beautiful picture of one who labors diligently with her hands to provide food for her household. Cooking is a vital skill that we learn, because throughout our lifetime we will need food. However, it can be more than just a necessity—as maidens at home, we can look at cooking as an opportunity to serve our families by planning the menus, making grocery lists within a budget, and developing healthier recipes for a productive lifestyle. This will be a rich blessing to our household.

We find in Titus 2 that the Lord desires young ladies to learn from older women whose wisdom is priceless (Proverbs 31:25). I encourage you to learn from your mother in the kitchen; sit under her teaching day by day and learn from her experience. Seek to record her favorite family recipes. We have included a section in the back of this cookbook for you to write some of these memory-filled heirlooms your mother can share with you.

A cookbook can be like a journal; as you try new recipes, write the date, any adjustments made, to whom you served it, any interesting or fun experiences, and how you liked the recipe. As you record your own cooking journey, your cookbooks will become a special heritage to pass down to your own daughters, when they begin the journey of being their family's cook.

May the Lord Jesus Christ, the true Bread of Life, fill your heart with His love as you joyfully serve the family He has blessed you with today—for truly *"He satisfieth the longing soul, and filleth the hungry soul with goodness"* (Psalm 107:9).

Feasting at the King's Table,

Sarah Lee Bryant

Editor of "The King's Blooming Rose Magazine"

introduction

by maggie

What a joy to be able to introduce to you a cookbook that includes a delightful selection of recipes for delicious meals from the home kitchens of "The King's Blooming Rose Magazine" readers! You will find over 360 recipes for favorite main dishes, delicious desserts, vegetable side dishes, salads and dressings, snacks and breakfast dishes, plus a whole section of healthy, white sugar-free and gluten-free desserts—even recipes for alternatives to store-bought items! In addition, you will find a handy selection of "sample menus" that may give you some quick ideas for preparing a meal for a special occasion. And last, but certainly not least, I hope you'll enjoy hearing from many young ladies in interviews about home- and kitchen- related subjects. The art of knowing how to prepare a healthy, well-balanced meal for your family is one that will be helpful to you throughout your life, especially if you run your own home someday.

Your efforts in the kitchen can be a huge blessing to your family. The atmosphere of the home kitchen will largely be the deciding factor about whether or not your family will want to spend time there. When they come to the kitchen, are they encouraged, or do they come to see a pile of dirty dishes and cluttered counters? Just as you enjoy being made welcome in this room, others do, too. Add "little extras" like a fresh bouquet of flowers on the tabletop for others to enjoy. When your family members enter for a snack or a meal, make them welcome and attend to their needs.

With gluten intolerances, diabetes and genetically engineered foods on the rise, it is much healthier to cook your own meals at home. With a little ingenuity, you can create your own recipes that are easy to prepare. To make your eating even healthier, you can buy food through co-ops, farmers markets, and you can also grow your own food; even if you have a small yard, you can grow lettuce for salads or start a cherry tomato plant. The more clean, pure foods we eat that have been grown the way our Maker intended, the healthier we will be as His people. It should be our desire to be well-equipped to serve Him with a healthy, able body, for we are bought with a price (I Corinthians 6:20). And you can help your family do this, with His help, as a daughter at home.

Creativity can be mixed in with your cooking—don't be shy about making subtle substitutions for different flavors and healthier ingredients. The amount of sugar called for can often be cut back, and you can make a recipe gluten-free by substituting gluten-free flours. Another way to make food "fun" is by learning to garnish and present your meal beautifully. Using antique platters or crystal serving bowls can be elegant, but this is only one method that you can use to dress a meal up and make it special for your family.

As daughters, we can use our time in the kitchen to encourage our family. When you are visiting over the breakfast dishes or making lunch, ask your brother or sister what the Lord has been teaching them. Share verses with them by posting them on a cabinet, the refrigerator, or in their favorite cookbook. Memorize verses together and make it a habit to recite verses while you are washing dishes or making a meal together.

May our Heavenly Father bless you as you seek to serve your family! *"And whatsoever ye do, do it heartily, as to the Lord, and not unto men; knowing that of the Lord ye shall receive the reward of the inheritance: for ye serve the Lord Christ"* (Colossians 3:23-24). Happy cooking!

Maggie Bullington

Editor of the "Cook's Cuisine" Column in "The King's Blooming Rose Magazine"

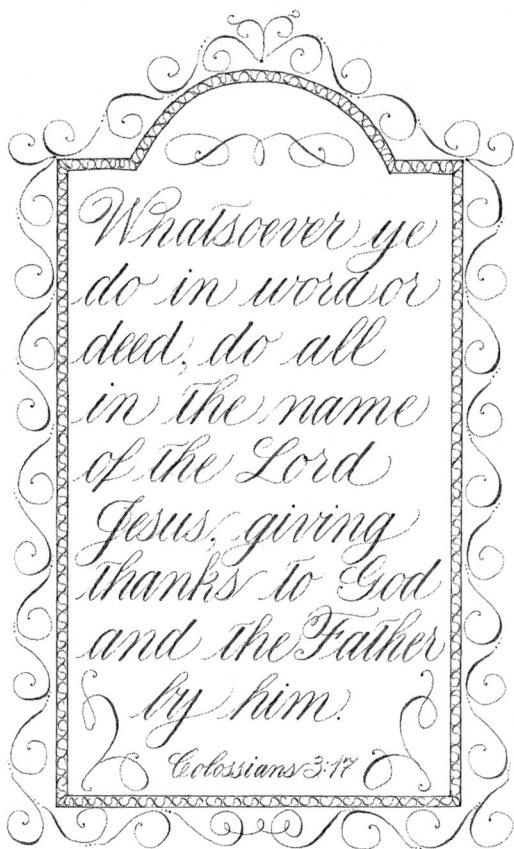

Whatsoever ye do in word or deed, do all in the name of the Lord Jesus, giving thanks to God and the Father by him.

Colossians 3:17

menu planning
for home & health

as you page through these recipes shared by young women across the country, let's consider ways to incorporate them into nutritious, inviting meals. What a blessing it is to have a new treasure of menu ideas in hand for sustaining the bodies God gave us to serve Him.

What to use

· A plan! Choose a helpful way of planning meals for your household. Does it help to plan a week's meals at once? Many families use this method. Or, you can simply write down a few recipes or food combinations to try during the week ahead. Know that planning ahead and allotting time to cook will be a great blessing in your schedule and your home.

· Take a look at what you already have on hand in your fridge, freezer, and pantry. If you buy in bulk, that stock will be a main factor of your meal plans. What's in your garden? Plan on incorporating it. Depending on how much you rely on your garden, its bounty can be overrun with food from the grocery store, and the garden won't be fully utilized. Use any leftovers you have in your menu planning.

· Use a cookbook, like this one, to give yourself ideas for tasty meals that others have designed, and their families have enjoyed. Making up recipes as you cook can be a good exercise; however, dishes will often turn out better if you follow a prewritten plan! Look for wholesome ingredients, and get to know your preferred sources for reliable recipes—books, friends, or websites. We want to be efficient in our search for recipes we use.

- Plan variety for the course of each week: a variety of meats and fish, a variety of whole grains and legumes, and a variety of vegetables and seeds. A diverse array of food choices helps prevent allergies and nutrient deficiencies, not to mention adding more interest to your cuisine. A wide color spectrum of fresh produce will ensure that you get the range of vitamins and phytonutrients.

- If you make great choices to start with, both in the healthfulness of food, and your family's appreciation of it, you can go back to the same standbys every week. For instance, have an egg casserole every Sunday morning, so you always know what to make. Or, choose a framework for meal themes, such as having soup on Monday night, stir-fry on Tuesday, steak on Wednesday, salad on Thursday, and so on.

What to have
throughout the day

- Always eat a hearty breakfast. This is the most excellent way to level blood sugar and weight gain. Eat protein and good fats for breakfast to carry you longer while you work or study. Plan your breakfast the night before, if not at the start of the week, so that you are ready in the morning.

- Lunch should be one of the larger meals of the day. Eat a variety of wholesome, real foods, informed by the seasons and your energy needs. To maintain even metabolism, small snacks can be eaten mid-morning and mid-afternoon. Plan ahead to have healthy, easy snack options available.

- Eat a lighter or smaller meal in the evening. The counterpart to eating a hearty breakfast, a lighter meal in the evening is more easily digested before bedtime and suits the way we burn calories.

What to eat at each meal

- You do not need every food group at every meal, but it is wise to have a protein-rich food at every meal. If it is meat, it will be a complete protein. If you are eating beans and rice for complete protein, it's fine to eat them at different meals within the same day. Proteins should not necessarily be eaten with carbohydrate-rich foods in order to get "all the food groups." Protein or carb foods are best when only one is the primary focus of a meal.

- Eat good fats at every meal and snack. Good fats consist of coconut oil, extra-virgin olive oil, avocados, nuts, and of course, real butter. Eat as much as you want! Cut back on refined carbohydrates and sugar, never on wholesome fats. Fats are necessary for every bodily function; they help in the assimilation of protein and of fat-soluble vitamins in vegetables. When eaten in accompaniment to sugar, fats prevent a drastic spike in blood sugar.

· Showcase flavorful beverages for refreshment at midday, or for a treat in the evening, not at mealtimes. Mealtimes should focus on food, not on liquid, for better digestion. Drink only a bit of water with meals if you need to. Many beverages are diuretic, so try to choose healthier, unrefined beverages or else make sure you are flushing your body with plenty of water surrounding the drinking of sweet or caffeinated beverages.

· To add great health benefits, eat probiotic and enzyme-rich foods at every meal. Probiotics are found in cultured foods and add good bacteria into the gut. Good bacteria is depleted by the consumption of processed foods. Examples are plain yogurt, homemade sauerkraut, water kefir, and more. Enzymes are found in living foods—fresh or cultured fruits and vegetables, and raw foods. Enzymes help your stomach to digest food so that your body doesn't draw from itself in order to digest. Eat raw vegetables or smoothies often.

· In summary, we need more vegetables in our diet, even cooked ones. Keep dessert to a minimum even though it can be a fun item to bake. Eat whole foods, as simple, fresh and local as possible. Many of the recipes herein are from ladies who cook "from scratch," which is wonderful.

Above all, make the time to enjoy your food and express thankfulness while you gather around the table to partake. Savor it, and promote happy memory-making during your family mealtimes. Use good ingredients and good recipes and enjoy them immensely, as God's gifts, with family and friends.

Renèe DeGroot is an author and enjoys studying health and nutrition. Writing from Montana, she desires to encourage others to live healthy, integrated, faithful lifestyles for God's glory.

menus *for special events*

special days call for special cooking. It can be so much fun to plan an extraordinary meal to celebrate an event or family milestone. With just a little extra effort, this can be a sweet and special way to let your family members and friends know how much you care for them. Here are some sample menus and suggestions that can aid you in your planning; feel free to insert extra dishes or replace dishes to suite your family's tastes.

Tea Party for Friends

Tea – your favorite flavor!

Cranberry Buttermilk Scones – Page 138

These are really simple to make and the cranberries are just the perfect ingredient to put in scones! Serve these with fresh, homemade lemon curd, raspberry jam or even cranberry sauce!

Herb Batter Bread – Page 131

To make it extra special, bake your bread in a round loaf shape and serve with fresh butter, cream cheese or brie cheese. Delicious and elegant!

Finger Jello – Page 231

Make this ahead and then serve the chilled squares in tiny glassware dishes.

Fresh Fruit

Grapes, strawberries, pears or freshly sliced peaches are delicious. Serve plain or with your favorite dip for fruits.

Mother's Day Breakfast in Bed

Bryant Breakfast Casserole – Page 41
> With eggs and meat included, this casserole is great to make for a "breakfast in a dish." Make it the night before and then bake it in the morning for easy preparation!

Melt-In-Your-Mouth Strawberry Muffins – Page 147
> A special breakfast needs a special muffin; this goes great with your "berry themed" smoothie.

Pineapple Berry Smoothie – Page 34
> A perfect fruit smoothie! Serve it cold in a tall glass with a straw and fresh berries on the side.

Mother's Day Tea

Hearty Potato Soup – Page 66
> Creamy potato soup is just right served in bowls of small cups. To make it special, crumble cooked bacon over each serving.

Fresh Lettuce and Spinach Salad with Basic Basil Dressing – Page 63
> This simple addition to a meal is healthy and raw, which provides many nutrients. Making the salad with a home-grown mix of greens makes it even better.

Aunt Phyllis' Cucumber Tea Sandwiches – Page 116
> Tiny tea sandwiches are so elegant...treat your mother!

Mile-High Raspberry Pie – Page 170
> This recipe is delicious—make more than one batch!

Father's Day Supper

Pepper Steak – Page 99
> This beef and pepper sauce over rice is sure to be enjoyed by your daddy.

Cut Veggies with Sun-Dried Tomato Dip – Page 226
> Use the vegetables that you have on hand to add a fresh and healthy side to your

Father's Day meal. Try cutting broccoli florets, cauliflower florets, carrot sticks, cucumber slices, thin slices of colorful peppers, and celery stalks to make a colorful veggie tray to serve with this amazing dip.

Fudgy Brownies – Page 153

Chocolate is just the thing to finish off a Father's Day supper!

Grandparent's Day

Rosemary Roasted Chicken with Potatoes – Page 106

Roasted chicken is delicious paired with herbs and potatoes.

Fantastic Green Beans – Page 80

A favorite recipe for green beans—very easy and goes with many dishes.

Italian Herb Muffins – Page 144

Serve with garlic butter.

Gluten-Free Angel Food Cake – Page 217

For dessert, serve this treat with fresh fruit or a strawberry sauce.

Parent's Anniversary

Marinated Steak – Page 97

This steak is perfect for any occasion. Make it in bite-sized pieces or whole steaks.

Crunchy Romaine Strawberry Salad – Page 54

This is sweet, crunchy, and fresh.

Three-Grain Pan Rolls – Page 134

Dinner rolls with the addition of flavorful herbs are so wonderful. You could also switch the herb seeds used to create your own unique flavor.

French Silk Chocolate Pie – Page 174

Treat your parents to a beautiful homemade pie. For a special touch, sprinkle the top with delicate shavings of semisweet chocolate.

host *a tea party!*

tea parties can be such an elegant, and yet simple, way to visit together and encourage others. Whether at home with your mother or sister, or with a group of young lady friends—this can be such a special time. There are so many ways to make your gathering unique, beautiful and elegant. Here are some tips for planning your own special tea party.

- The menu is an important part of your tea party! Plan ahead and carefully research what you'll serve; try make-ahead dishes that will free you up to do last-minute preparations in other areas. Making fancy sweets is fun, but do not limit yourself to this. Other menu suggestions are home-canned figs, grapes or orange sections, veggie dip with broccoli and carrots, tiny tea sandwiches using homemade bread (remove crusts) and filled with pimento cheese or chicken salad, crackers with spreads or cheeses, homemade pretzels, tiny bagels or English muffins served with jelly or lemon curd.

- You can choose to make a whole pot of a single variety of tea, or bring your teapot to the table with hot water and provide different kinds of tea bags for your guests to choose from. Provide sugar cubes, granulated sugar or honey, and milk or cream. Additionally, you can slice fresh lemon wedges to right into the tea. You could ask guests to bring their own special tea cup and share the story behind it. Also, consider having an alternative to tea for your guests; "Holiday Punch" is an easy beverage: 1 can of frozen juice concentrate and a bottle of ginger ale.

· A simple white or cream cloth can lend such an elegant feel to your tea table. Add individual place cards with a verse on each and a uniquely folded napkin for each place setting. To help create a cozy and welcoming atmosphere, play soft music in the background and arrange a beautiful centerpiece, using candles or a vase of fresh flowers.

· Part of the hostess' job is to see that everyone has a good time, but sometimes it may be difficult to keep the conversation going, especially if not all your guests know each other. For such times as these, provide yourself with a list of questions or conversation starters that you can use throughout the party, or play a simple game to help everyone get to know each other.

· Make simple foods look very elegant by making them bite-size or adding a pretty garnish of edible flowers, parsley, carrot swirls, or chocolate curls.

· It may be fun to provide each of your guests a "guest gift" to thank them for making the day special. Some simple ideas include a Scripture bookmark, a bar of sweet-smelling soap, a sachet, a package of either handmade or purchased note cards, a book of poetry or a cookbook, a tall taper candle tied with ribbon, flowers, or a box of tea.

· Do something meaningful during your tea, such as singing hymns or having a devotional. Hospitality is mentioned in the New Testament and we are commanded in Romans 12:13 to be *"distributing to the necessity of saints; given to hospitality."* Hospitality is a powerful tool; through such a simple thing as a tea party, we can be a light for Jesus.

– Maggie Bullington, Sara Fraser,
& Hannah Schoenfelder

Tea Party Printed in
Volume 8, Issue 2 of KBR

Special Serving
tips

· Dust cocoa powder or powdered sugar over a simply iced cake.

· Add a skewer full of fresh fruit to each family member's plate at breakfast.

· Serve slices of chicken or beef over a bed of lettuce.

· Brush melted butter over warm, homemade rolls and sprinkle them with favorite dried herbs.

· Use colorful garnishes like thinly sliced lemons, cherry tomatoes or purple cabbage.

· Make and serve iced tea to your family instead of sugary sodas. Add frozen strawberries or grapes to the glass for an unique look.

menus *for the road*

When traveling, especially on extended road trips, cooking your meals ahead can save money and time. Homemade cooking is also a healthier alternative to fast food. When our family takes long trips, I love to prepare meals to take along.

When planning menus to eat on the road, provide foods that are easy to heat at a gas stop, and do not make a large mess. Consider any special dietary needs of your family members; for example, be sure to include sufficient protein sources for high energy levels. Wrap each serving individually in plastic wrap, if possible. Here are some foods that we have enjoyed while traveling:

> ### yummy snack
> *"Take bread dough and press it into your muffin pan. Fill these pockets with a ground buffalo mixture, and bake. This makes a delicious snack on the road!"*
> —*Sara Boggs*

Breakfast Cereal – Page 37

Chunky Breakfast Granola – Page 36

Sunday Rolls for Sandwiches – Page 135

Pizza Crusts (pack precooked small crusts, pizza sauce and cheese; make pizzas and heat in a microwave) – Page 133

Oatmeal Crackers – Page 139

Pigs in a Blanket – Page 252

Homemade Fish Sticks

Homemade Muffin Corn Dog

Bean Burritos or Chicken & Rice Burritos

Pepperoni & Cheese Pockets

May the Lord bless your travels and the fruits of your labor!

—*Sarah Lee Bryant*

hospitality *a ministry*

Did you know that hospitality is a powerful witnessing tool—a vivid way to share the love of Jesus Christ and to minister to others? Opening our homes to share fellowship and food is one of the greatest mission fields a family can have; in fact, a Biblical guideline for a church elder is that he be a lover of hospitality, as I Timothy 13:2 reads, "*A bishop then must be blameless, the husband of one wife, vigilant, sober, of good behavior, given to hospitality.*"

Seeing that the Lord blesses and delights in hospitality, how can we, as daughters, assist our parents in presenting a comfortable atmosphere and delicious meal to visitors? First, we must learn our parents' vision in reaching others through hospitality. How, and to whom, do your parents desire to be hospitable? Seek to further and enable their vision in accordance with their expressed wishes. Once you know how to work with your parents in this area of hosting others, your support in preparing the menu can enable your parents to more easily serve others in the church or community. The following are several helpful tips to keep in mind when preparing for guests and showing them a reflection of Christ.

· It is not necessary to provide a gourmet meal for your guests— plan a menu that is within your abilities. Consider having a standard menu which you are efficient in preparing for company. If you are relaxed in your preparation of a meal, your joyful spirit will be a blessing to your family and guests.

· If fresh flowers or savory herbs are available, they are a simple and elegant way to spice up the table and kitchen, contained in a simple vase. Pumpkins, pine cones, and pine greenery are pretty decorations in the fall, while

wreaths, lights, and candles add a cheery feeling during the winter months.

· Tablecloths are an easy way to make plain tables more fancy—have different color tablecloths to go with the season: bright green, pink, yellow, and white are cheery for the spring season.

· Have a peaceful, homey atmosphere by playing calming music in the background.

· Serve any home-grown foods your family has produced, if possible; this makes the meal a special treat for those who live in an urban area.

· For a sit-down dinner, set the table beforehand and use small placecards at each setting so as to organize the seating arrangements.

· Be sure to make guests feel comfortable and welcome with an inviting atmosphere: clean and declutter main areas and have toys available for any children who may be coming. Remember your guests' interests and ask them thoughtful questions.

There are different seasons in each family's life when extending hospitality may not be a feasible option because of finances, busy schedules, or abilities. Be creative with the opportunities that arise to serve in your own family; a daughter can seek to find economical options for hospitality if finances are limited.

If your family is unable to invite others into your home, you could instead take a meal to the ill or elderly. Proverbs 31:20 says the virtuous woman *"stretcheth out her hand to the poor; yea, she reacheth forth her hands to the needy,"* and through this service of kindness, we as daughters can shed Christ's love and bring honor to our father's name, furthering his reputation. Seek to honor the Lord through embracing opportunities in which your family can extend the love of Christ—and in so doing, share the Gospel (Romans 1:16).

May we as daughters be a blessing to our parents in their efforts to share the Lord with others through food and hospitality.

—*Sarah Lee Bryant*

measurements

A pinch....................⅛ teaspoon or less
3 teaspoons ....1 tablespoon
4 tablespoons ....¼ cup
8 tablespoons ....½ cup
12 tablespoons ....¾ cup
16 tablespoons ....1 cup
2 cups ....1 pint
4 cups ....1 quart
8 quarts ....1 peck
4 pecks ....1 bushel
16 ounces ....1 pound
32 ounces ....1 quart
8 ounces liquid ....1 cup

Celsius to Fahrenheit
conversions

120°C.........................250°F
140°C ....275°F
150°C.........................300°F
160°C.........................325°F
180°C.........................350°F
190°C ....375°F
200°C.........................400°F
220°C.........................425°F
230°C.........................450°F

the maiden's
apron

this tutorial will show you how to craft an apron that is perfect for all your kitchen work—why not make yourself and your sisters matching aprons to wear while cooking together for your family? You can customize your apron, adding a ruffle, using embroidery, lace, buttons or appliqué; the options are endless!

—*Maggie Bullington*

1 You'll need to take measurements to ensure that your finished apron fits you perfectly. Stand straight and measure from shoulder to shoulder. This will be the width of the finished apron, so that it will fit comfortably across the top. Add 1 inch to this measurement for seam allowances. Next, measure from the shoulder seam of the blouse you are wearing down to the length you wish your finished apron to be. I like mine to extend below the counter that I am working on, so I decided to make my apron 27-inches long. Add ¾ inch to this measurement for seams.

1.

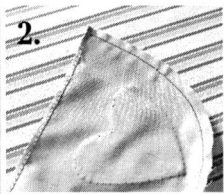

2.

3.

2 Cut your pieces out of pre-washed cotton fabric. The width of my apron is 18 inches + 1 inch for seams = 19 inches. The length for my apron is 27 inches + ¾ inch for seams = 27 ¾ inches. So, I cut two pieces 19 inches wide by 27 ¾ inches long. One piece is the back and one is the front. To complete cutting the front and back pieces, line them up at the top and cut a shallow half circle out of the top, leaving about 4 inches at each side (shoulders). (Photo 1) This is for the neck opening. Next, you will need four ties for the apron. I cut mine 18x2 inches. Finally, the pocket: you may cut whatever size you wish—I used a contrasting fabric for interest.

3 For pocket, press under ¼ inch along the top and then press under ¼ inch again to create a hem. Sew across top. Next, stitch a ¼ inch all the way around the unfinished sides of the pocket and then press under along the stitching. (Photo 2) Sew pocket to the front of apron.

4 Make each tie by pressing ¼ inch under to the wrong side of fabric on all sides of tie. (Photo 3) Fold tie in half lengthwise, matching pressed edges and stitch along pressed edge. (Photo 4)

5 On apron body pieces, press under ¼ inch, then another ¼ inch, on the curved neck opening. (Photo 5) Topstitch this in place. Matching right sides together, pin front and back together at shoulder seams. (Photo 6) Stitch with a ¼ inch seam and finish raw edge with zigzag stitch, if desired. Press under ¼ inch all the way around the outside of the apron and then press another ¼ inch under; topstitch.

6 Secure a tie to each of the four edges at your waist.

enjoy your new apron!

Nevertheless he left not
himself without witness,
in that he did good, and
gave us rain from heaven,
and fruitful seasons,
filling our hearts with
food and gladness.

Acts 14:17

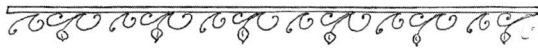

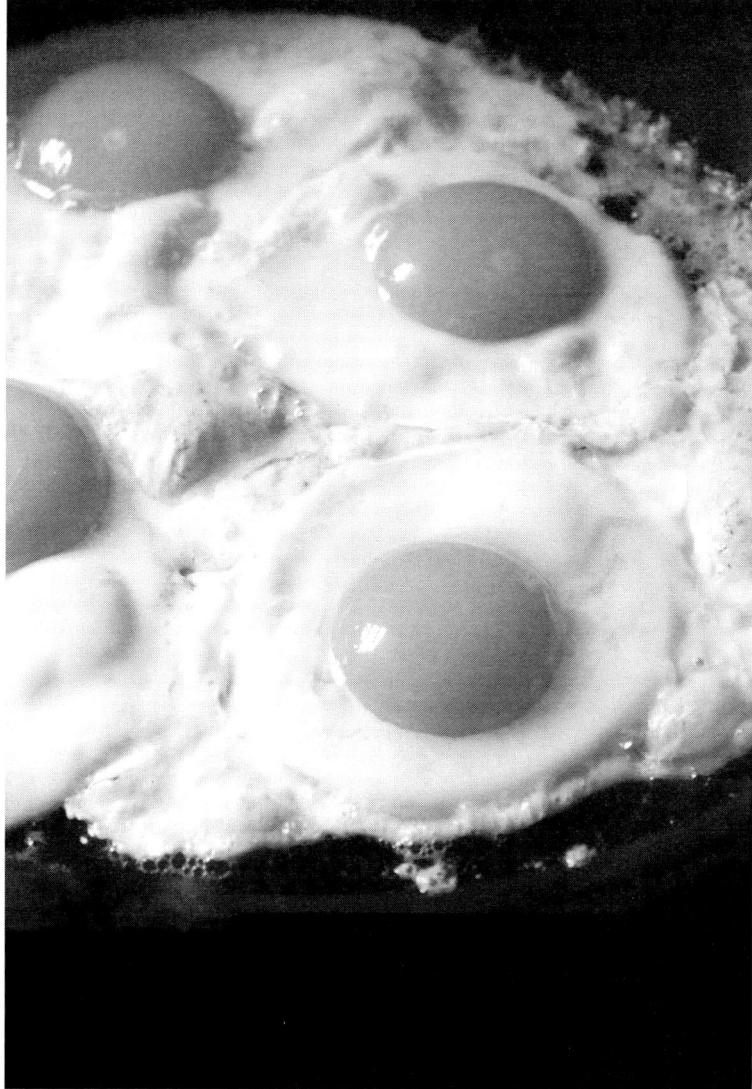

wholesome
breakfasts

in the
kitchen
with rachael

🌿 **How can daughters bless their families by creating wholesome menus?**

Food is a special way that we as maidens can bless our families. Everyone needs to eat, and by helping with cooking, we can demonstrate our appreciation for our family. I personally like to make special treats for my family and for neighbors. It is important that we learn to make healthy and nutritional meals, that we might be equipped to serve God to the fullest of our ability. Dividing cooking responsibilities between our sisters and mother can help lighten the cooking load for everyone, and bless each with the opportunity to develop proper cooking skills. For example, I usually cook our family's breakfasts, my sister makes our lunches, and my mother cooks dinner. In this way, my sister and I are also preparing ourselves for the responsibility one day we may undertake as wives and mothers.

🌿 **What is your favorite breakfast recipe?**

German Pancakes

8 eggs	1 teaspoon salt
1 ⅓ cups flour	¼ cup butter
1 ⅓ cups milk	1 teaspoon vanilla
2 tablespoons sucanat	

Mix well in blender. Pour into three greased and floured 9-inch cake pans. Bake for 20 minutes at 400°. Reduce heat to 350° and bake for 5-10 minutes. Cut into squares to serve with butter.

❧ How do you like to decorate for special occasions or birthdays?

I really like to have a pretty centerpiece on the table, and tablecloths are also wonderful to use. Using different colors for the appropriate season or event adds interest; for example, use orange, red, yellow, brown, and other darker colors for the autumn season. We also like to fold napkins for special events; this is a simple and wonderful skill to have. The flower/silverware holder is an easy way to fold a napkin—make a simple dinner elegant!

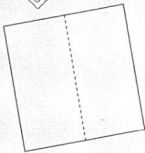

Open napkin. Fold in half on dotted line, bringing up the left side from bottom.

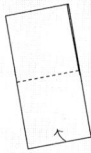

Fold in half on dotted line, bringing up to right side from bottom.

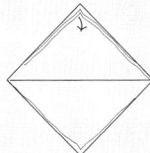

Turn down three points in succession, each higher than the last.

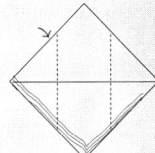

Fold side corners to back.

❧ Do you have any items saved in your hope chest for your future kitchen?

I love to store away kitchen utensils and books in my hope chest; it is exciting to think how I might one day be able to use it in my own home. Some of the things in my hope chest are handmade dishcloths, cloth napkins, a painted glass set, cook books, cake decorating tools, and many other things from family and friends.

❧ What verse does the Lord use to encourage you to serve food to your family cheerfully?

Philippians 4:13 always encourages me, *"I can do all things through Christ which strengtheneth me,"* as well as Ecclesiastes 9:10 *"Whatsoever thy hand findeth to do, do it with thy might."* We are the Lord's handmaidens in this world, given the mission of serving our families and others with His love, so let us do so to God's glory!

Rachael loves to serve her family delicious treats
and desires that the Lord would be glorified in
her life of service.

ℒ Smoothies & Shakes

Pineapple Berry Smoothie
Submitted by Sarah Bryant, KS

1 (10-ounce) can crushed pineapple
1 cup vanilla yogurt
1 ripe banana, quartered
1 cup pineapple juice
½ cup strawberries or raspberries
½ cup ice cubes

Combine pineapple, yogurt, juice, berries and ice cubes in a blender or food processor. Cover; blend until smooth. Garnish with strawberry and banana if desired.

Printed in Volume 1, Issue 3 of KBR

Cherry Vanilla Smoothie
Submitted by Megan Rippel, IL

1 cup apple juice
1 teaspoon vanilla
½ cup vanilla yogurt
1 ½ cups frozen cherries
1 tablespoon honey

Put all ingredients in blender and blend well. Enjoy!

Printed in Volume 2, Issue 2 of KBR

Green Tea Smoothie
Submitted by Mrs. Dana Bryant, KS

"For best results, make the smoothie in a food processor to avoid crushing the kiwi seeds, which may make it bitter."

1 cup green tea, chilled

2 cups honeydew melon
2 kiwi, peeled and diced
1 banana
1 tablespoon sugar (optional)
Dash of salt
6 ice cubes

In a food processor, combine ingredients and process until smooth. Serve immediately.

Printed in Volume 2, Issue 2 of KBR

Milkshake
Submitted by Emily Rebhan, WI

1 banana
1 cup milk
1 teaspoon vanilla
1 tablespoon peanut butter
1 egg

Blend all ingredients in blender and enjoy.

Printed in Volume 2, Issue 3 of KBR

Breakfast Dishes

Baked Oatmeal Breakfast
Submitted by Amanda Hahner, WA

2 eggs
½ cup sucanat or honey
½ cup oil
1 teaspoon vanilla
2 ½ cups oatmeal
½ cup coconut
2 tablespoons ground flax seeds
2 teaspoons baking powder
1 teaspoon salt
½ teaspoon cinnamon
Apples
Dried cranberries

Mix eggs, oil, vanilla, and sweetener together. Add remaining ingredients and stir until well mixed. Pour into greased 13x9-inch pan. Bake at 350° for 30 minutes. Serve with milk or your choice of canned or frozen fruit.

Chunky Breakfast Granola
Submitted by Rachael Bryant, KS

"We love this for special weekend breakfasts with farm fresh milk! You can also add chopped raisins, dates, and dried fruits to the finished granola."

6 cups rolled oats
½ cup sunflower seed
½ cup coconut
½ cup ground flax seed
⅔ cup honey
⅔ cup oil
1 teaspoon vanilla

Place rolled oats in ungreased 13x9-inch pan. Bake 10 minutes. Remove from oven and stir in sunflower seeds, coconut, and wheat germ. Add honey, oil and vanilla to mixture. Stir until thoroughly coated. Bake at 350° for 10-15 minutes. Stir every 3-5 minutes, until uniformly golden. Do not overbake. If you prefer, add about ½ cup peanut butter to the granola after baking, and stir evenly. Let cool in pan, then break into chunks. Makes 2 ½ quarts.

tip

journal cookbook
"Take notes in your cookbooks to record favorite recipes; write what you would change in it the next time you make it. These cookbooks will be a fun heritage to pass down to your future daughters!"

Raisin Bread Pudding
Submitted by Sarah Bryant, KS

"A great breakfast pudding."

2 slices bread, cut into cubes
1 cup milk
2 tablespoons sucanat
¼ cup butter
1 cup raisins (to taste)

Place bread cubes into 13x9-inch casserole dish. Heat milk, sugar and butter until butter melts. Pour over bread cubes and raisins. Sprinkle cinnamon over top. Bake at 325° for 25 minutes.

Peanut Butter Granola
Submitted by Laura Newcomer, ME

10 cups old-fashioned oats
1 cup wheat germ
1 cup ground flax seed
2 cups coconut
1 ½ cups brown sugar
1 teaspoon salt
½ cup oil
½ cup honey
½ cup peanut butter
2 teaspoons vanilla

Stir together dry ingredients in a large bowl. Mix peanut butter with heated oil and honey. Add vanilla. Mix well. Add to the dry ingredients. Spread on two large pans. Bake at 250° for 30-35 minutes. Stir occasionally.

Breakfast Cereal
Submitted by Mrs. Dana Bryant, KS

6 cups flour
3 cups plain yogurt or buttermilk
¾ cup coconut or 1 cup applesauce
1 cup honey (optional)
1 teaspoon salt
2 teaspoons baking soda
1 teaspoon vanilla extract
1 tablespoon ground cinnamon

Mix freshly ground flour and yogurt or buttermilk in large bowl. Cover and rubberband; leave on counter for 24 hours. Mix remaining ingredients into soaked batter. Pour into two 13x9-inch pans and bake at 350° for 30 minutes, until toothpick comes out clean. Do not overbake. Let cool and crumble the mixture into small pieces. Dehydrate at 200° for 12-18 hours. Turn cereal pieces every few hours to dry evenly. Store in airtight containers in fridge. Serve with milk or apple juice.

Blender Cornmeal Waffles
Submitted by Laura Newcomer, ME

1 egg
¾ cup milk
¼ cup oil
1 cup whole wheat flour
2 tablespoon cornmeal
2 teaspoon baking powder
2 teaspoon sugar
¼ teaspoon salt

Place ingredients in blender, starting with wet ingredients. Blend until smooth. Cook in a waffle iron.

Delicious Healthy Waffles
Submitted by Tiffany Schlichter, TX

4 large eggs
4 cups whole wheat flour
3 ½ cups milk
1 cup canola oil
2 tablespoons brown sugar, packed
8 teaspoons baking powder
½ teaspoon salt
Blueberries (optional)

Mix dry ingredients well. In a large bowl, beat eggs with whisk until smooth. Beat in remaining ingredients just until smooth. Add blueberries, if desired. Cook per waffle iron instructions. Makes approximately 12 large waffles.

Dad's Awesome Waffles
Submitted by Jenny Berlin, TN

"My dad enjoys making these waffles on Saturday mornings. They are certainly the best!"

1 cup flour
1 tablespoon baking powder
¼ teaspoon salt
1 tablespoon sugar
3 eggs
1 cup milk
4 tablespoons oil
1 teaspoon vanilla

Mix together dry ingredients. Next add the wet ingredients; mix well. Pour ¾ cup of batter into hot waffle baker and cook 3-5 minuets or until golden brown. Enjoy warm with butter, maple syrup, and powdered sugar!

Family Favorite Pancakes
Submitted by Christy & Abigail Mothershed, WV

"These pancakes are so simple and disappear quickly. You can serve them with jam, peanut butter, or just plain syrup and butter!"

4 cups unbleached all-purpose flour (can use part whole wheat flour)
2 tablespoons baking powder
2 teaspoons salt
4 eggs
4 cups milk
2 teaspoons vanilla
½ cup oil
½ cup sugar

tip

breakfast scramble
"In a skillet, melt butter and add cubed potatoes, sweet peppers and onions cut into strips. Cook until vegetables are tender and then add beaten eggs that have been mixed with a little milk or sour cream. Salt and pepper the mixture. Cook while stirring until done—a delicious breakfast!"

Mix dry ingredients together. Add wet ingredients and combine thoroughly. Pour about ⅓ cup of batter for each cake onto an oiled and preheated skillet on stove top. Cook on both sides until golden and fluffy. This recipe can be halved or doubled as needed with great success.

Wonderful Blueberry Pancakes
Submitted by the Bryant Family, KS

3 separated eggs
1 ½ cups wheat or spelt flour
1 teaspoon baking soda
¾ teaspoon salt
1 tablespoon sucanat
1 ⅔ cup buttermilk
2 tablespoons melted butter
1-2 cups blueberries

> **easy buttermilk** *tip*
> "Use a mixture of sweet milk and a teaspoon of apple cider vinegar or lemon juice to create 'buttermilk.' Let sit until it curdles slightly and use in recipe."

Separate eggs; beat egg yolks. Sift dry ingredients; add alternately with buttermilk to the beaten egg yolks. Add melted butter. Fold in beaten egg whites and blueberries. Bake in hot griddle until bubbles rise—about 3 minutes. Flip and cook another 2 minutes or until golden brown. Serve immediately with butter or fruit cream cheese (recipe following).

Strawberry Breakfast Cream Cheese
Submitted by Mrs. Dana Bryant, KS

"Delicious served over warm pancakes!"

1 ½ cups frozen strawberries
1 tablespoon honey, maple syrup or molasses
1 cup yogurt or cream cheese, homemade works well

Blend all together in food processor and serve over warm pancakes or toast.

Freda's Egg Casserole
Submitted by Esther Lang, WI

½ tablespoon butter
1 cup shredded cheese, divided
12 eggs
1 cup ham (optional)
Salt and pepper, to taste

Grease a 13x9-inch baking pan with the butter. Sprinkle ½ cup cheese evenly into pan. Break eggs unto cheese. Break yolks with a fork, but *do not* stir. Sprinkle on the ham, if desired, then the remaining ½ cup cheese. Sprinkle with a little salt and pepper. Bake at 325° for 30 minutes or until done.

Bryant Breakfast Casserole
Submitted by the Bryant Family, KS
"Our favorite recipe for weekend breakfasts or when guests are visiting."

1 pound sausage or hamburger, browned and drained
6 eggs
2 cups milk
2 cups bread cubes
1 cup grated Cheddar cheese
1 teaspoon salt
1 teaspoon dry mustard

Add salt and mustard to beaten egg-milk mixture. In a 13x9-inch casserole dish, layer bread cubes, sausage, and cheese. Pour egg mixture on top. Refrigerate 6-8 hours or overnight. Bake at 350° for 45 minutes and serve warm.

Camping
Bacon-Potato Breakfast
Submitted by the Schlichter Ladies, TX

"This recipe was first created by our grandmother during our mom's camping trips as a child. It's a treat on special occasions."

2 pounds bacon
1 onion, chopped
5 pounds potatoes

Cook potatoes, wrapped in foil, in embers of fire overnight. Next morning, cut up the cooked potatoes; set aside. Cook bacon until almost crispy; set aside. Sauté onion in bacon grease, then return bacon and potatoes to pan to warm it all together.

Ham & Cheese
Buttermilk Breakfast Muffins
Submitted by Laura Newcomer, ME

3 cups flour
1 tablespoon baking powder
½ teaspoon baking soda
Dash of pepper
¼ teaspoon salt
2 large eggs
1 ⅓ cup buttermilk
5 tablespoon oil
1 cup diced onion
1 cup diced ham
1 cup grated Cheddar cheese

Heat oven to 400°. Mix together dry ingredients. In a separate bowl, risk together the wet ingredients. Add the onions, ham, and cheese. Add the wet ingredients to the dry ingredients and mix well. Dish into prepared muffin tins (approximately 24). Bake for 20-25 minutes.

Early Morning Cinnamon Rolls
Submitted by Kimberly Vanderford, CO

"This is the topping recipe for pecan caramel rolls, for one loaf of breads' worth of dough. I use a 9x9-inch pan."

Icing: Put approximately 2 tablespoons of molasses in a clear two cup measuring cup, then fill cup a little past ¼ cup with honey, then fill it up to the ½ cup line with maple syrup. (You only use ½ cup total of sweetener; I have found that the above combination best competes with brown sugar.) Combine your sweetener with ¼ cup melted butter and 1 cup chopped pecans. Pour caramel pecan mixture in bottom of your 9x9-inch pan.

Rolls: Take your bread dough and roll it out in a rectangle, spread with a thin layer of butter, drizzle a small amount of honey over the butter, then sprinkle with generous amounts of cinnamon. Roll up and cut into rolls, place rolls on top of topping. I then put in the freezer to stop the rising; in the early morning I pull out to start rising in the oven then bake them at 350° for 45 minutes. Serve warm.

Pumpkin French Toast
Submitted by Megan Rippel, WI

5 eggs
1 cup pumpkin with pumpkin pie spice to taste
¼ cup milk
1 ½ tablespoons cornstarch
12 slices bread
Butter for skillet

Combine the first four ingredients in a blender until smooth. Pour into a shallow dish. Heat a skillet and melt a little butter to coat the surface of the skillet. Dip the bread slices into the pumpkin mixture and place them on the skillet. Cook until golden brown, then flip to cook other side. Serve with maple syrup or sautéed apples, which are sautéed in butter with sugar and cinnamon for a special fall treat!

Biscuits

Stir and Roll Biscuits
Submitted by Kathleen O'Connell, PA

2 cups flour
1 teaspoon salt
3 teaspoons baking powder
⅓ cup vegetable oil
⅔ cup milk

Mix flour, salt and baking powder. Add milk to oil; then add to dry ingredients. Mix well with fork. Knead slightly. Roll out and cut biscuits. Bake on a cookie sheet at 400° for 10-15 minutes.

Biscuits Supreme
Submitted by Christy & Abigail Mothershed, WV

"In our household of ten, we always double or triple this recipe. We usually replace 1-1½ cups of the all-purpose flour with freshly-milled whole wheat flour. We also replace the dairy milk with almond milk with wonderful results."

2 cups unbleached all-purpose flour
4 teaspoons baking powder
2-3 teaspoons sugar
½ teaspoon cream of tartar
½ teaspoon salt
½ cup shortening
⅔ cup of milk

Preheat oven to 450°. Stir together flour, baking powder, sugar, cream of tartar, and salt. Cut in shortening until mixture resembles coarse crumbs. Make a well in the center; add enough milk (stirring with a fork) to make your batter slightly sticky. Knead gently in the bowl or on a very lightly floured surface for about 10 to 12 strokes. Pat or roll out on a very lightly flour dusted surface with a lightly floured rolling pin to around ½-inch thickness. Don't over flour your surface or your biscuits will turn out dry. Cut out with cookie or biscuit cutter, being careful not to twist, and place on an ungreased cookie sheet. Gently place in preheated oven and cook for 10 to 12 minutes or until golden. Makes 10 to 12 delicious biscuits.

Delicious Breakfast Biscuits
Submitted by Rachael Bryant, KS

"My brothers love these at any meal, especially with eggs!"

2 ½ cups whole wheat flour
1 tablespoon baking powder
½ teaspoon salt
½ cup cold butter
¾ cup milk
¼ cup sucanat or natural sweetener of choice

Combine flour, baking powder, salt. Cut the butter into mixture until resembles course crumbles. Add milk and sucanat. Form dough into balls of desire shape, or roll out on floured surface and cut into 2-inch circles. Bake on ungreased cookie sheet at 375° for 10-15 minutes. Serve warm with honey and homemade butter!

Quick Buttermilk Biscuits
Submitted by Maggie Bullington, AL

"My favorite biscuit recipe!"

½ cup butter, slightly softened
2 cups self-rising flour
¾ cup buttermilk
Butter, melted

Cut ½ cup butter into flour with a pastry blender until mixture resembles coarse meal. Add buttermilk, stirring until dry ingredients are moistened. Turn dough out onto a lightly floured surface, and knead lightly about 3 or 4 times. Roll dough out to ¾-inch thickness, or desired thickness, and cut with a 2-inch biscuit cutter. Place on a lightly greased cookie sheet and bake at 425° for about 13-15 minutes or until delightfully golden-browned.

Having food and raiment

let us be
therewith
content.

I Timothy 6:8

salads & soups

in the
kitchen
with amanda

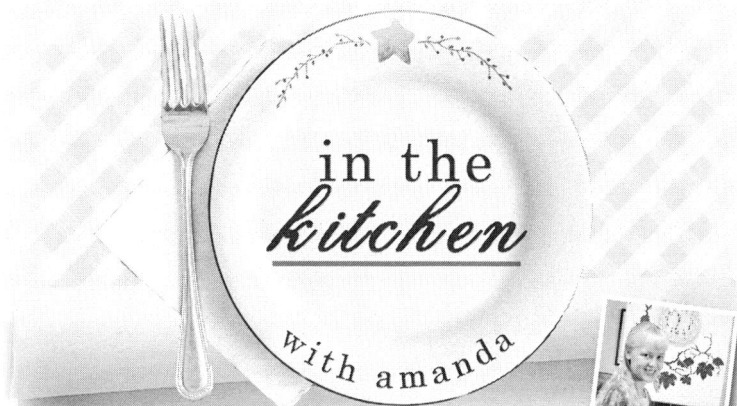

What is your most used kitchen "staple"?

Besides all of the various spices and herbs in our spice cupboard, one of my most used kitchen "staples" is frozen chickens that we butcher each year. I love to cook them—either by baking them in the oven, or boiling them and using the meat and the nutritious broth.

What are your favorite toppings for a simple salad?

Our family likes to add a combination of red or green onions, mushrooms, green peppers, cheese, dried cranberries, sunflower seeds, hard boiled eggs, or sliced almonds. We also enjoy homemade Italian Dressing (page 62) and Ranch dressing.

Ranch Dressing
⅔ cup buttermilk (or combination of milk and sour cream)
⅓ cup mayonnaise
1 ½ teaspoons salt
1 ½ teaspoons garlic powder
1 teaspoon onion powder
Pepper, to taste
Oregano, to taste

Mix together thoroughly in a quart jar, chill, and enjoy!

What colors are in your kitchen?

Currently, our kitchen is white, and we are in the process of stenciling grapevines and grape clusters on the wall. We also plan to stencil "I am the vine, you are the branches" above our sink. Some centerpieces we have made include placing a small candle in the middle of a mini wreath, arranging a vase of flowers, or even just a bright candle in the middle of the table makes it more inviting.

Do you have a special place to save up kitchen and home-related tools to use in your future home?

I love collecting kitchen and home-related items! It is exciting to plan for my future home in this way. I was blessed to receive a hope chest a couple of years ago, and since then, have filled it with many things, including a pie dish, a homemade tea cozy and washcloths from a friend, heart-shaped teaspoons, cookie cutters, a food processor, an apron, tea cups and a photo book that I am filling with favorite recipes from pen-pals.

What is your favorite main dish?

Apricot Chicken

½ cup apricot preserves	¼ teaspoon ground ginger
2 tablespoons soy sauce	1 pound chicken,
1 tablespoon chicken broth	cut into strips
1 tablespoon oil	1 green pepper, chopped
1 tablespoon cornstarch	½ cup cashews
2 cloves garlic, minced	Hot cooked rice

Sauté chicken in oil until no longer pink. Add green pepper. In a large bowl, combine the first seven ingredients. Add to chicken and heat to thicken. Add cashews and serve over rice.

What ways have you found to bless your family through the kitchen?

Besides trying to keep my family healthy by preparing wholesome meals, it is fun to surprise a family member with their favorite dessert or snack. Also, including a sibling during cooking time can grow wonderful relationships, which is a blessing!

Amanda loves living with her family of ten and enjoys healthy cooking and learning homemaking skills; her desire is to serve the Lord fully and love Him with all of her heart.

nutritious salads

To make a deliciously balanced salad, have a variety of greens. Iceberg lettuce adds a fresh, cool flavor to your salad, but is devoid of nutritional value. To make your salad as healthy as possible, add dark green lettuces. Home growing your greens with organic fertilizers and heirloom seeds is the best option—spinach, kale, and a variety of lettuces are easily grown.

You can add a lot to a simple salad just by adding a variety of delicious toppings—organic raisins, dried cranberries, sliced bell peppers, grated carrot, green peas, roasted sunflower seeds, mandarin orange slices, sliced fresh strawberries, diced fresh tomatoes, pomegranate seeds, olives and grated cheese.

washing veggies
"When washing delicate greens, rinse with cold water. This keeps them crisp and fresh, whereas warm water makes them wilt. After washing, either shake the leaves dry or pat dry on a kitchen towel."

~ Salads

Summer Corn Salad
Submitted by Rebecca Cahill, KS

⅓ green pepper, chopped
⅓ purple onion, chopped
Kernels of 5 ears of corn
1 large tomato
1 can chopped chili peppers, drained
1 can black beans, drained and rinsed
1 tablespoon chopped cilantro (optional)
Cayenne pepper, to taste
½ teaspoon salt
2 garlic cloves, crushed
8 ounces feta cheese

Dressing:
2 tablespoons apple cider vinegar or rice vinegar
2 tablespoons olive oil
2 tablespoons lemon juice
½ teaspoon chili powder

Mix dressing ingredients together and pour over salad. Toss well and serve.

Printed in Volume 1, Issue 3 of KBR

Easy Vegetable Salad
Submitted by Jonathan Bryant, KS
"This salad is simple, easy and fast for lunch."

Fresh cubed tomatoes
Fresh cubed cucumber
Fresh cubed zucchini

Stir together in a bowl with a little mayonnaise, salt and pepper.

Printed in Volume 1, Issue 4 of KBR

Taco Salad
Submitted by Emily Rebhan, WI

3 pounds ground beef
3 envelopes taco seasoning
3 heads lettuce, shredded
3 cups shredded Cheddar cheese
3 cups chopped tomatoes
2 cups chopped onion
3 (4 ¼-ounce) cans chopped or sliced olives, drained
2 (15-ounce) cans ranch or chili beans, drained
1 (16-ounce) package corn chips
1 (16-ounce) bottle Catalina salad dressing
1 (12-ounce) jar salsa

Brown beef; drain. Add taco seasoning. Cool. Toss with remaining ingredients in a large plastic bag or container.

Printed in Volume 2, Issue 3 of KBR

Garden Shell Salad
Submitted by Megan Rippel, WI

"This is a delicious pasta salad that's wonderful to bring to gatherings!"

8 ounces small pasta shells, uncooked
2 cups frozen peas
1 cup thinly sliced celery
½ cup chopped sweet red pepper
¼ cup chopped onion
⅔ cup mayonnaise
1 tablespoon vinegar
Salt, to taste
1 tablespoon minced fresh basil

Cook pasta according to package direction, adding the peas during the last 2-3 minutes of cooking time. Drain and rinse in cool water. In a large bowl, combine pasta, peas, celery, pepper and onion. In a small bowl, whisk the mayonnaise, vinegar and salt. Pour over pasta mixture and toss to coat. Cover and refrigerate for at least an hour before serving.

Printed in Volume 2, Issue 3 of KBR

Summer Cole Slaw
Submitted by Esther Lang, WI

14-16 ounces shredded cabbage
½ cup shredded carrots
½ cup raisins (optional)
¼ cup plain yogurt
2 tablespoons white sugar
2 tablespoons brown sugar
1 tablespoon lemon juice
¼ cup mayonnaise or salad dressing
1 tablespoon milk, more as needed

Combine first three ingredients. Combine dressing ingredients and mix well in another bowl; pour over salad and stir to coat salad well. Let sit at least an hour in refrigerator before serving for best flavor.

Printed in Volume 5, Issue 3 of KBR

Cabbage Slaw
Submitted by Grace Shewmaker

2 ½ ounces sliced almonds
16 ounces coleslaw mix
½ cup chopped green pepper
½ cup chopped red pepper
5 green onions, chopped
8 ounces water chestnuts (optional)
1 (3-ounce) package Ramen noodles

Dressing:
½ cup oil
¼ cup sugar
1 teaspoon salt
2 teaspoons vinegar
½ teaspoon pepper

Scatter almonds on baking sheet and toast at 350° for 8 minutes. Just before serving, combine almonds, vegetables, crushed noodles and dressing.

Printed in Volume 5, Issue 3 of KBR

Cucumber Salad
Submitted by Megan Rippel, WI

"We make this salad many times throughout the summer! It's a delicious way to use the cucumbers from our garden."

    2 medium-sized cucumbers, thinly sliced
    ⅓ cup white vinegar
    ⅓ cup water
    2 tablespoons sugar
    ½ teaspoon salt
    ⅛ teaspoon pepper

Place the cucumbers in a bowl. Whisk together remaining ingredients and pour over cucumbers. Cover and refrigerate at least 3 hours to blend flavors. Drain salad and store covered in refrigerator.

Received for Volume 5, Issue 3 of KBR

Crunchy Romaine Strawberry Salad
Submitted by Maggie Bullington, AL

"We served this at my brother's graduation party. It has crunchy, sweet, and well-balanced flavors. You can easily make it without the nuts if you wish."

    1 (3-ounce) package ramen noodles
    1 cup chopped walnuts
    ¼ cup butter
    ¼ cup oil
    ¼ cup organic sugar or 2 tablespoons honey
    2 tablespoons red wine vinegar
    ½ teaspoon soy sauce
    8 cups torn romaine lettuce
    ½ cup chopped green onions
    2 cups fresh strawberries, sliced

Break plain ramen noodles into small pieces. Sauté noodles and walnuts in the butter until golden; cool. For dressing combine oil, sugar or honey, vinegar and soy sauce in a jar with a tight fitting lid; shake well. Just before serving, combine lettuce, onions, strawberries, and noodle mixture. Drizzle with dressing and toss gently.

Received for Volume 5, Issue 3 of KBR

Orange Cream Fruit Salad
Submitted by Victoria Steiner, IL

"This is such an easy, simple recipe to make."

1 (20-ounce) can pineapple chunks, drained
1 quart peaches, drained
1 (11-ounce) can mandarin oranges, drained
2 firm bananas, sliced
1 apple, chopped
1 (3.4-ounce) box instant vanilla pudding
1 ½ cups milk
⅓ cup frozen juice concentrate
¾ cup sour cream

In a bowl, mix all the fruit. In another bowl, beat the pudding mix, milk and orange juice for 2 minutes. Add sour cream; mix well. Mix into fruit. Cover and refrigerate. Serves 8-10 people.

Printed in Volume 5, Issue 3 of KBR

tip

quick cool snack

"Wash fresh grapes, put them into a plastic freezer bag and freeze. Frozen grapes are a delicious summer snack!"

Roasted Beet Salad
Submitted by Sara Boggs, NC

"A lovely salad that is a perfect addition to those special events or summer dinners on the porch."

Preheat oven to 350°. Cut off the green tops and roast the beets whole for 45-60 minutes. Allow to cool, then peel by rubbing the surface with a paper towel. Slice into wedges and serve warm over salad greens. Top with nuts, dried cranberries and feta cheese tossed in a balsamic vinegar/honey/garlic dressing. This is also delicious with diced avocado or peaches added!

Printed in Volume 5, Issue 3 of KBR

Broccoli Salad
Submitted by Beth Cragun, IN

1 large bunch broccoli or ½ a bunch each of broccoli and cauliflower
8 ounces shredded Cheddar cheese
1 pound bacon
¼ onion, minced
Dressing:
1 cup mayonnaise
½ cup sugar
2 tablespoons white vinegar

Cut broccoli in small pieces. Fry bacon until crisp and crumble. Mince onions and mix with broccoli. Add dressing. Stir in cheese and bacon just before serving.

Printed in Volume 5, Issue 3 of KBR

Strawberry-Raspberry Salad
Submitted by Christine Neufeld, ON

1 head of salad lettuce, any kind
½-1 ½ quarts strawberries
Dressing:
1 cup raspberry vinaigrette dressing
¼ cup sugar
½ cup olive oil
¼ teaspoon Worcestershire sauce
1 tablespoon poppy seeds
1 tablespoon sesame seeds

Cut strawberries into medium-size pieces. Layer in the salad. Mix first two ingredients of dressings until dissolved, then add remaining ingredients. Toss dressing and lettuce together. Enjoy!

Printed in Volume 5, Issue 3 of KBR

Pomegranate Fruit Salad
Submitted by Elizabeth Adams, IA

1 pomegranate
1 orange
1 grapefruit
1 kiwi (other fruits are delicious as well)
Honey, if desired

In a large bowl, mix orange, grapefruit and kiwi slices. Add the pomegranate seeds to the bowl of fruit and mix well. Add honey.

Printed in Volume 5, Issue 3 of KBR

tip

preparing pomegranates

"Fresh pomegranates are rich in color—and so good for you! Perfect served on top of a summer salad, fruit salad, yogurt snack, or just plain. To prepare the pomegranate, slice off each end and submerge the fruit in a bowl of water. Peel the skin off with your hands, letting the seeds fall to the bottom of the bowl. Drain the water and throw away the pomegranate skin."

7-Layer Salad
Submitted by Susan Miller, OH

1 large head lettuce
1 pound bacon
1 ½ cups frozen peas
2 cups shredded cheese
8 hard-boiled eggs
2 cups salad dressing
2 tablespoons sugar
1 teaspoon salt

Layer first 5 ingredients in order given in 13x9-inch pan or glass plate. Combine dressing, sugar and salt; pour over salad. Sprinkle bacon and cheese on top.

Printed in Volume 5, Issue 3 of KBR

Purple Cabbage Salad
Submitted by Ashley Caldwell, CA

"The cabbage tends to become bitter with sitting overnight, so do not prepare this the day before serving."

Head of purple cabbage, thinly sliced
2 tablespoons orange juice concentrate
¼ teaspoon curry powder
¼ teaspoon dried mustard
½-¾ cup pineapple chunks
¼ cup pecan halves

Mix cabbage with orange juice concentrate. Toss all ingredients together lightly. Serves five.

Printed in Volume 5, Issue 3 of KBR

Summer Salad
Submitted by Mrs. Lori Rippe, TX

4 large firm ripe tomatoes, chunked
¼-½ cup crumbled feta cheese
2-3 tablespoons chopped fresh basil
1 teaspoon fresh oregano, or ¼ teaspoon dried
Dressing:
1 tablespoon olive oil
2 tablespoons lemon juice
1 teaspoon minced garlic
Salt and pepper, to taste

Mix together well, cover, and chill. Makes 8 cups.

Cranberry Salad
Submitted by Elisha Winslow, NH

1 pound ground, raw cranberries
2 cups sugar
1 large can crushed pineapple

2 cups miniature marshmallows
1 pint whipping cream

Soak cranberries, pineapple, marshmallows, and sugar overnight. In morning, whip the cream and combine all ingredients. Pour into mold and freeze. Take out of freezer just before serving. Serves 12.

Received for Volume 8, Issue 4 of KBR

Salad Dressings

Easy Ranch Dressing
Submitted by Naomi Holter, SK
2 cups sour cream or cultured buttermilk
Parsley, onion/garlic powder, and sea salt, to taste

Mix together. If your dressing is too thick, add cream or milk. If it's too thin, add more sour cream or buttermilk. Do the adding in moderation, or you will end up with a lot of dressing.

Printed in Volume 3, Issue 4 of KBR

Lovely Lemonarette
Submitted by Maggie Bullington, AL
"This dressing is great for the lemon lover—it's a bit tart!"

½ cup extra virgin olive oil
½ cup fresh lemon juice
1 teaspoon Dijon mustard
1 tablespoon raw honey
1 teaspoon salt

Dash of freshly cracked pepper
Pinch of garlic powder
(or one clove, crushed)
½ teaspoon herb of choice

Place all ingredients in a jar and shake vigorously. Place in a nice bottle and refrigerate.

Printed in Volume 3, Issue 4 of KBR

Cane Creek Dressing
Submitted by Catherine Taylor, TN
"This dressing tastes great on any summer salad and baked potatoes!"

½ cup apple cider vinegar
½ cup olive oil
½ cup water
½ teaspoon parsley

½ teaspoon basil
½ teaspoon thyme
½ teaspoon garlic
½ teaspoon Italian seasoning

Put vinegar, water and oil in salad dressing bottle. Mix each of the seasonings in; put the cap on and shake.

Printed in Volume 3, Issue 4 of KBR

Homemade Italian Dressing
Submitted by Angela Masloske, IL

1 teaspoon salt
1 teaspoon pepper
1 teaspoon mustard powder
1 teaspoon celery salt
3 tablespoons red wine vinegar
3 tablespoons olive oil

Put above ingredients in a jar and shake well, then add:

3 tablespoons red wine vinegar
12 tablespoons olive oil
2 crushed cloves garlic

Printed in Volume 3, Issue 4 of KBR

Vinaigrette Dressing
Submitted by Shaynie Migchelbrink, TN

⅓ cup vegetable oil
2 tablespoons, plus 1½ teaspoons red or cider vinegar
1½ teaspoons sugar

½ teaspoon Italian seasoning
½ teaspoon lemon juice
1 minced garlic clove
Salt and pepper, to taste

In a jar with a tightly-fitting lid, combine all ingredients and shake well. Chill or serve.

Printed in Volume 3, Issue 4 of KBR

Olive Oil & Garlic Dressing
Submitted by Cassie Whitaker, MO

1 cup olive oil
1 tablespoon apple cider vinegar
1 teaspoon Italian seasoning
3 garlic cloves

Put ingredients into blender and blend for 40 seconds. Store in refrigerator.

Printed in Volume 1, Issue 3 of KBR

Delicious Spicy French Dressing
Submitted by Maggie Bullington, AL

1 cup vegetable oil or olive oil
½ cup tomato ketchup
½ cup honey
⅓ cup apple cider vinegar
½ teaspoon paprika
¼ teaspoon garlic powder
¼ teaspoon celery salt
⅛ teaspoon onion powder or garlic powder

Combine ingredients in blender and blend until smooth—about a minute. Cover and chill thoroughly. Stir before serving over your favorite salad!

Caesar Salad Dressing
Submitted by Martha Joy Bullington, AL

"This is our absolute go-to recipe for salad dressing! We also use this recipe for mayonnaise; the difference in making a dressing and a mayonnaise is the blender speed you use. If you want a dressing, add the oil slowly while blending at a low speed; if mayonnaise is desired, use a very high speed while adding your oil."

1 teaspoon salt
3 farm-fresh eggs
1 ½ teaspoons sugar or honey
¾ teaspoon dry mustard
1 tablespoon lemon juice or apple cider vinegar
1 teaspoon shredded Parmesan cheese
1-2 cloves of garlic, crushed
2 tablespoons balsamic vinegar
6 drops hot sauce
6 drops Worcestershire sauce
1 cup olive oil

Blend ingredients (except oil). *Slowly* add oil while blending. Keep in refrigerator.

Italian Dressing
Submitted by Amanda Hahner, WA

¾ cup olive oil
⅓ cup vinegar
2 tablespoons finely chopped onion
1 teaspoon honey
1 teaspoon dry mustard
1 tablespoon fresh basil or 1 teaspoon dry basil
1 ½ teaspoons salt
2 teaspoons fresh oregano
    or ½ teaspoon dry oregano
1 teaspoon black pepper
2 cloves crushed garlic

Shake all ingredients in a tightly covered container. Shake well before using. Yields 1 ½ cups.

Basic Basil Dressing
Submitted by Maggie Bullington, AL

½ cup of olive oil
¼ cup apple cider vinegar
½ teaspoon garlic powder
1 teaspoon dried basil
Salt and pepper, to taste

Place all ingredients in a jar, mixing the dry ingredients in a small bowl first. Shake and serve.

French Dressing
Submitted by Megan Rippel, WI

½ cup ketchup
½ cup canola oil
¼ cup vinegar
2 tablespoons sugar
Few shakes of onion powder
¼ teaspoon Tabasco sauce, or more to taste

Add ingredients in a lidded container and shake until combined.

Printed in Volume 3, Issue 4 of KBR

Buttermilk Dressing
Submitted by Maggie Bullington, AL

1 cup mayonnaise, or Caesar Salad Dressing (page 62)
½ cup buttermilk
1 tablespoon dried parsley flakes
½ teaspoon onion powder or dried minced onion
¼ teaspoon garlic powder
¼ teaspoon freshly ground black pepper
⅛ teaspoon salt

Combine all ingredients in a pint jar and stir. Cover and chill. Serve with a green salad. Yields about 1 ½ cups of dressing.

✠ Soups & Stews

Parmesan Corn Chowder
Submitted by Julie Weaver, MI

2 cups water
2 cups diced and peeled potatoes
½ cup sliced carrots
½ cup sliced celery
¼ cup butter
¼ cup flour
1 teaspoon salt
½ teaspoon pepper
2 cups milk
1 (14-ounce) can cream-style corn or 1 cup frozen corn
1 ½ cups shredded Parmesan cheese

In large saucepan, combine first five ingredients. Bring to boil. Reduce heat; cover and simmer for 12-15 minutes or until vegetables are tender (do not drain). Meanwhile, melt butter in a small saucepan. Stir in flour, salt and pepper until smooth; gradually stir in milk. Bring to boil; cook and stir until thickened. Stir into vegetable mixture. Add corn and Parmesan cheese. Cook 10 minutes longer or until heated. Makes 7 servings.

Printed in Volume 5, Issue 2 of KBR

Homemade Chicken Vegetable Soup
Submitted by Beth Cragun, IN

"This is good with homemade bread!"

1 whole chicken
1 large onion
5-6 medium-sized potatoes
5-6 carrots
Chicken-flavored bouillon (optional)
1 can corn
1 can peas

Boil the chicken in a large pot until tender. While cooking, peel and dice the onion and potatoes; peel and slice the carrots. After chicken is done, remove from broth, pick the chicken from bones, and cut into desired sizes. Discard skin and bones. Strain chicken broth and cook vegetables in broth until tender. If richer flavor is desired, add the chicken-flavored bouillon. Add chicken in with vegetables and add the corn and peas. Salt and pepper to taste.

Printed in Volume 5, Issue 2 of KBR

Garden Chili
Submitted by Mary Roach, MN

½ pound dry kidney beans
¼ cup vegetable oil
2 chopped onions
1 pound steak, cut into ½-inch cubes
4 garlic cloves, minced
1-2 chili peppers, minced
3 tablespoons chili powder
2 teaspoons cumin
8 tomatoes, chopped
1-2 sweet peppers, diced
2 zucchinis, diced
¾ cup fresh corn kernels
1 ½ tablespoons fresh
    oregano, minced
¼ cup basil, minced

tip

transform your table

"For spring and summer, use small vases to create bouquets, or float single blossoms in a bowl of water. For fall and winter, try a large bowl of pine cones, cloves, cinnamon sticks and other spices. Use small branches, colorful leaves and tall candles."

Soak dry beans overnight. Before cooking chili, add enough water to cover beans and simmer 1½-2½ hours, until tender. In a large kettle, sauté onions in oil until soft. Add meat, garlic, chili powder and cumin. Sauté about four minutes. Add tomatoes, cover and simmer for one hour, stirring occasionally. Add remaining ingredients and simmer ½ hour longer. Enjoy!

Printed in Volume 5, Issue 2 of KBR

Hearty Potato Soup
Submitted by Sharilyn Halteman, PA

½-1 pound ground beef (optional)
1 cup thinly sliced carrots
1 tablespoon chopped green pepper
2 cups diced potatoes
2 cups tomato juice
2 cups milk
⅓ cup whole grain flour
1 ½ teaspoons salt
⅛ teaspoon pepper

In soup kettle, brown first five ingredients. Simmer, covered, until vegetables are tender—about 25 minutes. Combine last four ingredients together and add to soup, stirring constantly. Heat but do not boil. Serves six.

Printed in Volume 5, Issue 2 of KBR

Old-Fashioned Potato Soup
Submitted by Catherine Taylor, TN

8 potatoes, peeled and diced
1 onion, finely chopped
1 quart milk
1 tablespoon butter
Salt and pepper, to taste

tip

clean cooking pots

"Add enough water to cover the bottom of the scorched pan with a squirt of liquid dish soap. Bring this mixture to a boil; remove from heat and let cool before scrubbing clean."

Gently boil potatoes in water until done. Sauté onions with butter in a separate pan. Combine the onions and potatoes in large pot. Add milk, salt and pepper. Simmer for 30 minutes.

Received for Volume 5, Issue 2 of KBR

Taco Soup

Submitted by Victoria Steiner, IL

"This is a favorite with our family—especially nice for Sundays: make on Saturday, start the crock pot Sunday morning and, when you return from church, it is ready! We usually double this recipe for our family of eleven."

1 pound ground beef
1 (28-ounce) can crushed tomatoes
1 (15-ounce) can corn or 2 cups frozen corn
1 (15-ounce) can black beans, undrained
1 (15-ounce) can kidney beans, undrained
1 small onion or 2 teaspoons dry minced onion
2 teaspoons garlic powder
1 teaspoon salt
1 teaspoon onion powder
½ teaspoon red pepper
½ teaspoon cumin
¼ teaspoon pepper
1 teaspoon parsley

Toppings:

Tortilla or corn chips
Shredded Cheddar cheese
Sour cream

Combine all ingredients, except toppings in crock pot. Cover and cook on low for 4-6 hours. Serve with toppings.

Printed in Volume 5, Issue 2 of KBR

Authentic Mexican Tortilla Soup
Submitted by Christine Nuefeld, ON

2 chicken breasts, cubed
2 large onions, diced
6 jalapeño peppers, seeds and membrane removed
5 cups hot water
2 cups tomato juice
2 tablespoons each consomate and consome soup powder (found in Mexican stores)
6 cups corn
2 cups salsa

In a large frying pan, season chicken with seasoning salt. Fry chicken; add onions and peppers. In a large pot, heat water. Once the chicken is fried, add to the hot water. Add remaining ingredients and cook for 20 minutes. Serve with crushed tortilla chips, shredded cheese and a dollop of sour cream.

Received for Volume 5, Issue 2 of KBR

Santa Fe Stew
Submitted by Maggie Bullington, AL

"This recipe is perfect for feeding a crowd and is great for potlucks! Feel free to soak and cook your own beans, also."

2 (16-ounce) cans pinto beans
2 (16-ounce) cans navy beans
2 (16-ounce) cans black beans
2 (16-ounce) cans kidney beans
3 pounds cooked chicken or turkey
2-3 (6-ounce) packages frozen corn
1 (28-ounce) can diced tomatoes
1 cup onion, diced
4-5 stalks of celery, diced
½ teaspoon garlic powder
2 tablespoons chili powder
Chicken broth
Salt and pepper, to taste

Drain and rinse all beans; combine with remaining ingredients except broth in a 6-½-quart slow cooker. Add enough broth to cover ingredients. Cover and cook on low setting for 8 to 10 hours, or on high setting for 4 hours. Serves 10 to 12.

Printed in Volume 5, Issue 2 of KBR

Cream of Chicken Soup
Submitted by Vietta Wideman, ON

"My little brother calls this 'tummy-ache soup' because he is sure the mild soup makes his tummy feel better when he is sick."

¼ cup butter
5 tablespoons flour
3 teaspoons chicken soup base
3 cups boiling water

1 cup chicken broth
½ cup chicken chunks
1 cup rich milk
Pinch of salt

Melt butter in saucepan over low heat. Blend in flour. Gradually add the boiling water with soup base added. Stir until smooth. Add broth and bring to boil until thickened slightly. Stir in milk and salt.

Received for Volume 5, Issue 2 of KBR

Split Pea & Potato Soup
Submitted by Maggie Bullington, AL

½ cup chopped onion
1 cup split peas
2 large unpeeled potatoes, scrubbed and diced
5 cups water
½ cup Parmesan cheese (optional)
¾ teaspoon salt

In large saucepan, cook onions 3 minutes over medium heat. Add split peas, water, salt and potatoes. Bring to a boil; reduce heat; simmer 45 minutes. Puree soup and add cheese, if desired.

Creamy Potato Soup
Submitted by Emily Bow, NY

3 cans cream of potato soup
3 cans milk (measured in emptied soup cans)
2 cans mixed vegetables, undrained
1 can corn, undrained
2 tablespoons flour
½ cup mayonnaise
Dill, paprika, minced onion, to taste
Crumbled bacon or diced ham
Grated Colby-Jack cheese

Combine all ingredients except cheese in large pot. We add leftover vegetables occasionally. Bring to slow boil then cover and turn on low until thickened. Just before serving, add cheese. Serves 6-8.

Received for Volume 5, Issue 2 of KBR

Esther's Chili Soup
Submitted by Esther Lang, WI

1 pound ground beef, browned and drained
28 ounces diced tomatoes
6 ounces tomato paste
1 (30-ounce) can pinto beans, undrained
1 (15-ounce) can kidney beans, undrained
1 (15-ounce) can black beans, drained
1 (15-ounce) can corn, undrained
2-3 cups water
½ teaspoon salt
⅛ teaspoon pepper
1 tablespoon dry onion
½ teaspoon garlic
2 teaspoons chili powder
1 teaspoon cumin
½ teaspoon oregano
1 ½ tablespoons sugar

Heat on stove. Add ¼ teaspoon of baking soda to soup while it is bubbling to counteract the acid of the tomatoes, if desired.

Chicken Vegetable Soup
Submitted by Esther Lang, WI

2 cups cooked chicken, cut up
2 (32-ounce) cans chicken broth or homemade broth
2 pounds frozen mixed vegetables
1 ½ cups barley
1 teaspoon parsley
⅜ teaspoon sage
½ teaspoon thyme
¼ teaspoon curry powder
1-2 teaspoons salt
¼ teaspoon pepper
1 teaspoon dry onion
1 teaspoon celery salt

Mix all ingredients in a 7-quart crock pot. Add about 8 cups water to fill crock pot up to about 2 inches from the top. Cook on high about 6 hours, adding more water as needed if it gets too thick.

Italian Meatball Soup
Submitted by Brittany Schlichter, TX
"A tasty and healthy dinner!"

2 pounds ground beef, uncooked
½ cup bread crumbs
⅓ cup minced onion
2 teaspoons oregano
2 tablespoons parsley
¼ teaspoon salt
⅛ teaspoon pepper
4 quarts chicken broth
2 pounds spinach
2 pounds Piccolini mini farfalle noodles, cooked

Combine first seven ingredients. Shape into small meatballs. Brown in the oven on a foil-lined cookies sheet at 425° for about 10-20 minutes or until cooked through. Add meatballs to heated broth with spinach. Simmer until spinach is cooked. Add cooked noodles just before serving. Enjoy!

Bryant's Favorite Cheeseburger Soup
Submitted by the Bryant Family, KS

"In the winter, we like to make a huge pot of this soup and serve it for several meals. Vary it to suit your family's taste."

½ pound ground beef, browned
¾ cup shredded carrots
¾ chopped onion
¾ cup diced celery
1 teaspoon basil
1 teaspoon parsley
4 cups diced, potatoes
4 tablespoons butter, divided

3 cups chicken or beef broth
¼ cup wheat flour
¾ teaspoon salt
1 ½ cups farm fresh milk
¼ teaspoon black pepper
8 ounces cubed cheese
¼ cup sour cream

Sauté carrots, onion, celery, basil and parsley in 1 tablespoon butter until tender. Add broth, potatoes and cooked beef. Boil and reduce heat, cover and simmer 10-20 minutes until potatoes are tender.

In small saucepan, melt butter, add flour, cook and stir 3-5 minutes until bubbly, add to soup, boil 2 minutes. Reduce heat; add cheese, milk, salt and pepper. Heat through until cheese melts. Remove from heat and stir in sour cream before serving.

Chicken Soup with Herbs
Submitted by Tiffany Schlichter, TX

15 cups chicken broth
6 cups cooked chicken or turkey, shredded
6 carrots, diced
Celery
3 tablespoons dried parsley
1 ½ teaspoons cayenne pepper
1 ½ teaspoons dried thyme
1 ½ teaspoons black pepper
1 ½ teaspoons dried oregano
Garlic powder, to taste

Place all ingredients into a large pot. Bring soup to a boil. Cover and simmer for 20 minutes. Serve over rice.

Potato Soup
Submitted by Amanda Hahner, WA

6 cups potatoes, diced
1 cup celery, diced
1 cup carrots, diced
1 cup onions, chopped
3 cups chicken broth
2 cups sour cream

4 tablespoons flour
2 cups milk
2 teaspoons salt
½ teaspoon pepper
2 teaspoons parsley or fresh chives
1 cup grated Cheddar cheese

Combine vegetables with chicken broth in kettle. Cover and cook until just tender (not mushy)—about 20 minutes. Mix flour and milk with whisk, heat until it thickens, add sour cream, salt, pepper, and cheese. Whisk until smooth. Stir this into vegetable and broth mix, adding parsley. Stir until mixed. Heat on low until soup is hot. Do not boil. Serves 10.

Kale-Lentil Stew
Submitted by Rachel Abernathy, MO

4-6 cups chopped kale
1 medium-sized onion, finely chopped
3 garlic cloves, finely chopped
28 ounces tomato paste
1 ½ cups frozen green peppers, chopped
1 cup split red lentils, rinsed
5 cups water
½ teaspoon cumin powder
Dash of sea salt
⅓ cup sunflower or other vegetable oil
2 cups water

Heat oil in a thick-bodied pan until hot. Add onion, garlic, lentils, and salt. Stir over heat for five minutes. Add the cumin and stir over heat until mixture starts to brown. Add five cups water and boil until the lentils are done, stirring often. Add the tomato paste, kale, peppers, and 2 cups water. Boil for 5-10 minutes, stirring to prevent sticking. Serve with or on top of bread.

Winter Fish Stew
Submitted by Sarah Bryant, KS

"This recipe makes a quick and easy crockpot meal; it is hearty and delicious with homemade cornbread. The cheese variation is our favorite!"

3 (16-ounce) packages of your favorite kind of frozen fish fillets
8 medium-sized potatoes, chopped into ½-inch cubes
3 carrots, sliced
4 cups chicken broth
Water
2 tablespoons dried parsley
1 bay leaf
1 teaspoon salt, or to taste
1 teaspoon basil
1 (32-ounce) can diced tomatoes
1 cup frozen peas
1 cup frozen corn

In large pot, cook frozen fish, potatoes and carrots until almost done in chicken broth and sufficient water. Add the remaining ingredients and cook until done—about 10-15 minutes. Yields 8 servings.

Cheese Variation: Instead of adding tomatoes, add more water; add 2 cups shredded mozzarella cheese and 1 (16-ounce) package cream cheese at the end.

tip

freezing tomatoes

"When the tomato season is in full swing, preserve your crop! Wash and cut the cores out of each tomato and then freeze in plastic bags. To use in soups or chilies, run warm water over each frozen tomato. This will help peel the skin right off—chop and add to your soup."

NOTES & RECIPES

She is like the
merchants' ships;

she bringeth her
food from afar.

Proverbs 31:14

side *dishes*

in the
kitchen
with maurya

How can a daughter bless her family in the family kitchen?

Whether you are a chipper chef or an once-a-month meal maker, every mother enjoys a clean kitchen. The best way I can bless my family in the kitchen, besides preparing meals, is to keep it clean. Washing dishes, scrubbing the stove, or scouring the oven are the best ways to keep the "feel-clean" attitude in the family.

What is your favorite dinner menu to prepare?

When my parents brought our three new adopted siblings home from Colombia, South America, they brought home many ethnic traditions and foods, which have quickly become the "family favorite." The rather tall order includes Sancocho, Aji Picante, Empanadas, Rice, and Avocados.

How do you plan your meals in advance?

Our family's meals are planned two-weeks in advance. Typically, my mom and I will sit at the table and discuss what meals we would like to see on the menu. "Passer-by's" will usually shout out their favorite meals (hint for "I want this on the next menu"). Also, being the courier, I run through the house checking the pantry, refrigerator, and freezers taking note of anything extra we have to use in our upcoming menu. This assists our budget as well, making sure that we do not buy anything we really do not need.

Do you have any shopping tips?

My mom and I go grocery shopping together, and usually have two shopping carts; we separate fruits, vegetables, and breads from the meats and canned goods. Our grocery list is separated by categories according to the store's aisles. This way we can start shopping at one end of the store and finish at the other without having to run back and forth.

How can one add a special touch to an ordinary meal?

Simplicity is good; it can be inexpensive and efficient. But let's be honest, sometimes simplicity can be bland. If you feel bored or exhausted with a certain recipe, try experimenting with spices and extracts. Sometimes, a simple meal just needs a little more zing to it that a particular spice can add. On the same note, know your spices. If an entree seems too sweet, don't add Tarragon or Marjoram. Likewise, if a dish is too salty, do not add Bouillon or Cajon. Furthermore, try sautéing the spices in butter along with onion and/or garlic. This will enhance the spice's flavor incredibly!

How can a family practice hospitality?

I'll never forget when our family experienced true hospitality with some of our best friends. At first, our family was very anxious about having supper with a family we had just met. However, from the moment we walked into their house, we could sense the presence of the Holy Spirit. On the drive home, we discussed what had just occurred within our hearts and minds. "I felt... precious," someone whispered in the car. "Almost like I'd never felt godly love before." Unanimously, we agreed to strive for others to feel the exact same way with our family. That's true hospitality!

I love to do simple little things that honor our guests. Playing soft classical music during the meal, or placing a small bouquet of flowers by their bedside are great little extras that leave a bigger impression on their minds than we could ever imagine. These small things show our guests that we are truly striving to go the extra mile in making them feel welcome.

Maurya resides with her family, for whom she enjoys cooking elegant dinners. She is striving to bring glory to God in all things every day.

Fantastic Green Beans
Submitted by Rebecca Cahill, KS

"We are of the opinion that these green beans taste like candy! They are even better the second day."

> 4 cups green beans
> 1 tablespoon olive oil
> 2 garlic cloves, minced
> 3 tablespoons Bragg's Liquid Aminos or soy sauce

Mix ingredients in a saucepan and sauté until green beans are tender. Serves 6.

Editor's Note: *"We have tried these delicious beans on several occasions and they are our favorite way to prepare green beans!"*

Printed in Volume 3, Issue 2 of KBR

Three-Cheese Squash Casserole
Submitted by Maggie Bullington, AL

"This is the recipe we made up when we had an abundance of squash last summer. It's really delicious and uses a lot of fresh veggies! You can also use this as a main dish. Sprinkle a pound of browned ground beef over the top of the tomatoes, if you like."

> Yellow squash
> ½ onion, chopped
> 8 ounces softened cream cheese
> 2 eggs
> Salt and pepper, to taste
> 1 tomato, sliced
> Colby or Cheddar cheese, shredded
> Parmesan cheese, shredded

Slice yellow squash to fill bottom of a 15x10-inch pan. Sprinkle with onion. Combine in a bowl cream cheese and eggs. Spread over squash and add salt and pepper. Cover with sliced fresh tomatoes. Sprinkle cheese. Bake at 350° for 30 minutes. Remove from oven and sprinkle with Parmesan cheese.

Printed in Volume 6, Issue 3 of KBR

Maple Nut Crunch
Submitted by Sara Boggs, NC

"This is a very simple (though slightly labor-intensive if you don't have a food processor) snack or side dish. It's very colorful, sweet, and cool in the summer."

4-5 large apples
1-2 carrots
1 small fresh yam
¼ cup maple syrup (fresh, if available)
¾ cup almonds, slivered or chopped

Grate apples, carrots, and yam and place in bowl. Mix together with the remaining ingredients.

Printed in Volume 3, Issue 2 of KBR

Delicious Sweet Carrots
Submitted by Sarah Bryant, KS

"This is a favorite family recipe and is traditionally on our Thanksgiving menu."

12 large carrots, cut into ⅛-inch slices
3 tablespoons butter
2 tablespoons maple syrup or honey
1 tablespoon fresh or dried basil
¼ teaspoon salt

Steam carrots for 10 minutes, or until tender. In a large saucepan, melt butter. Add cooked carrots, maple syrup or honey, basil and salt. Stir well, thoroughly coating carrots with butter sauce. Serves 6.

Printed in Volume 2, Issue 1 of KBR

Stuffing
Submitted by Johanna Kautt, TX

1 cup chopped celery
½ cup chopped onion
6 tablespoons oil
7 cups cubed or crumbed bread (one medium or large loaf)
1 ½ cups chicken or turkey broth
½ cup walnuts
Salt and pepper, to taste

Sauté the celery and onion in oil until soft. Toss with bread in a bowl. Add warmed broth, walnuts and seasonings. Mix until well blended. Stuff bird or bake in a covered casserole at 350° for 20 minutes.

Printed in Volume 7, Issue 1 of KBR

Tomato Tart
Submitted by Maggie Bullington, AL

"This is delicious. Can even be used as a main dish in the summertime tomato season."

1 (9-inch) pie crust
6 fresh medium-sized tomatoes, cut into wedges
¼ cup fresh basil, chopped
1 clove of garlic, minced
¾ cup Parmesan cheese, shredded
1 cup mozzarella cheese, shredded
½ cup mayonnaise
½ cup onion
½ cup mushrooms
1 tablespoon butter
1 tablespoon parsley, chopped
Pepper, to taste

Preheat oven to 350°. Bake pie crust about 15 minutes, Sauté onion and mushrooms in one tablespoon of butter until onions are translucent. Set aside. Mix together cheese, mayonnaise, garlic and basil. Stir in cooled onion and mushrooms. Place tomatoes into pie crust, with the skin down. Spoon cheese mixture evenly over tomatoes. Sprinkle parsley and pepper on top. Bake for about 30 minutes, or until brown and bubbly.

Cauliflower Mashed Potatoes
Submitted by Sarah Bryant, KS

"We try to minimize the carbs in our daily diet, replacing that with more nutritious vegetables. One week, we had an abundance of cauliflower available, and as I prepared lunch, I had the idea to make 'cauliflower mashed potatoes.' We all loved it and now make it frequently in substitution for a starch side dish. We use all cauliflower for this recipe by substituting a second head of cauliflower for the potatoes."

1 head of cauliflower, divided in small portions
6-8 medium-sized potatoes, peeled and sliced in quarters
¼ cup butter
½ cup of milk or chicken broth
1 cup cheese
Salt and pepper, to taste

Boil the cauliflower and potatoes until tender, then mash or blend them until desired consistency. Add remaining ingredients and mix well. Serve warm. Serves about 8.

Raw Cranberry Sauce
Submitted by Courtney Minica, TX

"This is the healthiest (not to mention yummiest) cranberry sauce you'll ever find. If you like a chunky, sweet/tart cranberry taste, this is for you!"

12 ounces cranberries
4 apples, peeled and chopped
8 ounces raisins, soaked

In a food processor, blend the cranberries with two apples. Remove from processor and fold in the remaining two apples and raisins. Serve cold. If you want a smoother cranberry sauce, blend everything at once. I like to replace the raisins with agave nectar to taste.

Received for Volume 8, Issue 4 of KBR

Mashed Potatoes with Garlic
Submitted by Kaitlyn Ford, MO

3 pounds potatoes, peeled and quartered
3 cloves garlic, peeled and quartered
1 teaspoon salt
2 tablespoons olive oil

Cook potatoes until tender, then mash and add other ingredients. Blend well and enjoy!

Printed in Volume 7, Issue 1 of KBR

Cajun Fries
Submitted by Rebecca Ann Morgan, LA

1 ½ cups milk
2 cups flour
2 teaspoons black pepper
½ tablespoons cayenne pepper

3 tablespoons Tony Chachere's seasoning mix
3 teaspoons seasoned salt

Pour milk in bowl. Add flour and seasonings in a separate bowl and stir. Cut up potatoes. Place your cut potatoes in milk then coat in flour mixture. Fry in cooking oil and enjoy.

Onion Rings
Submitted by Maggie Bullington, AL

"My family really enjoys these!"

Large onion
2 egg yolks
½ cup milk

¾ cup flour
½ teaspoon salt

Cut onion crosswise into ¼-inch slices. Separate all the slices into rings. Beat the egg yolks and add milk. In a separate bowl, sift the flour and salt together. Add flour mixture to egg mixture and stir together until blended. Coat the onion rings in this batter and fry in a pan of palm oil heated to 395°. Enjoy soon after fried—delicious!

Baked Rice Pilaf
Submitted by Amanda Hahner, WA

1 ¾ cups water	3 tablespoons parsley
1 cup shredded carrots	2 tablespoons onion
1 cup chopped celery	2 tablespoons butter
¾ cup rice, uncooked	1 tablespoon dried herbs

Mix together. Bake at 375° for 45-60 minutes, or until rice is tender.

Green Bean Casserole
Submitted by Esther Lang, WI

3 tablespoons butter	⅜ teaspoon pepper
3 tablespoons flour	1 teaspoon dried onion
1 teaspoon salt	1 ½ cups yogurt
1 ½ teaspoons sugar	4 cans green beans

Melt butter. Stir in flour and seasonings. Add a little yogurt at a time and stir carefully—not too much stirring or the yogurt will get runny. Pour over drained beans. Bake in an uncovered 3-quart casserole dish at 350° for 30 minutes. This may also be topped before baking with shredded cheese, cornflake crumbs (½ cup cornflakes, crushed and mixed with 1 tablespoon butter), or French fried onions.

Roasted Herb Potatoes
Submitted by Tiffany Schlichter, TX

"This makes an excellent side dish; my brothers also like us to make it for them to take on their camping trips!"

20 potatoes, chopped	1 ¼ teaspoons dried thyme
5 onions, chopped	1 ¼ teaspoons salt
10 tablespoons olive oil	1 teaspoon pepper
10 teaspoons Italian seasoning blend	

Heat oven to 450°. Grease bottom and sides of large roasting pan with shortening. Mix all ingredients and spread in pan. Bake, uncovered, until cooked, turning occasionally.

Vegetable Stir-Fry
Submitted by Nathan Bryant, KS

½ cup fresh tomatoes, cubed
½ cup cucumber, cubed
½ cup zucchini, cubed
¼ cup onion, cubed
½ cup mushrooms, sliced

Mix all vegetables; in a frying pan lightly cook in soy sauce.

Editor's Note: *"Stir-fry makes a wonderful meal when served with rice. Cook brown or basmati rice using chicken or beef broth for extra flavor."*

Printed in Volume 1, Issue 4 of KBR

Aunt Ede's Cornbread Casserole
Submitted by Sarah Bryant, KS

"This was my great-aunt's recipe and is a traditional Thanksgiving favorite!"

1 cup cornmeal
½ teaspoon salt
1 ½ teaspoons baking powder
2 cups fresh or frozen corn
3 eggs
1 cup sour cream
½ cup cooking oil

Mix all ingredients and pour into 2-quart casserole. Double recipe for 13x9-inch casserole. Bake at 375° for 25 minutes or until brown on top.

tip

perfect pasta

"Add a couple tablespoons of oil or butter to your water before adding pasta. This will help the pasta keep from sticking together. Also, add your salt to the boiling water to make sure your noodles will be seasoned evenly. Boil on high heat so that the noodles do not use their flavor."

Kale Pasta Dish

Submitted by Rachel Abernathy, MO

"This is a recipe of my Dad's invention, and it is a great way to use kale. This can be an entire meal—and, if your family enjoys onion, add more than four!"

8-12 ounces uncooked pasta (not noodles)
4 medium-sized onions
⅛ cup olive oil
1 tablespoon basil
½ teaspoon salt
1 bunch of fresh, chopped kale

Cook pasta according to package directions and drain. In a large skillet, sauté onions in olive oil, salt and basil until tender. Add kale on top of onions and cook, covered, for 5 minutes on medium heat. Stir in pasta and serve. Salt to taste. Serves 2-4.

Mom's Garden Pasta Salad

Submitted by Jenny Berlin, TN

"My mom loves to serve this light side dish with hamburgers. It is always delicious!"

1 package uncooked tri-color spiral noodles
½ cup thinly sliced carrots
2 stalks celery, chopped
½ cup chopped green bell pepper
½ cup cucumbers, peeled and thinly sliced
2 large tomatoes, diced
¼ cup onion, chopped
1 bottle Italian dressing
½ cup grated Parmesan cheese (optional)

Cook pasta according to directions until al dente. Rinse under cool water and drain. Mix chopped carrots, celery, cucumbers, green peppers, tomatoes, and onion together in a large bowl. Add the noodles and dressing, mix well. Top with Parmesan and chill several hours or overnight before serving.

Spicy Squash Pasta
Submitted by Maggie Bullington, AL

"When we get butternut squash from the garden or from local vegetable stands during the fall harvest time, this is the perfect dish to make! Since butternut squash keep for so long, it's a great dish for anytime of the year."

1 butternut squash
1 pound of your favorite dry pasta (spaghetti works fine)
Olive oil
2 cloves garlic, finely minced
¼ teaspoon red pepper flakes (optional)
Fresh herbs of choice—thyme, sage and rosemary
1-2 cups fresh ricotta cheese
Salt and pepper, to taste

Roast the butternut squash as follows: Slice in half lengthwise and remove all the seeds by scraping with a spoon. Place both halves cut-side up on a cookie sheet, salt and pepper to taste and roast at 400°. After 10 minutes, turn the cut-side down and bake until fork-tender.

Cook pasta according the package, making sure to salt your cooking water. While pasta cooks, heat a couple tablespoons of olive oil and add garlic, salt and pepper flakes, if desired. Cook slightly, not allowing garlic to burn. Add about ½ teaspoon each of fresh, chopped thyme, sage and rosemary. While cooking, scoop out the flesh of the cooked butternut squash and add to the herb and garlic mixture. Chop squash slightly with a wooden spoon to incorporate squash and herbs.

In another skillet, add a couple more tablespoons of olive oil. When pasta tests done, drain and add to warm oil. Sprinkle more chopped herbs and a bit of salt into the pasta. Toss to coat.

On your serving platter, dollop desired amount of ricotta cheese in the center and top with squash mixture, covering the cheese completely. Over this, add your pasta. Enjoy!

Printed in Volume 7, Issue 4 of KBR

NOTES & RECIPES

Be thou diligent to know the state of thy flocks, and look well to thy herds... Thou shalt have goats' milk enough for thy food, for the food of thy household, and for the maintenance for thy maidens.

Proverbs 27:23, 27

main *dishes*

in the
kitchen
with samantha

♪ If you were coming home late from an outing, what would you make for a quick supper?

Here is a recipe we enjoy:

Taco Salad

2 pounds ground beef
1 onion
2 (15-ounce) cans tomato sauce
1 ½ teaspoons chili powder
½ teaspoon garlic powder
¼ teaspoon ground cumin
¼ teaspoon oregano
Salt, to taste
2 ½ cups shredded Cheddar cheese
3 hearts of romaine lettuce, torn into small pieces
2-4 tomatoes, chopped small
1 (2 ¼-ounce) can sliced ripe olives, drained
Large bag of tortilla chips
Salsa
Sour cream

Brown beef with onion in a large frying pan. Add tomato sauce and seasonings to browned ground beef mixture. Bring to a boil; lower heat and simmer for 15 minutes to blend flavors, stirring occasionally. Meanwhile, assemble remaining ingredients in separate serving dishes. To serve, spread sauce over chips and top with lettuce, tomatoes, cheese, olives, salsa, and sour cream. We let each family member fix their own plate. Serves 6-8.

🌿 Does your family grow a garden?

Yes, our family does have a garden. My top three favorite garden veggies would be sweet potatoes, tomatoes, and cucumbers. I love almost all fresh produce, especially when it comes from your own land and the fruit of your labors!

🌿 Do you have any entertainment tips that your family has found useful when showing hospitality to others?

One big thing that makes a difference when you are showing hospitality is preparing ahead of time. Plan ahead what meals you will have, what ingredients you need, and how you will have things set up when your guests arrive. If possible, prepare some of the food ahead of time. If you do not have time to plan ahead, just be flexible in order to truly bless your guests. I have to constantly remind myself of this! I have learned that it makes a big difference when you arrive at someone else's home and they drop everything to greet you and make you feel welcome. If your hosts are running all around doing last minute things when you arrive, you don't feel as welcome, but more as if you are in their way. It is wonderful to seek to serve others our best food on our best dishes, but it is more important that we spend time with our guests—even if we end up serving them leftovers on paper plates! We should strive to be more like Mary and less like Martha. I would much rather have a simple and relaxed meal with friends, than have a fancy meal on fine china that I felt rushed to prepare.

That being said, I think it is a blessing when we can prepare beautiful and tasty dishes for our guests. Presentation makes a difference. Practice artfully arranging cut veggies and other things on platters. I try to make it a goal to cook healthy, tasty, and visually appealing food. Each one of those things is important. Do that for your family, too—not just your guests. Show your family how much you love them by the food you prepare for them!

The more often we have people into our home, the easier we find it to show true hospitality. Here are a few things we do before having families into our home:

· Prepare food ahead of time, if possible.

· Make sure our main bathroom is clean.

· Give our home a quick vacuum to freshen things up.

· Possibly make a dessert or sweet treat of some type (cookies or brownies make our home smell really good).

· If we are having younger children over, we make sure there is not anything hazardous in their reach that they can get into. Mom used to have us crawl around on our hands and knees looking for things that were at a childs' eye level!

What colors are in your kitchen?

Maroon is the main color we have used in our kitchen, with a splash of green, brown, and cream. Our family hasn't done a lot of centerpieces, but we do use a vase of flowers (fresh or silk) occasionally. I think centerpieces are beautiful, as long as they are not too tall, so they block you and your guests from seeing each other.

Do you have a favorite kitchen tool or gadget you reach for again and again?

My favorite kitchen tool would be our Pampered Chef Measure-All® Cup. You can measure liquids in one side, and thick, sticky things like honey and peanut butter in the other side. I use it all the time!

In what ways do you bless your family through cooking?

A few years ago, my two sisters and I split up each day's meals—one of us makes breakfast, one makes lunch, and I make dinner. Each of us are in charge of planning that meal for the week, making a shopping list, and preparing that meal every day. That system has been a blessing to our family (especially to Mom). It has also given each of us great real-life practice!

Everyone has to eat—why not treat your family to a nice meal once in a while? It will bless your Dad, Mom, brothers, and sisters!

Samantha enjoys living with her family and delights in preparing healthy, tasty, appealing food; her utmost goal is that Christ would be honored and glorified through her life.

Beef Main Dishes

Three-Cheese Penne Bake
Submitted by Sarah Bryant, KS

1 pound penne pasta, cooked
½ pound beef
1 (26-ounce) can tomato sauce
1 (15-ounce) package ricotta cheese
1 cup mozzarella cheese, shredded
¼ cup Parmesan cheese

Preheat oven to 350°. Cook beef until brown. Add pasta sauce. In bowl, combine ricotta, mozzarella and Parmesan cheese. In pan, layer penne, beef/sauce, and cheese mixture. Repeat layers. Sprinkle additional mozzarella cheese on top and bake at 350° until cheese is melted and it is heated through. Serves 6.

Printed in Volume 1, Issue 2 of KBR

Company Casserole
Submitted by Samantha & Rebekah Parker, VA

"This recipe can be prepared ahead of time and refrigerated or frozen. It is a favorite with all ages and goes a long way. Enjoy!"

2 pounds ground beef
⅓ cup chopped onions
1-2 jars of spaghetti or tomato sauce
8 ounce package fine spaghetti noodles
15 ounces cottage cheese
8 ounces cream cheese
8 ounces sour cream

Brown the ground beef with the onions. Drain grease. Stir in the spaghetti sauce. Cook the noodles according to the package directions. Combine the cottage cheese, cream cheese and sour cream in a bowl. In a 2 ½-quart baking pan prepared with non-stick spray, layer—ground beef mixture, noodles and cheese mixture—two times. Bake at 350° for 1 hour or until heated through. Serves 6.

Printed in Volume 7, Issue 1 of KBR

Honey-Baked Lentils
Submitted by Maggie Bullington, AL

"This is one of my favorite potluck dishes; it can easily be doubled for a crowd!"

1 pound (2 ⅓ cups) lentils
1 small bay leaf
5 cups water
2 teaspoons salt
1 teaspoon dry mustard
¼ teaspoon powdered ginger
1 tablespoon soy sauce
½ cup chopped onion
1 cup water
½ pound browned ground beef, or sausage or 4 slices of bacon
⅓ cup honey

Combine first four ingredients in a Dutch oven or saucepan. Bring to a boil. Cover tightly and reduce heat. Simmer 30 minutes. Do not drain. Discard bay leaf. Preheat oven to 350°. Combine separately and add the next five ingredients. Stir in most of the meat into lentils and transfer to an ovenproof dish. Sprinkle the remainder of the meat over the top. Pour honey on top; cover tightly. Bake one hour in preheated oven. Uncover last 10 minutes while cooking. Serves 8.

Printed in Volume 7, Issue 1 of KBR

Pizza Burgers
Submitted by Esther Lang, WI

"A quick and easy meal."

8 hamburger buns or English muffins
1 pound ground beef, browned and drained
1 (15-ounce) can black beans, drained
16 ounces pizza sauce
Shredded mozzarella cheese

Open buns and arrange on one or two cookie sheets. Mix meat, sauce and beans together; place on top of buns. Spread out meat mixture to cover buns; sprinkle top of each with about 1 tablespoon of cheese. Bake at 400° until heated through and the cheese is melted.

Enchiladas

Submitted by Samantha Parker, VA

"A family favorite and great easy dinner!"

1 bottle or can enchilada sauce
16 ounces tomato sauce (optional)
3-4 packages tortilla shells
3 pounds ground beef
½ onion, chopped
1 pound Mexican cheese
2 (15-ounce) cans of refried beans, or pinto beans, heated and mashed
Sour cream for topping

Coat your pan(s) with non-stick spray. We use a 15½x10½-inch glass pan and a 9x9-inch glass square pan. Mix the enchilada sauce and tomato sauce together. Spread about ½ cup of mixture on the bottom of your pans. Cook beef in frying pan with onions. Add beans and a little bit of cheese. Put about ¼ cup of this mixture in each tortilla shell, roll up and place in your glass pans. Pour the rest of sauce on top and sprinkle with cheese. Bake at 350° for 25-30 minutes. Serve with sour cream. Enjoy! Serves 8.

Marinated Steak

Submitted by Maggie Bullington, AL

"Absolutely delicious...this is what Mommy uses a lot for making steaks. The marinade is very versatile and can be used for T-bone steaks out on the grill or for cooking sirloin steaks in a skillet indoors. Try it today—it's very easy!"

3-4 pounds of steak
¼ cup ketchup
¼ cup Bragg's Liquid Aminos or soy sauce
1 teaspoon ground oregano
2 cloves garlic, minced
2 tablespoons olive oil
½ teaspoon pepper

Trim meat of excess fat and cut into desired serving pieces. Mix marinade ingredients and marinate meat for an hour or overnight. Cook meat to desired doneness.

Popover Pizza
Submitted by Maggie Bullington, AL

"One of my favorites."

1 pound ground beef
1 large onion, chopped
1 (1 ½-ounce) package spaghetti sauce mix
1 (15-ounce) can tomato sauce
½ cup water
2 cups shredded mozzarella cheese
2 eggs
1 cup milk
1 tablespoon vegetable or olive oil
1 cup all-purpose flour
¼ teaspoon salt
½ cup grated Parmesan cheese

Cook ground beef and onion in a large skillet until meat is browned, stirring to crumble meat; drain. Add sauce mix, tomato sauce and water, stirring well; simmer 10 minutes.

Spoon meat mixture into a lightly greased 13x9-inch pan; sprinkle with mozzarella cheese. Beat eggs, milk and oil until foamy. Add flour and salt and beat until smooth. Pour batter over meat mixture, spreading evenly. Sprinkle the Parmesan cheese right over the top of this. Bake at 400° for 30 minutes or until the top is puffed and golden brown. Cut into squares and serve hot. Yields 6 servings.

Deep in the Woods Beef & Sausage Dip
Submitted by Maggie Bullington, AL

¾ pound ground beef
¾ pound mild pork sausage
½ large yellow onion, chopped
1 cup ketchup
4 teaspoons chili powder
1 tablespoon sweet paprika
2 (15-ounce) cans kidney beans, undrained

2 cups shredded Cheddar cheese
1 cup sliced black olives
½ cup chopped green onion

Preheat oven to 350°. Brown beef, sausage and onion in a medium skillet. Drain excess fat. Add ketchup, chili powder, paprika and beans. Mix well. Place mixture in a 13x9-inch baking dish. Bake 15 minutes. Sprinkle cheese, olives and green onions on top. Bake an additional 5 to 10 minutes, until cheese melts. Serve with your favorite chips. Makes about 10 cups.

Pepper Steak
Submitted by Maggie Bullington, AL

"This recipe was sent to my mother by a friend of hers and we have enjoyed it ever since. Serve over rice for a delicious meal."

¼ cup butter
½ cup chopped onion
2 green peppers, cut into strips
2 pounds beef, cut into strips
⅛ teaspoon garlic powder
1 teaspoon salt
2 cups tomatoes, chopped
1 beef bouillon cube
1 tablespoon cornstarch
¼ cup water
3 tablespoons soy sauce
1 teaspoon sugar

instant burn relief

"Keep an Aloe Vera plant by your kitchen window in case of burns. Cut the tip off one of the leaves and apply the gel on the burn for relief."

Melt butter in skillet. Add onion and peppers. Sauté 5 minutes. Set aside. Add beef. Sprinkle with garlic powder and sauté, stirring slightly until browned. Add tomatoes and bouillon cube and simmer about 10 minutes. Blend cornstarch, water, soy sauce, sugar and salt. Stir into meat mixture and cook until thickened. Add onion and green pepper mixture and combine. Serve with rice. Serves 6.

New Country Pie

Submitted by Laura Newcomer, ME

Crust:

    1 pound ground beef
    ¼ cup chopped onions
    ¼ cup chopped green peppers
    1 teaspoon salt
    ½ cup tomato sauce
    ½ cup bread crumbs
    ¼ teaspoon oregano

Filling:

    1 ⅓ cups minute rice
    1 cup water
    1 ½ cups tomato sauce
    1 cup grated cheese, divided
    ½ teaspoon salt

Combine crust ingredients and mix well. Pat mixture into bottom of 9-inch or 10-inch pie pan and pinch 1-inch fluting around the edge. Set aside.

Combine all of the filling ingredients except for ¾ cup cheese. Spoon into meat shell. Cover with foil. Bake at 350° for 25 minutes, uncover and sprinkle with remaining cheese. Return to oven and bake 10-15 minutes more. Serves 5-6.

Beef Stroganoff Casserole

Submitted by Jenny Berlin, TN

"This is one of my favorites to make for my family on busy weekday nights!"

    1 pound lean ground beef
    ¼ teaspoon salt
    1 teaspoon black pepper
    1 teaspoon vegetable oil
    8 ounces can sliced mushrooms
    1 large onion, chopped
    3 cloves garlic, chopped

¼ cup dry white cooking wine
1 can cream of mushroom soup
½ cup sour cream
1 tablespoon Dijon mustard
4 cups cooked eggs noodles
Chopped fresh parsley (optional)

Preheat oven to 350°. Spray 13x9-inch baking dish with nonstick cooking spray. Place beef in large skillet; season with salt and pepper. Brown beef over medium-high heat until no longer pink, stirring to separate beef. Drain fat from skillet; set beef aside.

Heat oil in same skillet over medium-high heat until hot. Add mushrooms, onion, and garlic; cook and stir until tender. Add cooking wine. Reduce heat to medium-low and simmer 3 minutes. Remove from heat; stir in soup, sour cream and mustard until well combined. Return beef to skillet.

Place noodles in prepared dish. Pour beef mixture over noodles; stir until noodles are well combined and coated. Bake, uncovered, 30 minutes or until heated through. Sprinkle with parsley if desired.

Chicken & Turkey Dishes

Chicken Breast Casserole
Submitted by Kathleen O'Connell, PA

4 uncooked chicken breasts
1 can cream of mushroom soup
1 cup sour cream
¼ cup butter, melted
1 package Ritz crackers, crumbled

Mix the soup and sour cream; put chicken in a medium dish and put the soup mixture on top. Mix the butter and crackers together; put on top. Bake at 350° for 1 hour and 5 minutes.

Chicken Pot Pie
Submitted by Shaynie Migchelbrink, TN

2-3 pounds cooked chicken
2 cups chicken broth or 2 cups water and 2-3 bouillon cubes
1 ½ cups frozen peas, thawed
1 ½ cups frozen corn, thawed
1 tablespoon onion powder
3 potatoes, peeled and diced
2-3 carrots, sliced
1 can mushroom soup

Batter:

1 cup self-rising flour
½ cup butter, melted
½ teaspoon pepper
1 cup buttermilk

Simmer potatoes and carrots in a small amount of water until almost soft. Place chicken in the bottom of a 13x9-inch pan. Add peas and corn. Drain potatoes and carrots, and add to pan. Mix broth, onion and soup. Pour over ingredients in pan. Mix batter ingredients and pour evenly over the top. Bake at 425° for 30-40 minutes, until top is browned.

Printed in Volume 2, Issue 4 of KBR

Cashew Chicken Toss
Submitted by Hannah Heinritz, WI

"This is my favorite recipe to pamper friends and family with when I have them over for a summer luncheon. Cool, nutritious, refreshing and so good!"

1 (16-ounce) can pineapple chunks
3 tablespoons sugar
2 teaspoons cornstarch
2 teaspoons orange peel
¼-½ teaspoon dry basil
Dash pepper
1 pound boneless, skinless chicken breasts, cooked
4 cups salad greens

11 ounces canned mandarin oranges, drained
⅓ cup cashews

Drain pineapple, reserving the juice. Set pineapple chunks aside. In a saucepan, combine the sugar, cornstarch, orange peel, basil and pepper. Slowly
stir in pineapple juice until well blended. Bring the mixture to a boil and
stir occasionally until thickened. Cut the cooked chicken breasts into cubes.
Arrange the salad greens, chicken, oranges and pineapple chunks on individual plates. Drizzle with warm dressing and sprinkle with cashews. Serves
5 main-dish portions.

Received for Volume 8, Issue 3 of KBR

Chicken Tetrazzini
Submitted by Samantha Parker, VA

4-5 cups cooked chopped chicken
16 ounces whole wheat fusilli noodles
1 cup unsalted butter
¾ cup white flour
3 ½ cups milk
2 cups chicken broth
1 teaspoon salt
½ teaspoon pepper
¼ teaspoon nutmeg
16 ounces frozen peas
    or 1-2 cups fresh mushroom slices
½ cup Parmesan cheese

rubber bands to the rescue

*"When you are having company, mark
each person's glass by using assorted color
rubber bands. Put a different color, or a
combination of colors, around each glass."*

Cook pasta according to package directions until tender and drain. Make
sauce by melting butter in a large frying pan. Stir in flour and cook one
minute or until bubbly. Slowly blend in milk and chicken broth. Cook and
stir until thickened. Stir in salt, pepper, nutmeg, peas or mushrooms, and
chicken. Combine cooked noodles and sauce/chicken mixture in a greased
10 ½x15 ½-inch casserole dish. Top with Parmesan cheese. Bake at 350° for
20-30 minutes or until bubbly. This makes a great freezer meal.

Parmesan Chicken Fingers

Submitted by Megan Rippel, WI

"These bake quickly, which make them great for lunch. Any leftovers are delicious cut up and served cold over a salad the next day!"

1 cup buttermilk
1 ½ teaspoons Frank's Red Hot pepper sauce
2 pounds boneless skinless chicken breasts, cut into strips
1 ½ cups Contadina® bread crumbs (Roasted Garlic & Savory Spices flavor)
⅓ cup Parmesan cheese

Combine buttermilk and pepper sauce in a Ziploc bag. Add chicken strips and refrigerate for 30 minutes. Discard marinade. Combine bread crumbs and Parmesan cheese in another Ziploc bag. Add chicken strips and shake to coat. Place breaded chicken in a single layer in greased baking dishes. Bake at 450° for 15 minutes or until juices run clear. Enjoy with ranch dip!

Printed in Volume 3, Issue 3 of KBR

Biscuit-Topped Lemon Chicken

Submitted by Tiffany Schlichter, TX

2 large onions, chopped
10 carrots, chopped
10 celery ribs, chopped
Garlic powder
6-12 cups cooked chicken
    or turkey, shredded
1 cup butter, cubed
⅔ cup flour
8 cups milk
⅔ cup lemon juice
3 (10 ¾-ounce) cans cream of chicken soup
2 teaspoons pepper
1 teaspoon salt

Biscuit Ingredients:
7 ½ cups self-rising flour
3 cups milk
3 ½ cups Cheddar cheese
6 tablespoons butter, melted

In a large stock pot, sauté onions, carrots, celery and garlic powder in butter. Stir in flour until blended; gradually add milk. Bring to a boil; cook and stir until thickened. Add chicken, soup, lemon juice, pepper and salt; heat through. Pour into two greased 13x9-inch pans; set aside. In a large bowl, combine biscuit ingredients just until moistened. Turn unto a lightly floured surface. Knead 8-10 times (do not over-knead). Pat or roll dough out to a ¾-inch thickness. With a floured 2 ½-inch biscuit cutter, cut 30 biscuits. Place over chicken mixture. Bake uncovered at 350° for 35-40 minutes or until golden brown.

Chicken, Rice & Broccoli Casserole
Submitted by Amanda Hahner, WA

4 cups chicken broth
2 cups chicken pieces
Broccoli, fresh or frozen
2 teaspoons parsley

⅔ cup rice
¾ cup cheese
Onion, as much as desired

Put all ingredients in a casserole dish or roaster and bake 275° for 3 hours.

tip

self-rising flour

"Place 1½ teaspoons baking powder and ½ teaspoon salt in a measuring cup. Add all-purpose flour to measure 1 cup."
—*Tiffany Schlichter*

Delicious Chicken Burritos
Submitted by Sarah Bryant, KS

20 whole wheat tortillas (page 251)
2 cups cooked brown rice
2 hormone-free chicken breasts, cut into bite size pieces
1 package fresh mushrooms, sautéed
1 jar salsa (sweet pineapple-flavored salsa is best)
1 cup homemade cheese
Garlic powder, salt, and pepper, to taste

Combine all ingredients and place in tortilla wraps. Wrap and place in 13x9-inch baking pan, seam-side down. Sprinkle cheese on top. Warm in a 350° oven until cheese has melted. Serves 10.

Chicken & Vegetable Tortilla Wraps
Submitted by Mrs. Dana Bryant, KS
"This is delicious served with chopped almonds and sesame seeds."

Cooked and chopped chicken of desired amount
1 cup sliced mushrooms
2 zucchini, chopped
5-8 large carrots, chopped
1 onion, chopped
2 cups mozzarella cheese (optional)
Add any vegetables on hand

Stir vegetables, cheese and cooked chicken together and gently cook with soy sauce, adding water as needed. Place vegetable mixture on burrito and roll. Ready to eat! These can also be baked with cheese on top instead of cooking the cheese with vegetables.

Rosemary Roasted Chicken with Potatoes
Submitted by Martha Joy Bullington, AL

2 teaspoons paprika
1 ½ teaspoons crushed rosemary leaves
1 teaspoon minced garlic
½ teaspoon ground black pepper
1 teaspoon salt
2 tablespoons olive oil
6 chicken thighs
1 ½ pounds small potatoes, cut into 1-inch cubes

Mix oil, spices and salt in large bowl. Add chicken and potatoes; toss to coat well. Arrange chicken and potatoes in single layer on greased, foil-lined 15x10-inch baking pan. Roast in preheated 425° oven, turning occasionally, for 30 minutes or until chicken is cooked through and potatoes are tender.

fried chicken *tip*
"When making fried or baked chicken, put all dry ingredients in a large plastic bag. Put chicken in the bag and shake to coat with the flour mixture. This eliminates mess and you can just throw the bag away!"

Chicken Dish
Submitted by Kimberly Vanderford, CO

1 ½ -2 pounds cooked chicken
2 (10-ounce) packages frozen broccoli or mixed vegetables
1 cup mayonnaise or mayonnaise substitute
    or ½ cup mayonnaise and ½ cup plain yogurt
1 can cream of chicken soup or 2 cups white sauce
½ cup bread crumbs
¼ teaspoon curry powder (omit if using mixed vegetables)
1 tablespoon lemon juice
½ cup grated cheese
1 tablespoon melted butter

Cook and chop chicken. Grease 11x7-inch casserole dish. Mix mayonnaise, soup, curry powder, and lemon juice. Mix chicken with vegetables, pour mayonnaise mixture over it and toss well. Mix cheese, breadcrumbs, and butter. Sprinkle over casserole. Bake at 350° for 30 minutes. Serves 6.

Mashed Potato Casserole
Submitted by Esther Lang, WI

2 cups cooked chicken, cubed
1 can corn, drained
1 (15-ounce) can pinto beans, drained
1 can green beans
2 tablespoons dry onion
1 teaspoon salt
½ teaspoon pepper
8 ounces tomato sauce
1 (14-ounce) can diced tomatoes
3 cups mashed potatoes
1 egg, beaten
½ cup cheese

Mix first nine ingredients together and place in a 13x9-inch casserole container. Set aside. Stir potatoes, egg and cheese together. Spoon over casserole and spread to cover it evenly. Bake at 350° for 30-40 minutes or until hot and browned at the edges.

Chicken Enchiladas
Submitted by Nicole Gross, PA

"This is one of my all-time favorite recipes; my family loves it. We like to make this recipe for others in need. You can make it the day before and refrigerate until ready to cook. I make this dish healthier by making my own cream of chicken soup (recipe on page 243)."

1 (16-ounce) can refried beans
10 (8-inch) flour tortillas
1 (10.75-ounce) can condensed cream of chicken soup, undiluted
1 cup sour cream
3 cups cubed cooked chicken
3 cups shredded Cheddar cheese, divided
1 (14.5-ounce) can enchilada sauce
¼ cup sliced ripe olives
Shredded lettuce

Spread about 2 tablespoons of beans on each tortilla. Combine soup and sour cream; stir in chicken. Spoon ⅓ to ½ cup down the center of each tortilla; top with 1 tablespoon cheese. Roll up and place seam side down in a greased 13x9x2" baking dish. Pour enchilada sauce over top; sprinkle with olives and remaining cheese. Bake, uncovered, at 350° for 35 minutes or until heated through. Serve over shredded lettuce with tortilla chips. Makes 10 enchiladas.

Chicken Mozzarella
Submitted by Jenny Berlin, TN

"Very yummy and super easy!"

6 chicken breasts
1 package shredded mozzarella cheese
2 cans cream of mushroom soup
½ cup white cooking wine (optional)
2 cups stuffing
½ cup butter

Place chicken on bottom of large pan. Cover with cheese and soup. Moisten stuffing with butter and cooking wine and spread on top. Bake at 350° for 45 minutes.

Coconut Chicken
Submitted by Martha Joy Bullington, AL

1 large onion, thinly sliced
2 mangos, peeled and sliced or 5-10 dried apricots, cut into cubes
1 whole chicken, cut into pieces
2 tablespoons melted coconut oil or butter
1 teaspoon sea salt
½ teaspoon freshly ground pepper
¼ teaspoon paprika
Pinch of ground nutmeg (optional)
Grated rind of 1 lemon
1 cup chicken broth
Juice of 1 lemon
1 can whole coconut milk

Preheat oven to 350°. Lay onion slices in a large stainless-steel baking dish. Arrange mango slices in a layer on top of onions and place chicken pieces, skin side up, over mango. Mix together coconut oil, salt, pepper, paprika, nutmeg, and lemon rind in a small bowl and brush on chicken pieces. Bake for about 1 ½ hours, or until chicken is nicely brown. Remove chicken and mango slices to a heated platter. Pour chicken broth (or stock) into the dish and bring to a boil over high heat, scraping up coagulated juices. Reduce heat and simmer, stirring in lemon juice and coconut milk. Strain into a small saucepan and continue to simmer to allow the liquid to reduce and thicken slightly. Serve gravy with chicken.

tip

handy charts
"Keep a chart with standard measurements and weights handy by affixing it right inside your kitchen cabinet. This can also be done with highly-used recipes to keep them readily available when needed."

No-Meat Main Dishes

Cheese-Lover's Pasta Roll-Ups
Submitted by Tiffany Schlichter, TX

1 egg, beaten
1 (15-ounce) container ricotta cheese
2 cups mozzarella cheese
4 green onions, chopped
1 tablespoon Italian seasoning
1 can spaghetti sauce
16 lasagna noodles, cooked
¼ cup Parmesan cheese

Heat oven to 375°. Mix first five ingredients until well blended. Spread 1 ½ cups spaghetti sauce in the bottom of a 13x9-inch baking dish. Spread each noodle with 3 tablespoons of the cheese mixture; roll up. Place in dish, seam-side down. Top with remaining sauce and Parmesan cheese; cover. Bake 40-50 minutes or until heated through, uncovering last 10 minutes.

Sloppy Lentils
Submitted by Samantha Parker, VA

"A tasty and healthy lunch; this is like sloppy joes without the meat!"

2 cups lentils
2 cups chopped onions
3 tablespoons olive oil
1 (30-ounce) can diced tomatoes
3 (6-ounce) cans tomato paste
2 cloves garlic, minced
½ cup ketchup
1 teaspoon mustard powder
1-2 tablespoons chili powder
¾ cup honey or molasses
1 tablespoon white vinegar
Salt and pepper, to taste
At least 16 hamburger buns

16 slices of Cheddar cheese

Soak lentils for 4 hours or overnight in filtered water. Rinse lentils and put in a pot with 6 cups of filtered water. Season to taste with salt, if desired. Bring to a boil, then reduce heat and cover. Simmer until tender—about 30 minutes—stirring occasionally.

Meanwhile, cook onions with olive oil in a large skillet until onions have softened and turned translucent—about 4 minutes. Add tomatoes, garlic, tomato paste, ketchup, mustard powder, chili powder, honey/molasses, vinegar, salt and pepper. Simmer 5-10 minutes until thickened. Drain lentils. Stir lentils into sauce mixture, adding a little water if needed to obtain desired "sloppy joe" consistency. Serve on buns with a slice of cheese. Some people like to have it open-faced, while others like it as a sandwich. Enjoy!

Black Bean Burgers
Submitted by Maggie Bullington, AL

"You can also use a food processor to mash the beans. This is a delicious lunch!"

3 (16-ounce) cans black beans, rinsed and drained
    or 1 (1-pound) bag of dried black beans, cooked
1 ½ cups uncooked oats
1 medium-sized onion, chopped
2 jalapeño peppers, diced (optional)
¾ cup fresh cilantro (optional)
2 eggs, beaten
1 teaspoon salt
¼ cup flour
¼ cup cornmeal
1 tablespoon oil
Homemade buns

Mash beans with a fork until they become a very smooth mixture. Combine with next six ingredients, mix and form into patties. Stir together the flour and cornmeal. Dredge bean patties in mixture. Cook in oil in skillet on medium-high heat for 5 minutes on each side. Serve on buns with toppings of your choice.

Perfect Patties

Submitted by Christy & Abigail Mothershed, WV

"These vegetarian patties are a wonderful quick and easy, healthy alternative to meat patties and the serving possibilities are so varied (sandwiches, wraps, over a bed of rice or mashed potatoes with gravy)."

4 cups water
4 cups rolled oats
1 onion, finely chopped
½ cup walnuts, chopped
½ cup raw sunflower seeds
2 tablespoons vegetable salt
1 tablespoon molasses
3 tablespoons nutritional yeast flakes
1 tablespoon Italian seasoning
½ tablespoon oregano
½ tablespoon basil

Boil the 4 cups of water. Mix with other ingredients; let sit in bowl for 20 minutes. Shape into patties using ⅓ cup measure or wide-mouth mason jar lid and ring. (To form patties, use a lid; place lid inside ring, spray or rub with oil, fill with patty mix, pressing firmly. Invert ring and lid on cookie sheet. Place fingers around ring and put both thumbs on the lid, then press lid down through the ring. It will form a perfect patty!) Bake on oiled cookie sheet at 350° for about 25 minutes on one side, then 20 minutes on the other. Time may vary according to patty size and oven heat. Let cool a bit on rack. These patties also freeze well.

tip

menu journal

"When cooking for the family, you may find that you are cooking the same things over and over. One idea that helps is keeping a food journal. Arm yourself with a notepad, journal, or calendar/planner and begin recording what you have for meals every day. When you start to repeat meals, look back on what you've had in the past! If you decide to keep your records in a journal, you can also easily make notes about any changes you made in a recipe."

Squash Enchiladas
Submitted by Keturah Wahl, AL

4 tablespoons butter
4 tablespoons flour
2 teaspoons chili powder
2 cups milk
2 cups grated cheese
6 cups diced summer squash
2 tablespoons vegetable oil
1 ½ cups diced onion
3 minced garlic cloves
1 ½ teaspoons minced hot peppers (optional)
16 tortillas
3 cups diced tomatoes
Cheese for topping

Preheat oven to 400° and grease a 13x9-inch baking pan. Melt the butter and stir in the flour and chili powder. Add the milk stirring continuously to prevent lumps. Add the cheese and keep heating until melted. Season to taste with salt and pepper. Steam the squash about 5 minutes or until tender. Heat the oil and sauté the garlic, onion and hot peppers until limp. Mix with the steamed squash and the sauce. Spoon filling onto each tortilla and roll to form the enchiladas. Place seam side down in your prepared pan. Top with the left over sauce mixture and chopped tomatoes. Sprinkle with cheese. Bake at 400° for half an hour.

Sandwiches

French Bread Subs
Submitted by Bethany Ward, TX

One loaf of French bread
Sliced cheese
Lunch meat

Cut the French bread in half lengthwise. Put a layer of cheese and then a layer of meat, then another layer of cheese. Put on a cookie sheet and put into the oven for 10-15 minutes on 350°. Cool, cut and enjoy!

Fresh Garden Tomato Sandwiches
Submitted by Megan Rippel, WI

"These are quick to make for a delicious lunch! We make them often when our tomato plants are full of big ripe tomatoes."

8 slices bread
8 slices from a large tomato
8 thin slices from a large onion
8 slices of your favorite cheese

Place the bread slices side by side on a baking sheet. Layer a tomato slice, onion slice, and cheese slice on each piece of bread. Broil until cheese is melted and bread is toasted. Serves 4.

Printed in Volume 3, Issue 2 of KBR

Unbelievable Chicken Salad
Submitted by Emily Parish, MO

4 skinless, boneless chicken breasts
1 small package chopped walnuts or pecans
½ cup dried craisins
1 tall stick celery, chopped small
½ cup red onion, chopped
Mayonnaise
Salt and pepper to taste

Boil chicken until tender; drain and cool completely. Dice chicken into small bits. Stir in craisins, walnuts, onions and celery. Mix in enough mayonnaise to make salad spreadable, using 4-5 tablespoons. Salt and pepper lightly. Refrigerate about 1 hour; stir again before serving on homemade bread. Serves 6.

Printed in Volume 6, Issue 1 of KBR

Summer Garden Sandwiches
Submitted by the Bryant Family, KS

"Makes a fun picnic; vary to your family's tastes!"

Sliced tomatoes, cucumbers, peppers, squash, or zucchini
Two fresh homemade slices of bread made
of freshly-ground wheat, potato, spelt, or rye flour

Cut sandwich diagonally and serve to your family with mayonnaise and/or mustard spread, a glass of iced fruit tea, and slices of apple and carrot. Enjoy a fun picnic lunch!

Printed in Volume 3, Issue 3 of KBR

Black Bean Rollups
Submitted by Victoria Steiner, IL

"We really enjoy these for lunches! They are also very easy to make."

8 ounces softened cream cheese
8 ounces sour cream
1 cup shredded Cheddar cheese
½ cup or more of black beans
Garlic powder, seasoning salt, cumin and chili powder, to taste

Beat all together. Refrigerate the mixture to make it a little firmer, if desired. Spread a couple scoops of the mixture on a tortilla. Roll up. Enjoy!

Printed in Volume 6, Issue 1 of KBR

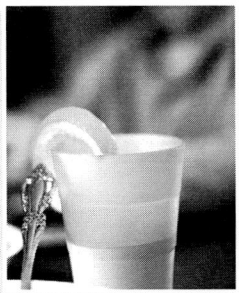

Aunt Phyllis'
Cucumber Tea Sandwiches
Submitted by Elizabeth Adams, IA

"A recipe passed from my aunt to grandmother to myself, this is an easy, delicious addition to a tea or special lunch!"

1 (8-ounce) package cream cheese
½ package zesty Italian dry dressing mix
1 clove garlic, minced
Slices of rye bread
Cucumber, sliced with sections of ½-inch peeled off the edges lengthwise, leaving some green remaining
Dill weed

Mix first three ingredients together and spread on square bread or cookie-cutter sliced bread. Top each with a thin slice of cucumber. Sprinkle with dry or fresh dill weed. Enjoy!

Printed in Volume 8, Issue 2 of KBR

Open-Faced Tuna Melts
Submitted by Kira Saxton, OH

1 tomato (optional)
5 cans tuna, drained
1 cup mayonnaise
⅔ cup jalapeños, chopped
⅔ cup pickles, chopped
⅔ cup fresh chopped onion
5 slices bread
½ cup shredded cheese per slice of bread

Open and drain each can of tuna. Put tuna into a bowl and add the mayonnaise, jalapeños, pickles and onion. Mix well. Divide the tuna mixture evenly on the slices of bread. Broil on low in the oven for about 1 minute. Take it out and add the cheese over each slice. Put it back in the oven until the cheese melts. Slice the tomato and put some on top of each melt, if desired.

Received for Volume 8, Issue 3 of KBR

Party Pastries
Submitted by Briana & Becky Balmez, TN

½ cup butter or margarine, softened
1 (3-ounce) package cream cheese, softened
1 cup all-purpose flour
Dash of salt
Leaf lettuce
Chicken Salad Filling (recipe following)

Combine butter and cream cheese in a mixing bowl; beat at medium speed of an electric mixer until smooth. Add flour and salt; mix well. Divide dough into 30 balls. Place in ungreased miniature (1 ¾-inch) muffin pans, pressing dough on bottom and up sides to form shells. Prick bottoms and sides of shells with a fork. Bake at 400° for 10 minutes or until lightly browned. Remove from pans, and cool on wire racks. Line shells with lettuce. Spoon Chicken Salad Filling evenly into shells. Cover and chill. Yields 2 ½ dozen.

Chicken Salad Filling
Submitted by Briana & Becky Balmez, TN

"For a change of pace, make a pizza filling for these pastries instead of chicken salad. You'll need ⅓ cup pizza sauce and ½ cup (2 ounces) shredded mozzarella cheese. Omit the lettuce and simply spoon the pizza sauce evenly into the shells, and top with cheese. Bake at 350° for 5 minutes or until cheese melts. Serve warm."

¾ cup finely chopped cooked chicken
⅓ cup mayonnaise
¼ cup finely chopped celery
2 tablespoons finely chopped green bell pepper
2 tablespoons finely chopped dill pickle
⅛ teaspoon ground white pepper

Combine all ingredients; stir well. Cover and chill. Yields 1 ½ cups.

Seafood Main Dishes

Salmon Patties
Submitted by Sarah Bryant, KS

"This is our family's favorite lunch meal; it's a great source of protein. I usually serve it with stir-fried vegetables and herb-seasoned couscous."

2 cans salmon, drained
2 cups rolled oats
1 cup mayonnaise (page 249)
½ teaspoon salt

Mix all ingredients together and form patties. Heat frying pan and cook each patty in oil or pork lard for several minutes on each side, until golden brown and slightly crispy. Serves 6.

Chive-Studded Fish Fillets
Submitted by Maggie Bullington, AL

"This fish is just as fast and easy as it is delicious! The sauce can easily be mixed while the fish is cooking, so this main course can be thrown together in a flash. When my family tried this for the first time, it tasted like something that you could get at Red Lobster."

2 pounds fish fillets
2 tablespoons lemon juice
½ cup Parmesan cheese, grated
¼ cup melted butter
3 tablespoons chives
3 tablespoons mayonnaise
¼ teaspoon salt
Dash of hot sauce

Lay thawed fish fillets on a well-greased baking sheet and brush with lemon juice. Broil for 6 minutes or until flakey. Combine remaining ingredients and spread over cooked fish. Broil another 2 minutes until light brown.

Shrimp Crostini
with Creole Cream Sauce
Submitted by Hannah Schoenfelder, MN

1 French baguette
½ cup plus 2 tablespoons butter, divided
1 pound medium fresh shrimp, peeled and de-veined
2 tablespoons, plus 2 teaspoons Creole seasoning, divided
1 red bell pepper, chopped
1 tablespoon minced garlic
¼ cup lemon juice
2 teaspoons Worcestershire sauce
1 ⅓ cups heavy whipping cream
2 teaspoons hot sauce (optional)
2 tablespoons chopped fresh parsley
¼ cup chopped green onion

Preheat oven to 350°. Cut baguette into 24, ½-inch, slices. Spread both sides of slices with butter. Place on a baking sheet and bake 5-10 minutes or until golden around the edges; set aside. Combine shrimp and 2 tablespoons of Creole seasoning in a small bowl; set aside. In a large skillet, melt 2 tablespoons butter over medium heat. Add red pepper and garlic; cook 2-3 minutes until pepper becomes soft. Add shrimp and cook 2 minutes on each side; remove shrimp. Add lemon juice, 2 teaspoons Creole seasoning, Worcestershire sauce, heavy cream and hot sauce, if desired. Simmer for 5 minutes. Remove from heat; stir in green onions and parsley. To serve, spoon 3-4 shrimp onto each crostini; top shrimp with about 2 tablespoons of sauce. Garnish with parsley and green onions, if desired. Serves 12.

Printed in Volume 8, Issue 2 of KBR

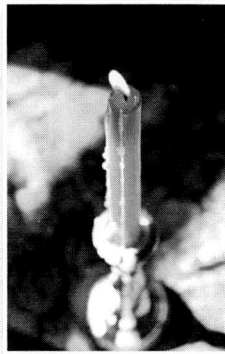

Tuna Noodle Casserole
Submitted by Esther Lang, WI

16 ounces rotini, cooked and drained
3 cans tuna, drained
16 ounces frozen peas, or peas and carrots
3 tablespoons butter
3 tablespoons flour
¾ cup milk
1 cup yogurt
1 teaspoon salt
1 ½ teaspoons sugar
⅜ teaspoon pepper
1 teaspoon dry onion
1 teaspoon chives
¼ teaspoon garlic powder

Melt butter, add flour, salt, sugar and seasonings. Stir in milk and yogurt until smooth. Cook until thickened. Stir in drained tuna and frozen peas. Pour over noodles and stir to mix well. Place in a 15x10-inch casserole container. Add 1 cup water (or the noodles will dry out during baking). Bake, covered, at 350° for 1 hour.

tip

homegrown hospitality
"My family enjoys extending hospitality to others. We like to give our guests a full picture of what it is like to live in the country by serving a farm-fresh meal, with our homegrown meat such as venison or chicken, and then lots of homegrown vegetables. Of course, we top everything off with homemade bread along with homemade butter and jam. It is so much fun to serve our guests in this way and watch their faces as they discover that the potatoes and corn were just harvested from our garden! It is such a blessing to show hospitality."
—Jenny Berlin

NOTES & RECIPES

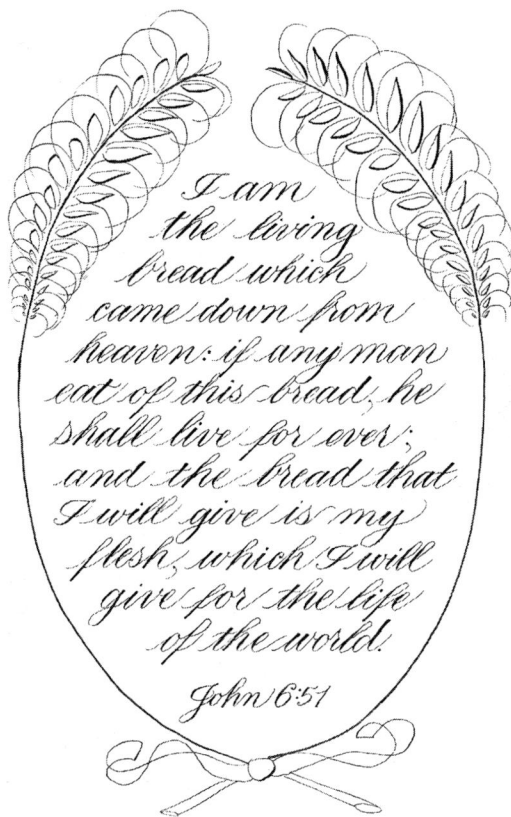

I am
the living
bread which
came down from
heaven: if any man
eat of this bread, he
shall live for ever;
and the bread that
I will give is my
flesh, which I will
give for the life
of the world.

John 6:51

breads & muffins

in the
kitchen

with jessica

🌿 **What is your favorite dish to make?**

I like making Oven-Fried Chicken. It is nice because it is easy to make, very tasty and can go with many side dishes. It's one of my Dad's favorites because he loves pepper.

Oven-Fried Chicken

3 chicken breasts
¼ cup flour
½ teaspoon salt
⅛ teaspoon paprika
⅛ teaspoon pepper
1/6 cup butter
¼ cup shortening

Defrost meat. Cut each chicken breast into quarters. In a plastic bag, mix flour, salt, paprika and pepper. Place a few pieces of chicken at a time inside of bag and coat to shake. Heat oven to 400°. Place a 13x9-inch pan in the oven containing the butter and shortening; heat until butter and shortening are melted. Remove pan and place the chicken chunks in it. Bake, uncovered, for 30 minutes. Turn chicken and bake for another 30 minutes. Enjoy!

🌿 **Do you have any entertainment tips that your family has found useful when showing hospitality to others?**

We like to have at least one bouquet of flowers around, perhaps some unscented candles lit and plenty of places to sit. Large floor pillows are handy when there are a lot of children. Also, if we are eating outside, it is a good idea to make sure the table is on even ground, otherwise it can make for an interesting meal!

Do you have a favorite kitchen tool or gadget that you reach for again and again?

It would be our bench knife—we got ours from King Arthur flour. It is handy for cutting the bread dough into loaf sizes, and is great for scraping the sticky dough parts off the table when you are done kneading and shaping.

Do you have any kitchen tips that you have found helpful when making meals?

Clean as you go—it makes things so much easier in the end! Also, have pre-chopped celery or onion in the fridge and then you don't have to stop and chop them while you are cooking.

Who taught you how to cook? Do you remember anything that you loved to make as a little girl?

My mom and older sister were the ones who taught me, although I also did a lot of trial and error. I remember my favorite thing to bake was chocolate chip cookies—by the dozen.

What ways have you found to bless your family through cooking?

I try to have some sort of cookie or muffin for my dad to take to work, or make dinner when Mom has had a long day. I also enjoy having my young nieces help me in the kitchen—and hope it will be a blessing to them someday as they grow up.

Jessica lives with her parents in Minnesota and enjoys cooking, Bible study, sewing, gardening, and other domestic arts.

Breads

Oat Bread
Submitted by Cassie Whitaker, MO

1 cup oats, ground in blender
1 cup flour
4 teaspoons baking powder
1 cup milk
½ teaspoon salt
2 tablespoons honey
2 beaten eggs
¼ cup oil

Mix together oatmeal, flour, salt and baking powder in a medium-sized bowl. Make well and add remaining ingredients. Stir until smooth. Pour into greased 9x9-inch pan; bake for 25 minutes at 350°.

Printed in Volume 1, Issue 2 of KBR

Zucchini Bread
Submitted by Megan Kunkel, WI

3 cups flour
1 teaspoon salt
1 teaspoon baking soda
¼ teaspoon baking powder
1 tablespoon cinnamon
2 cups sugar
3 eggs
1 cup oil
1 tablespoon vanilla
2 cups grated zucchini
⅓ cup chopped nuts

In a medium-sized bowl, combine flour, salt, baking soda, baking powder, cinnamon and sugar. In another bowl, mix the eggs, oil and vanilla together until well blended. Mix into dry ingredients. Add zucchini and nuts and mix to incorporate. Pour into greased loaf pans. Bake at 325° for 1 hour or until done. Makes 2 loaves.

Printed in Volume 1, Issue 4 of KBR

Late-Night Breadsticks
Submitted by Rebekah Wall, SK

½ cup grated Parmesan cheese
¼ cup finely shredded Cheddar cheese
½ teaspoon Italian seasoning
½ teaspoon garlic powder
⅛ teaspoon onion powder
1 (1-pound) loaf of frozen bread dough, thawed
¼ cup butter or margarine, melted

In a shallow bowl, combine first five ingredients; set aside. Divide dough into 16 pieces; roll each into a 6-inch rope. Dip ropes in melted butter then roll in cheese mixture. Place 2 inches apart on a baking sheet. Let rest for 10 minutes. Bake at 400° for 10-12 minutes or until golden brown. Yields 16 breadsticks.

Printed in Volume 4, Issue 3 of KBR

Monkey Bread
Submitted by Mrs. Gloria Wall, SK

3 (10-count) cans biscuits
Cinnamon and sugar
½ cup margarine
1 cup brown sugar

Cut biscuits into fourths. Roll each piece in cinnamon and sugar mix. Layer pieces in a bundt or tube pan. Melt margarine and brown sugar; bring to boil. Pour over biscuits. Bake at 350° for about 30 minutes. Turn onto plate right away after you take them from the oven.

Printed in Volume 4, Issue 3 of KBR

Cheese Corn Bread
Submitted by Maggie Bullington, AL

4 cups flour
½ cup sugar
6 tablespoons baking powder
1 ½ teaspoons salt
2 eggs, slightly beaten
2 cups milk
1 cup shredded cheese
1 (14-ounce) can whole kernel corn, drained
½ cup oil

Combine all ingredients in a bowl and stir until flour is moistened. Batter will be lumpy. Spread in a greased 13x9-inch pan. Bake at 400° for 35 minutes or until golden brown.

Printed in Volume 7, Issue 1 of KBR

Gluten-Free Brown and White Bread
Submitted by Elizabeth Miller, NY

"You can substitute buckwheat flour for the brown rice flour and milk instead of water and dry milk powder if you like. The Xanthum or Guar (sounds like "GWa") gum acts like gluten in gluten-free baking. You can buy it through food co-ops or health food stores."

2 cups white rice flour
1 ¼ cups brown rice flour
1 tablespoon active dry yeast
2 ½ teaspoons Xanthum or Guar gum
1 ½ teaspoons salt
½ cup dry milk powder
3 tablespoons sugar
3 eggs
¼ cup oil
1 ⅔ cups water
1 teaspoon apple cider vinegar

In mixer bowl, beat wet ingredients together. In separate bowl, combine all dry ingredients. With mixer running, slowly add dry to wet, and beat about ten minutes. Pour batter into two greased loaf pans and let rise for one hour. Bake at 375° for about 40-45 minutes, or until toothpick comes out clean. Cool in pans 10 minutes, then on rack 1 hour before cutting.

Printed in Volume 7, Issue 3 of KBR

Oatmeal Cinnamon Bread

Submitted by Alexxus Hall, TX

"We started making this bread a year ago and it's now a favorite among our family—perfect all-year round!"

1 cup quick cooking oats
1 ½ cups water
1 ¾ cups whole wheat pastry flour
1 teaspoon baking soda
½ teaspoon salt
1 teaspoon cinnamon
½ cup butter, softened
2 cups applesauce
2 large eggs
1 teaspoon vanilla extract
½ cup ground flax seed

tip

breadbox organizing
"Use a nice antique breadbox that will go with your kitchen décor, and store seasonings, supplement or vitamin bottles, or table linens inside. This will keep them off the counter and neatly put away."

Preheat the oven to 350°. Grease and flour a 9x5-inch loaf pan. Place oats in a small heatproof bowl. Place water in a small saucepan and bring to a boil. Pour boiling water over oats. Set aside. Combine the flour, baking soda, salt and cinnamon in a small bowl and mix well. Place butter in a large bowl. Beat with an electric mixer at high speed until creamy. Add applesauce gradually, beating constantly until well blended. Add eggs, one at a time, beating well after each addition. Beat in vanilla extract. Gradually add flour mixture to creamed mixture and beat until smooth. Stir oats into mixture. Spoon batter into prepared pan. Bake about an hour or until a toothpick inserted in center of loaf comes out clean. Cool for 10 minutes in loaf pan, and then transfer bread to a wire rack to cool completely.

Printed in Volume 7, Issue 4 of KBR

Spiced Pumpkin Prune Bread
Submitted by Esther Lang, WI

4 eggs
⅔ cup oil
1 cup sugar
2 cups pumpkin
1 ⅓ cups prune juice
3 cups white flour
1 cup wheat flour
1 teaspoon salt
½ teaspoon cream of tartar

2 teaspoons baking soda
1 teaspoon cinnamon
1 teaspoon ginger
1 teaspoon cloves
1 teaspoon nutmeg
12 ounces (about 2 cups)
   prunes, cut into quarters
½ cup chopped nuts

Mix eggs, oil, sugar, pumpkin and prune juice; set aside. Mix all remaining ingredients except nuts and prunes; add to pumpkin mixture and stir until blended. Stir in chopped nuts and cut-up prunes. Pour into 3 greased 8x4-inch loaf pans. Bake at 350° for 1 hour. Let cool 10 minutes, then remove from pans.

Printed in Volume 8, Issue 1 of KBR

Homemade Bread
Submitted by Kimberly Vanderford, CO

"One of our special treats is to put butter on a slice of fresh, warm bread as soon as it comes out of the oven."

3 ¾ cups warm water
⅓ cup oil
⅓ cup sweetener (molasses or honey)
3 cups flour
1 tablespoon yeast
1 egg
2 heaping tablespoons gluten
2 teaspoon salt
⅛ teaspoon vitamin C

Mix warm water, oil, sweetener, flour; add tablespoon yeast. Mix slightly. Let the mix rest for 12 minutes. Add flour until the dough pulls away from, or cleans, the sides of the bowl. Knead for 10-20 minutes. After the bread is kneaded, let it rise on the counter or in a bowl until it doubles in size. Shape it into loaves and put in pans. Bake at 350° for 15 minutes and then 325° for 25 minutes.

Herb Batter Bread

Submitted by Tiffany & Brittany Schlichter, TX

"If you have fresh herbs on hand, you can double the dried herb amount called for. The following directions are for use with a Kitchen Aid mixer, but batter bread can certainly be made by hand as well!"

3 cups flour
1 tablespoon sugar
1 teaspoon salt
1 (2 ¼-teaspoon) package yeast
1 ¼ cups warm water (120-130°)
1 tablespoon dried chopped parsley

2 tablespoons shortening
¼ teaspoon dried thyme
½ teaspoon dried oregano
Butter
Italian seasoning blend
    or fresh herbs

Using shortening, grease bottom and sides of an 8 ½x4½x2½-inch or 9x5x3" loaf pan. Mix 2 cups of the flour, sugar, salt and yeast in bowl. Add water, parsley, shortening, oregano and thyme. Using flat beater, beat with Kitchen Aid on low speed (speed 1) for 1 minute, scraping bowl frequently. Beat on medium speed (speed 2 or 2 ½) 1 minute, scraping bowl frequently. Stir (stir setting) in remaining 1 cup flour until smooth. Spread batter evenly in pan and pat into shape with floured hands. Cover with towel and let rise in warm place 40 minutes or until doubled. Heat oven to 375°. Bake 20-45 minutes or until done. Immediately remove from pan to wire rack. Brush top of loaf with butter and sprinkle with Italian seasoning or fresh herbs. Best served warm. Enjoy!

Egg Bread
Submitted by Sarah Miller, WA

12 cups whole wheat flour
4 cups water
6 eggs, beaten
½ cup honey
½ cup fat of choice (olive oil or lard)
3 tablespoons yeast
4 ½ teaspoons salt
2-4 cups unbleached flour

Combine flour and water; cover and let sit for 12-24 hours (this step is optional). Combine the honey and fat; heat until warm. Add the yeast and salt. Beat in eggs. Pour over the flour and water mixture. Mix well with hands. Knead in 2-4 cups of unbleached flour. Let rise until doubled. Punch down. Shape. Let rise. Bake at 350° for 30-40 minutes, or until the bread sounds hollow when thumped.

Whole Wheat Bread
Submitted by Sarah Miller, WA

12 cups freshly ground whole wheat flour
4 cups milk
½ cup water
½ cup honey
½ cup fat of choice (olive oil or lard)
4 teaspoons salt
4 tablespoons yeast
About 1 cup unbleached flour

Combine flour and milk; cover loosely and let set for 12-24 hours (this step is optional). Combine the water, honey, and fat; heat until warm. Mix in yeast. Pour into the bowl with the flour/milk mixture; add salt. Mix well. Knead in ½-1 cup of unbleached flour to make a fairly stiff dough. Cover, sit in a warm place. Let rise until doubled. Punch down, shape and let rise again. Bake at 350° for 30-40 minutes. Makes 3 loaves.

Pizza Crust
Submitted by Sarah Bryant, KS
"This makes one crust, so we usually make 5-6 recipes for one meal."

1 cup warm water
2 ¼ teaspoons yeast
2 tablespoons oil

2 tablespoons sugar
1 teaspoon salt
2 ½ cups flour

Mix ingredients together in large bowl and let rise for about 30 minutes. Roll out thinly on floured pans.

tip

personal pan pizzas
"Have a special dinner for your family by making 'personal' pizzas, which each person tops with their favorite pizza toppings, such as sausage, pineapple, peppers, mushrooms, olives, or homemade mozzerella cheese!"

Rolls

Moist Pumpkin Rolls
Submitted by the Bryant Family, KS

1 cup sugar
½ cup warm water
2 cups warm milk
¼ cup butter, softened or melted
2 cups mashed cooked pumpkin
2 teaspoons salt
½ cup wheat germ
10-12 cups all-purpose flour
7 teaspoons dry yeast

In large mixing bowl, combine sugar, water, milk, butter, pumpkin, and salt. Mix well. Add wheat germ, 7-8 cups of the flour, and yeast. Mix, and then continue adding flour and kneading until dough is elastic and not sticky. Place dough in greased bowl; grease top of dough, cover with a towel, and set in a warm place until doubled—about 1 hour. Punch dough down and divide into thirds. Divide each third into 16 pieces and shape into balls. Place on greased baking sheets, and grease tops. Cover and let rise until almost doubled; about 30 minutes. Bake at 350° for 15-18 minutes, until tops are golden. Remove wire racks and cover with a towel. Serve warm with fresh homemade butter or soup! Yields 4 dozen rolls.

Three-Grain Pan Rolls
Submitted by Amanda Hahner, WA

2 cups water
½ cup bulgur
1 tablespoon active dry yeast
1 cup warm milk
½ cup quick cooking oats
⅓ cup honey
2 eggs
1 teaspoon salt

¾ teaspoon pepper
5-6 cups whole wheat flour
2 tablespoons olive oil
2 teaspoons celery seed
2 teaspoons fennel seed
2 teaspoons sesame seed
1 teaspoon poppy seed

In a saucepan bring water to a boil. Stir in bulgur. Reduce heat; cover and simmer for 15 minutes. Drain. In large mixing bowl, dissolve yeast in warm milk. Add the oats, honey, eggs, salt, pepper, bulgur and ½ of the flour. Beat until smooth. Stir in rest of flour to form soft dough and knead until elastic—about 6-8 minutes (dough will be lumpy). Place in a greased bowl, turning once to coat top. Cover and let rise in a warm place until double—about 1 ¼ hours. Punch dough down. Turn onto a lightly floured surface; divide into 22 pieces. Roll into balls. Arrange 11 balls in one 9-inch round greased pan. Put the other balls into another round pan. In a bowl, combine seeds. Brush roll tops with oil and sprinkle seeds over top. Cover and let rise in a warm place until double—about 40 minutes. Bake at 375° for 18-22 minutes or until golden brown. Remove from pans to wire racks to cool. Yields 22 rolls.

Overnight Sticky Buns
Submitted by Sarah Miller, WA

Sauce:
    1 cup butter
    ⅔ cup sorghum, or ¼ cup molasses and ½ cup honey
    ⅓ cup honey

Rolls:
    1 tablespoon yeast
    2 eggs
    ½ cup honey
    ¾ cup butter

2 ½ teaspoons salt
2 ½ cups water
7 cups whole wheat flour

Mix sauce ingredients, boil for 1½ minutes, and pour into two 13x9-inch pans. Sprinkle ¾ cup nuts over sauce. Mix together flour and water. Let sit 12-24 hours (this step is optional). Melt butter and honey together. Beat together the eggs and add to butter mixture. Add yeast and salt. Mix into flour and water mixture. Let rise. Divide into half. Roll each out to a ½-inch thickness. Spread with butter and drizzle with honey. Sprinkle with cinnamon. Roll out and cut into 1½-inch rounds. Place on top of sauce/nut mixture in pans. Bake at 350° for 20-30 minutes; turn out onto a plate and serve warm.

Sunday Rolls
Submitted by Maurya Petrick, TN

4 ½ teaspoons yeast
Pinch of sugar
2 cups warm water
2 eggs, beaten
½ cup sugar or honey
½ cup oil
2 teaspoons salt
6-7 cups flour

Activate yeast with warm water, sugar, and oil. Whisk eggs, sugar together; mix in with yeast. Stir 3 cups of flour into the egg/yeast mixture; add flour ½ cup at a time. When dough becomes too stiff to stir by hand, turn it out onto a floured surface and knead until smooth, but still soft, adding flour a little at a time if dough is too sticky. Place dough in a bowl coated with oil or shortening; cover dough and let rise in a warm area until doubled in size—about 1-1½ hours. Punch dough down and gather into a ball. With floured hands, shape pieces of dough into balls. Arrange rolls about ½-inch apart on a greased baking sheet(s). Cover rolls with a damp towel and let rise again until doubled in size—about 45 minutes. Preheat oven to 350°. Bake rolls 25-30 minutes, or until golden, then top with grated Parmesan, sesame, poppy seeds or kosher salt as desired. Do not overbake. Makes about 40 3-inch rolls.

Best Dinner Rolls
Submitted by Jenny Berlin, TN

"These simply are the best dinner rolls!"

4 ½ -5 cups all purpose flour
¼ cup sugar
1 tablespoon yeast
1 teaspoon salt
1 cup milk

½ cup water
2 teaspoons butter
2 eggs
1 egg, lightly beaten

In a large bowl, combine 2 cups flour, sugar, yeast, and salt. In a small sauce pan, heat the milk, water, and butter to 120-130°. Add to dry ingredients; beat on medium speed for 3 minutes. Add two eggs; beat on high speed for 2 minutes. Stir in enough remaining flour to form a soft dough (dough will be sticky). Knead for 6-8 minutes or until dough is smooth and elastic. Place in a greased bowl, turning once to grease top. Cover and let rise in a warm place for about 1 hour. Punch dough down and turn onto a lightly floured surface; divide into 24 portions. Shape into balls. Divide the balls between two greased 13x9-inch pans. Cover with clean cloth and let rise until doubled. Brush with beaten egg, and sprinkle with topping of your choice. Bake at 375° for 10-15 minutes or until tops are golden brown. Yields 24 dinner rolls.

Optional Roll Toppings

Parm-Garlic: 2 tablespoons Parmesan cheese and ½ teaspoon garlic powder.

Almond-Herb: 2 tablespoons chopped sliced almonds and ½ teaspoon each salt, dried basil and dried oregano.

Everything: 1 teaspoon each of poppy seed, salt, dried garlic powder, sesame seeds and dried minced onions.

tip

dough ball sizes
"A dinner roll should be a bit larger than a golf ball, a cocktail bun is about the size of a Ping-Pong ball, and a hamburger bun is slightly smaller than a baseball."

Scones

Chocolate Chip Scones
Submitted by Tessa Blackstad, WA
"A wonderfully rich scone that my mom and I enjoy on special occasions!"

2 ½ cups pastry flour, cake flour, or all-purpose flour
½ teaspoon salt
¼ cup sugar
2 ¼ teaspoons baking powder
6 tablespoons unsalted butter, cut into pats
¾ cup cream—half and half, light, heavy, or whipping cream
2 large eggs
2 teaspoons vanilla
1 ½ cups chocolate chips
Coarse white sparkling sugar, for topping

Preheat oven to 400°. Lightly grease a baking sheet. In a medium-sized bowl, whisk together the flour, salt, sugar and baking powder until thoroughly combined. Add the butter, working it in until the mixture is unevenly crumbly. Whisk together the cream, eggs and vanilla. Set aside 2 tablespoons and add the rest to the dry ingredients, along with the chocolate chips. Mix to form a moist dough. Transfer the sticky dough to a heavily floured surface. Gently pat and round it into an 8-inch circle. Brush the dough with the reserved egg/cream mixture and sprinkle heavily with coarse sugar. Cut dough into 16 pieces, like a pizza. Space the scones evenly on the prepared pan. Bake the scones for 20 minutes, until they are golden brown. Serve warm. Store in an airtight container. To reheat, wrap loosely in aluminum foil and bake in a preheated 350° oven for about 10 minutes.

Printed in Volume 8, Issue 2 of KBR

Basic Cream Scones
Submitted by Elizabeth Adams, IA

"This is my favorite basic scone recipe for tea time, originally learned from a mother and daughter who own a lovely tea room. I made these for my grandma's 80th birthday tea that my mom and I hosted. You can even press in blueberries on top for a special touch and then serve with blueberry jam, lemon curd and cream...delicious!"

2 cups flour
1 tablespoon baking powder
½ teaspoon salt
¼ cup sugar
5 ⅓ tablespoons butter
½ cup heavy cream
1 egg
1 ½ teaspoons vanilla

Preheat oven to 425°. In a bowl, combine the flour, baking powder, salt, and sugar. Cut the butter into the dry ingredients with a pastry blender. In a separate bowl, add the cream, egg and vanilla; mix well. Once the dry ingredients resemble little pebbles, add the cream/egg mixture to the dry. Gently incorporate the wet into the dry, being careful not to over-mix. Place the dough on a lightly floured surface and knead 8 to 10 times. Pat into two 6-inch circles; cut each circle into eight triangles (or use cookie cutters). Place on greased cookie sheet. Sprinkle large cut sugar on top, if desired. Bake for 11 minutes, or until golden. Enjoy!

Received for Volume 8, Issue 2 of KBR

Cranberry Buttermilk Scones
Submitted by Sara Barratt, MI

3 cups all-purpose flour
⅓ cup, plus 2 tablespoons sugar, divided
2 ½ teaspoons baking powder
¾ teaspoon salt
½ teaspoon baking soda
¾ cup butter
1 cup buttermilk

1 cup dried cranberries
1 teaspoon grated orange peel
1 tablespoon milk
¼ teaspoon ground cinnamon

In a bowl combine the flour, ⅓ cup sugar, baking powder, salt and baking soda; cut in the butter. Stir in buttermilk until combined. Fold in cranberries and orange peel. Turn onto a floured surface; divide dough in half. Shape each portion into ball and shape into six-inch circle. Cut each circle into six wedges. Place on lightly greased baking sheet. Brush with milk. Combine the cinnamon and 2 tablespoons sugar; sprinkle over scones. Bake at 400° for 15-20 minutes or until golden.

Received for Volume 8, Issue 2 of KBR

Crackers

Oatmeal Crackers
Submitted by Rachel Abernathy, MO

½ cup spelt flour, or alternative flours or mixtures of
    whole/white wheat, spelt, teff, quinoa, barley, or buckwheat
1 ½ cups oats, or alternative flakes like quinoa, barley, or spelt
½ tablespoon baking powder
½ teaspoon sea salt
⅛ cup sunflower oil
½ + cup water

Mix dry ingredients together. Add oil and mix well. Add water and mix until the dough forms a ball. Dough should not be sticky or too wet. Sprinkle flour on cookie sheets and roll out until desired thickness. Salt the top and run rolling pin over before cutting into small squares with a pastry cutter. Makes 1-3 cookie sheets, depending on thickness.

Wheat Crackers
Submitted by Michelle Whitaker, MO
"For square crackers, use a knife or pizza wheel to cut."

6 cups wheat flour
¼ cup honey
or ½ cup sorghum
2-3 cups cream, or 1 cup oil and 2 cups water
1 teaspoon salt

Mix honey, flour and salt in a large bowl. Add liquid. Kneed dough 2 minutes, then flour a place to roll it out on. Roll it out to desired thickness and use cookie cutters to cut out the shapes desired. Lay on a greased cookie sheet, sprinkle with salt and bake at 300° until crisp.

Printed in Volume 1, Issue 2 of KBR

Homemade Crackers
Submitted by Rachel Abernathy, MO
"Add ⅓ cup dried parsley flakes with the dry ingredients for an interesting twist!"

2 cups unbleached wheat flour
⅛ cup oil or melted shortening or butter
½ teaspoon sea salt
¾ cup water (the amount will vary depending on grain used)

Mix dry ingredients together. Add oil and mix well. Add water and mix until the dough forms a ball. Dough should not be sticky or too wet. Sprinkle flour on cookie sheets and roll out until desired thickness. Salt the top and run rolling pin over before cutting into small squares with a pastry cutter. Makes 2-3 cookie sheets of crackers.

Muffins

Pumpkin Muffins
Submitted by Rebekah Wall, SK

"These freeze well!"

4 eggs
2 cups sugar
1 ½ cups oil
1 (14-ounce) can pumpkin
3 cups flour
2 teaspoons baking powder
1 teaspoon cinnamon
2 teaspoons baking soda
1 teaspoon salt

Beat first 4 ingredients together, then blend in remaining ingredients. Put in muffin papers and sprinkle with white sugar and cinnamon. Bake at 400° for 12-14 minutes.

Printed in Volume 3, Issue 1 of KBR

Blueberry Muffins
Submitted by Katrina Backus, CA

"The pastry flour makes these wonderful!"

2 eggs
⅓ cup honey
1 cup buttermilk
2 cups pastry flour
1 teaspoon salt
½ teaspoon baking soda
1 cup fresh or frozen blueberries

Whisk eggs into buttermilk thoroughly. In separate bowl, blend dry ingredients. Blend into liquid until just mixed. Fold in blueberries. Fill greased muffin tins until almost full. Bake 20-25 minutes at 375°. Cool 5 minutes before removing from pans. Makes 10 large or 12 medium-sized muffins.

Printed in Volume 3, Issue 1 of KBR

Apple Strudel Muffins
Submitted by Emma Perrine, IA

8 cups flour
1 tablespoon baking powder
1 teaspoon baking soda
2 teaspoons salt
2 cups butter
4 cups sugar
8 eggs
1 tablespoon, plus 2 teaspoons vanilla
6 cups chopped apples

Topping:

1 ⅓ cups packed brown sugar
¼ cup flour
½ teaspoon cinnamon
¼ cup butter

Preheat oven to 375°. Grease muffin tins. In a bowl, mix flour, baking powder, baking soda and salt. In another bowl, beat together butter, sugar and eggs until smooth. Mix in vanilla. Stir in apples, and gradually blend in the flour mixture. Spoon the mixture into prepared muffin pans. In a small bowl, mix brown sugar, flour and cinnamon. Cut in butter until mixture is coarse like crumbs. Sprinkle over tops of mixture in muffin pans. Bake 20 minutes or until toothpick comes out clean. Let sit for 5 minutes before removing muffins from pan. Cool on wire rack. Yields 48 servings.

Printed in Volume 3, Issue 1 of KBR

Apple Muffins
Submitted by Anna Holt, TX

"This is a healthy, sweet-tooth killer snack! It also tastes great when served with honey, strawberry jelly or butter."

3 ½ cups whole wheat flour
5 teaspoons baking powder
1 ½ teaspoons salt
1 teaspoon ground cinnamon

2 beaten eggs
1 ½ cups milk
1 tablespoon cinnamon
⅔ cup oil
½ cup honey
2 cups peeled and chopped apple
¼ cup raisins (optional)

Topping:
4 tablespoons sugar or sucanat
1 tablespoon cinnamon

Stir together first 4 ingredients; make a well in the center. Blend eggs, milk, oil, honey, and raisins; add all at once to dry mixture. Stir just until moistened. Fill greased muffin tins ⅔ full. Sprinkle with topping mixture. Bake at 350° for 15-20 minutes or until golden. Makes 24 muffins.

Printed in Volume 3, Issue 1 of KBR

Banana Muffins
Submitted by Bonnie Faber, OH

1 ¾ cups all-purpose flour
½ cup sugar
2 ½ teaspoons baking powder
¾ teaspoon salt
1 well-beaten egg
¾ cup milk
⅓ cup cooking oil
1 cup chopped banana

Stir the first 4 ingredients together thoroughly; make a well in the center. Combine egg, milk and oil and add all at once to the dry mixture. Add banana. Stir just until moistened. Fill paper-lined muffin pans ⅔ full. Bake at 400° for 25-30 minutes. Yields 12 muffins.

Printed in Volume 3, Issue 1 of KBR

Oat Bran Muffins

Submitted by Katrina Backus, CA

1 egg	2 teaspoons baking powder
¼ cup honey	1 teaspoon cinnamon
1 cup buttermilk	½ teaspoon baking soda
¼ cup raisins, soaked and drained	½ teaspoon salt
2 ½ cups uncooked oat bran	¼ cup chopped walnuts

Preheat oven to 425°. Whisk egg and honey thoroughly together. Blend in buttermilk and raisins. In a separate bowl, mix the rest of the ingredients. Blend into liquid until just mixed. Fill greased tins until almost full. Bake 15-17 minutes; cool 5 minutes before removing from pan. Makes 10-12 medium-sized muffins.

Printed in Volume 3, Issue 1 of KBR

Italian Herb Muffins

Submitted by Heidi Lindsey, WI

"These are wonderful with a warm soup in the winter!"

2 cups flour
2 tablespoons grated Parmesan cheese
1 tablespoon sugar
1 tablespoon Italian seasoning
1 tablespoon baking powder
1 teaspoon salt
1 egg
¾ cup milk
½ cup oil
¼ cup butter, softened
½ teaspoon garlic powder

In a bowl, combine flour, cheese, sugar, seasoning, baking powder and salt. In another bowl, whisk egg, milk and oil. Stir into dry ingredients just until moistened. Bake at 400° for 15-20 minutes. Serve warm with butter and garlic powder. Yields 10 muffins.

Printed in Volume 3, Issue 1 of KBR

Chocolate Chip Muffins
Submitted by Rebekah Wall, SK

"*Very yummy when warm.*"

1 ½ cups flour
½ cup sugar
1 tablespoon baking powder
¼ teaspoon salt
⅓ cup oil
½ cup chocolate chips
1 egg
1 cup milk

Mix dry ingredients, add chocolate chips. Add remaining ingredients and stir until mixed. Do not beat. Bake at 375° for 20 minutes.

Printed in Volume 3, Issue 1 of KBR

Pumpkin Butterscotch Muffins
Submitted by Hayley Hobbs, AL

2 ½ cups wheat flour
1 tablespoon baking powder
1 teaspoon baking soda
½ teaspoon salt
1 ½ cups brown sugar
2 teaspoons cinnamon
¾ teaspoon nutmeg
1 ¾ cups pumpkin (15-ounce can)
4 eggs
½ cup oil
2 cups nuts (optional)
2 cups butterscotch chips

Mix dry ingredients. Add wet ingredients. Add pumpkin, nuts and butterscotch chips. Bake at 350° for 20 minutes or until done. Yields 18-24 muffins.

Printed in Volume 6, Issue 4 of KBR

Mississippi Spice Muffins
Submitted by Laura Newcomer, ME

"This recipe is a favorite in our household. The batter can be kept in the refrigerator for several weeks, making a quick and easy addition to a meal."

1 cup oil or margarine
2 eggs
2 cups applesauce
1 ½ cups sugar
4 cups flour
1 tablespoon cinnamon
2 teaspoons allspice
1 teaspoon cloves
2 teaspoons baking soda
½ teaspoon salt

Mix wet ingredients together. Sift dry ingredients and add to the wet mixture. Mix well. Fill greased muffin tins half full. Bake at 350° for 20 minutes.

Printed in Volume 8, Issue 1 of KBR

Millet Muffins
Submitted by Maggie Bullington, AL

2 ¼ cups flour
¼ cup millet
1 teaspoon salt
1 teaspoon baking powder
1 teaspoon baking soda
1 egg
½ cup oil
½ cup honey
1 cup buttermilk

Mix dry ingredients and wet ingredients separately, and then add together. Mix just until moistened. Fill prepared muffin tins or papers about ⅔ full. Bake at 400° for 15 minutes.

Melt-In-Your-Mouth Strawberry Muffins
Submitted by Martha Joy Bullington, AL

1 cup whole wheat flour
1 cup white flour
¼-½ cup honey
1 ½ teaspoons baking soda
2 eggs
1 cup yogurt
¼ cup butter, melted
1 teaspoon vanilla
1 cup chopped strawberries

Combine all ingredients. Pour into muffin tins and bake at 375° for 20-25 minutes. Makes about 12 muffins.

Spiced Banana Muffins
Submitted by Esther Lang, WI

"I like to make a double batch of these muffins. They freeze very well."

3 cups wheat flour
1 ½ teaspoons baking soda
¾ teaspoon salt
¼ teaspoon ground nutmeg
3 eggs
2 ¼ cups mashed bananas
1 cup sugar
6 tablespoons oil

Mix first four ingredients; set aside. Beat eggs, bananas, sugar and oil; add flour mixture and mix well. Bake at 400° for 20 minutes in greased or paper-lined pans. Makes 2 dozen.

He should have fed
them also
with
the
finest
of the
wheat: and with
honey out of the
rock should I
have satisfied thee.

Psalm 81:16

delicious *desserts*

in the
kitchen
with esther

℘ What is your favorite meal to make?

I always like to make salads, so almost any meal which includes a salad is a favorite! Recently we started making an enchilada casserole—it is very easy and fun to make:

Enchilada Casserole

"We make this in the morning and refrigerate it until the late afternoon. We bake it for 1 hour."

10 wheat tortillas
1 (24-ounce) jar salsa
2 cups cooked, cut-up chicken
1 can black beans, drained

8 ounces cream cheese
1 tablespoon dry onion
Cheese (optional)

Measure 1 cup salsa and set aside. Mix remaining salsa, chicken, beans, cream cheese and onion. Spoon chicken mixture down the center of each of the tortillas. Roll up and place in a row in a greased 15x10-inch pan. Top with the reserved 1 cup salsa and sprinkle with cheese, if desired. Bake, covered, at 350° until hot.

Corn Chip Salad

2 romaine hearts, washed and cut up
4 hard-boiled eggs, chopped
½ cup peanuts
½ cup raisins
Crushed corn chips or tortilla chips

Toss together and add dressing:

½ cup mayonnaise ¼ cup sugar
½ cup plain yogurt 2 tablespoons vinegar
¼ cup brown sugar

Do you have any entertaining tips that your family has found useful when showing hospitality to others?

We try to make simple meals that do not take much last-minute preparation. We try to do as much ahead as we can. Also, we consider the ages of the guests, to make it enjoyable for everyone.

Do you have a favorite kitchen tool you use often?

I have a favorite little whisk I frequently use. I also use our kitchen scissors on many things—chicken, lettuce, vegetables, or baked potatoes.

What method do you use to plan your meals?

We use a notebook with one week on each page, so that we can see more of "the big picture" when we're planning. I like to plan meals a week at a time. I think it is important to plan ahead and work ahead. This makes it much easier when it is time to put a meal on the table.

Who taught you how to cook?

My mom taught me how to cook, and my dad did too. I always loved to help Dad make homemade pizza!

What ways have you found to bless your family through the kitchen?

I like to bless my family by preparing foods they especially like. I love it when my dad says, "This is my favorite casserole!"

Esther loves to prepare nourishing meals for her
family, while ministering to their varied food needs.
She longs to be a joyful channel of Christ's love.

ℒ Brownies & Bars

Speedy Brownies
Submitted by Lydia Lewis, TX

2 cups sugar
1 ¾ cups white flour
½ cup baking cocoa
1 teaspoon salt

5 eggs
1 cup vegetable oil
1 teaspoon vanilla extract
1 cup chocolate chips

In mixing bowl, combine first seven ingredients; beat until smooth. Pour into greased 13x9-inch baking pan. Sprinkle chocolate chips over the top. Bake at 350° for 30 minutes or until toothpick comes out clean. Cool in pan on wire rack. Makes about 2 dozen bars.

Printed in Volume 1, Issue 3 of KBR

Chocolate Chip Cheese Bars
Submitted by Emily Rebhan, WI

2 ½ cups flour
1 teaspoon baking soda
½ teaspoon salt
½ cup butter, softened
½ cup shortening

1 cup packed brown sugar
½ cup sugar
2 eggs
1 ½ teaspoons vanilla
2 cups chocolate chips

Filling:
16 ounces cream cheese, softened
1 cup sugar
2 eggs

Combine flour, baking soda and salt. In a separate bowl, beat butter, sugar, shortening, eggs and vanilla. Stir in flour mixture and chocolate chips. Press enough dough to cover the bottom of a greased 13x9-inch pan. In mixing bowl, beat filling ingredients. Spread over dough. Crumble remaining dough on top. Bake at 350° for 35-40 minutes or until toothpick inserted near center comes out clean. Cool on wire rack and refrigerate.

Printed in Volume 1, Issue 3 of KBR

Fudgy Brownies
Submitted by Emma Perrine, IA

4 ounces chocolate
½ cup butter
2 cups sugar
2 teaspoons vanilla

4 eggs
1 cup all-purpose flour
¼ teaspoon salt

Glaze:
½ cup chocolate chips
1 tablespoon butter

Heat oven to 350°. Grease a 13x9-inch pan. In a small saucepan over low heat, melt chocolate and ½ cup butter, stirring until smooth. Remove from heat; cool 10 minutes. In medium-sized bowl, combine sugar, vanilla and eggs; beat until light and fluffy. Add flour, salt and chocolate mixture and blend well. Spread in greased pan and bake at 350° for 30-38 minutes. Do not over bake! Cool 1 hour or until completely cooled. In small saucepan, melt glaze ingredients over low heat, stirring constantly until smooth. Drizzle over cool brownies. Let stand until set, and cut into bars. Yields 24 bars.

Printed in Volume 2, Issue 1 of KBR

Peanut Butter Brownies
Submitted by Laura Mae Newcomer, ME

3 eggs
1 ½ cups sugar
¾ cup brown sugar
¾ teaspoon salt
2 cups flour
2 tablespoons baking powder
½ cup peanut butter
½ cup butter or ¼ cup shortening
1 ½ teaspoons vanilla

Combine first three ingredients and blend thoroughly. Add remaining ingredients and mix. Bake at 350° in a 13x9-inch pan for 25 minutes. Do not overbake; these are much better soft!

Printed in Volume 4, Issue 2 of KBR

Easy Chocolate Chip Bars
Submitted by Shaynie Migchelbrink, TN

1 cup butter, softened
1 cup packed brown sugar
1 teaspoon vanilla
2 cups flour
⅛ teaspoon salt
½-1 cup chocolate chips

Beat butter, sugar and vanilla with electric mixer on medium speed until well-blended. Mix flour and salt in a separate bowl. Add to butter mixture. Mix well. Stir in chocolate. Press mixture into an ungreased 15x10-inch pan. Bake at 350° for 20-25 minutes. Cool 5 minutes. Yields 20 servings.

Printed in Volume 4, Issue 2 of KBR

Pear Custard Bars
Submitted by Sara Barratt, MI

½ cup butter softened
⅓ cup sugar
¾ cup all-purpose flour
Filling/Topping:
1 (8-ounce) package cream cheese, softened
½ cup sugar
1 egg
½ teaspoon vanilla
1 (15 ¼-ounce) can pear halves, drained
½ teaspoon sugar
½ teaspoon ground cinnamon
¼ teaspoon vanilla extract
⅔ cup walnuts or macadamias

In mixing bowl, cream butter and sugar. Beat in the flour and vanilla until combined. Stir in nuts. Press into a greased, 8-inch baking pan. Bake at 350° for 20 minutes or until slightly browned. Cool on wire rack. Increase heat to 375°. In a mixing bowl, beat cream cheese until smooth. Add sugar, egg and vanilla; mix until combined. Pour over cooled crust. Cut pears into thin slices; Arrange in single layer over filling. Combine sugar and cinnamon; sprinkle over pears. Bake at 375° for 28-30 minutes—center will be soft set and become firmer upon cooling. Cool on a wire rack for 45 minutes. Cover and refrigerate for at least 2 hours before cutting. Store in refrigerator.

Printed in Volume 8, Issue 2 of KBR

Chocolate Chip Bars
Submitted by Esther Lang, WI

2 cups quick oats
1 cup brown sugar
½ cup sugar
1 cup flour
¼ teaspoon salt
1 teaspoon baking soda
¼ cup hot water
½ cup butter, melted
1 teaspoon vanilla

Frosting:
¼ cup soft butter
¼ cup creamy peanut butter
1 teaspoon vanilla
¼ teaspoon salt
2-2 ½ cups powdered sugar
4 tablespoons milk

Mix bar ingredients together. Press into a greased 13x9-inch pan. Press ½ cup chocolate chips into the dough. Bake at 350° for 20 minutes. Cool. Mix frosting ingredients together and frost bars, adding a few more chocolate chips on top.

Zucchini Dessert Squares
Submitted by Samantha Robinson, CA

Crumb crust:
    4 cups flour
    2 cups sugar (can reduce to 1 ½ cups)
    ½ teaspoon cinnamon
    ½ teaspoon salt
    1 ½ cups cold butter
Filling:
    8-10 cups cubed, peeled, and seeded zucchini
    ⅔ cup lemon juice
    1 cup sugar
    1 teaspoon cinnamon
    ½ teaspoon nutmeg

In a bowl, combine dry ingredients; cut in butter until crumbly. Reserve 3 cups. Pat remaining crumb mixture in a greased 13x9-inch pan. Bake at 375° for 10 minutes or until light brown. For filling, place zucchini and lemon juice in saucepan and bring to a boil. Reduce heat, cover and cook for 6-8 minutes until zucchini is crisp-tender. Stir in sugar, cinnamon, and nutmeg; cover and summer for 5 minutes. Spoon over crust. Sprinkle with reserved crumb mixture. Bake at 375° for 30 minutes. Serves 10-16.

Blackberry Bars
Submitted by Samantha Robinson, CA

1 cup all-purpose flour
¾ cup brown sugar, packed
¼ cup butter
½ cup sour cream
1 egg, beaten

¾ teaspoon baking soda
¼ teaspoon salt
1 teaspoon ground cinnamon
½ teaspoon vanilla
1 ½ cups fresh blackberries

Combine flour and brown sugar; cut in butter with pastry blender until mixture resembles coarse meal. Press 1 cup of mixture in bottom of an ungreased 8-inch square pan. Reserve ½ cup of mixture for topping. Combine remaining crumb mixture, sour cream, egg, baking soda, salt, cinnamon, and vanilla; blend well. Stir in blackberries. Spoon over crust, spreading evenly. Sprinkle on topping. Bake at 350° for 30-40 minutes. Cool; cut into bars.

Celestial Bars

Submitted by Jenny Berlin, TN

"These are my favorite dessert bars to make. They are always a hit!"

Cookie Layer:

½ cup butter, softened

2 cups packed brown sugar

3 eggs

1 teaspoon vanilla extract

½ teaspoon almond extract

2 cups all purpose flour

½ teaspoon salt

1-1½ cups chopped pecans (optional)

2 squares (1 ounce each) unsweetened chocolate, melted and cooled

Icing:

½ cup butter, softened

3 cups confectioners sugar

3-4 tablespoons milk

1 teaspoon vanilla

Glaze:

½ cup semisweet chocolate chips

2 teaspoons shortening

In a large mixing bowl, cream butter and brown sugar until light and fluffy. Add eggs, one at a time, beating well after each edition. Add extracts; beat well. Combine flour and salt; add to creamed mixture. Stir in pecans (batter will be thick; but be very careful not to over mix. Just combine until moist.) Divide batter in half; stir chocolate into one portion. Alternately spoon plain and chocolate batters into a greased 13x9-inch baking pan. Swirl with a knife. Bake at 350° for 16-20 minutes or until toothpick inserted near the center comes out clean. Cool completely on a wire rack.

For icing, in a large bowl, cream butter and confectioners sugar. Add milk and vanilla; beat until smooth. Spread over bars.

For glaze, melt chocolate chips and shortening in a heavy sauce pan or microwave; stir until smooth. Drizzle over bars. Refrigerate until chocolate is completely set before cutting into bars. Yields 4 dozen.

Nutella Rice Krispee Treats
Submitted by Tabea Hall, BC

4 cups mini marshmallows
¼ cup butter
½ cup Nutella
5-6 cups rice cereal

Topping:
1 tablespoon butter
½ cup milk chocolate chips
1 cup Nutella

Heat marshmallows, butter and Nutella in glass bowl in microwave (or use a pot on the stove top for approximately 5 minutes). Stir every thirty seconds until smooth. Pour marshmallow mixture over rice cereal. Stir to coat evenly. Press mixture into a greased 13x9-inch pan.

For topping, combine ingredients in a glass bowl and microwave on high, stirring every 15-30 seconds until chocolate is melted and mixture is smooth (or stir on the stove constantly for 5 minutes, or until smooth). Spread over pan of rice krispee treats. Chill for an hour before cutting into squares. This is best shared with family and served with a cold glass of milk!

Heath Bar Dessert
Submitted by Annie Jones, FL

6 egg whites
1¾ cups sugar
½ teaspoon cream of tartar
1 pint heavy whipping cream
1 tablespoon sugar
1 bag of Heath Bars, crushed

Beat the egg whites, sugar, and cream of tartar until stiff (this takes about 10 minutes). Divide and pour into two 13x9-inch pans lined with foil. Bake 45 to 50 minutes at 325°. Cool, then lift foil out. Carefully remove foil and put one meringue back into a pan. For the filling: whip the whipping cream and 1 tablespoon of sugar. Stir in the crushed Heath Bars and pour over the meringue in the pan. After the filling is spread evenly over the meringue, top with the remaining meringue. Cover and refrigerate overnight.

Cookies

Christmas Cookies
Submitted by Megan Rippel, WI

"These cookies can be made for any holiday; just use cookie cutters that match the occasion! We have had this recipe since I was little, and it's the best roll-out cookie recipe we have found!"

2 ½ cups flour
1 teaspoon baking powder
¼ teaspoon salt
½ cup butter
¾ cup sugar
1 egg
1 teaspoon vanilla
3 tablespoons milk

Frosting:
2 tablespoons butter
2 cups powdered sugar
1 teaspoon vanilla
Approx. 5 tablespoons milk

First mix together 2 cups flour, baking powder and salt in a bowl. In another bowl, cream together the butter and sugar. Then beat in the egg, vanilla and milk. Stir in the flour mixture and then gradually add enough of the remaining flour to make dough stiff enough to roll. Form the dough into a ball and chill for about 1 hour. Preheat oven to 375°. Roll out the dough to ⅛-inch thick. Cut out dough with Christmas cookie cutters and place on ungreased cookie sheets. Bake 8-10 minutes or until lightly browned. For the frosting, mix all the ingredients together. Add more sugar or milk as needed. Divide the frosting into different bowls and tint with the colors you would like using food coloring. Frost cookies once they are cooled.

Printed in Volume 2, Issue 1 of KBR

Jam-Filled Cookies
Submitted by Susanna Dorfsmith, CA

1 cup butter
2 cups sugar
4 eggs
2 teaspoons vanilla extract
5 cups flour
1 teaspoon salt
½ teaspoon baking soda
¾ cup jam

In a large bowl, cream butter and sugar. Beat in eggs and vanilla. In a medium-sized bowl, combine dry ingredients. Gradually stir in the creamed mixture. Cover and refrigerate 1 hour. On a lightly floured surface, roll out dough to ⅛-inch thickness. Cut half the dough with a round cookie cutter or biscuit cutter. Spread each round with about ½ tablespoon of jam. Cut remaining half of dough with a doughnut cutter. Place over round cookies and bake at 375° for 8-10 minutes. Cool on paper towels. Store in airtight containers. Makes about 2 ½ dozen.

Printed in Volume 2, Issue 1 of KBR

Peanut Butter No-Bake Cookies
Submitted by Mrs. Cheryl Schlichter, TX
& Kathleen O'Connell, PA

3 cups oats
⅓ cup peanut butter
⅔ cup butter
¾ cup sugar
½ cup milk
⅔ teaspoon vanilla

Set aside the first 2 ingredients. In a pan, mix the butter, sugar and milk over low heat on the stove. Let simmer for 2 minutes; add vanilla and stir well. Add oats and peanut butter, mix well. Drop by spoonfuls onto wax paper and let set until firm. You can add raisins.

Healthy Oatmeal Cookies
Submitted by Esther Lang, WI

½ cup applesauce
2 mashed bananas
or 1 cup applesauce
⅓ cup oil
1 ¼ cups sugar
1 teaspoon molasses
2 teaspoons vanilla
1 egg
1 ½ cups wheat flour
¾ cup white flour
1 teaspoon baking soda

3 cups quick oats
2 tablespoons wheat germ
2 tablespoons flax seeds
2 tablespoons wheat bran
¼ cup coconut
1 cup raisins
1 cup nuts
or ½ cup sunflower seeds
1 cup chocolate chips

Bake in two greased 13x9-inch pans at 350° for 30 minutes. Cool 10 minutes before cutting. Can be baked as drop cookies too. Delicious when served warm!

Printed in Volume 5, Issue 4 of KBR

Flax Cookies
Submitted by Mrs. Gloria Wall, SK

1 cup buttermilk
½ cup canola or olive oil
1 teaspoon vanilla
½ teaspoon salt
1 teaspoon cinnamon
1 ½ cups wheat flour
3 cups quick oats

½ cup applesauce
2 eggs
1 cup brown sugar
1 teaspoon baking soda
1 cup raisins
1 cup ground flax seeds

Preheat oven to 350°. Beat all wet ingredients with sugar, salt, soda and cinnamon. Add raisins, then add flour, flaxseed and quick oats. If necessary, gradually add more milk or water to get a "flowing" dough. Drop by teaspoons onto cookie sheet and bake for 15-18 minutes.

Received for Volume 5, Issue 4 of KBR

$250 Cookies
Submitted by Naomi Holter, SK

"A lady had these cookies at a restaurant, and asked for the recipe. The waitress said she could have it for $250. The lady thought the waitress meant $2.50, but when she got her bill, she discovered she had been charged $250! The lady paid her bill, then shared the recipe with her friends. I now share it with you."

2 cups butter
4-6 cups white flour
2 cups brown sugar
4 eggs
2 teaspoons vanilla
5 cups oatmeal, ground into course flour
1 teaspoon salt
2 teaspoons baking powder
2 teaspoons baking soda
24 ounces chocolate chips
3 cups chopped nuts (optional)

Cream butter and both sugars; add eggs and vanilla. Mix together with flour, oatmeal, salt, baking powder and soda. Add chocolate chips and nuts. Scoop with a cookie scoop or shape into balls; place 2 inches apart on ungreased cookie sheets. Bake for 10 minutes at 375°. Depending on size of cookies you make, this recipe makes approximately 100 cookies.

Printed in Volume 4, Issue 2 of KBR

Oatmeal Coconut Cookies
Submitted by Alida Royal, OR

3 cups wheat flour
1 cup butter
2 teaspoons baking powder
2 teaspoons baking soda
1 ½ cups raw sugar
1 teaspoon salt
4 eggs

4 cups oatmeal

2 cups dried and shredded coconut

2 cups almonds, chopped

Combine flour, baking powder, baking soda, sugar, and salt. In a large bowl, beat the butter, sugars and eggs. Gradually blend in dry ingredients. Fold in last three ingredients. Shape into balls. Bake at 350° for 10-12 minutes.

Printed in Volume 5, Issue 4 of KBR

Whole Wheat Sugar Cookies
Submitted by Esther Lang, WI

1 ½ cups sugar

1 cup melted butter

¼ cup milk

2 teaspoons lemon peel

2 teaspoons vanilla

2 eggs

4 cups wheat flour

2 teaspoons baking powder

1 teaspoon baking soda

1 teaspoon salt

1 teaspoon nutmeg

Cinnamon sugar for dusting/rolling

Mix first 6 ingredients in order given, then add dry ingredients and mix well.

Pan variation: Press dough onto greased 18x14-inch cookie sheet; sprinkle with cinnamon sugar. Bake at 350° for 25 minutes. Cool 10 minutes and then cut into 64 pieces.

Drop cookie variation: Refrigerate dough 1 hour. Shape into small 1-inch balls and roll in cinnamon sugar. Bake on an ungreased cookie sheet at 375° for 8-10 minutes or until done. Cool 1 minute and then remove.

Printed in Volume 8, Issue 1 of KBR

Healthy Chocolate Cookies
Submitted Tessa Blackstad, WA

"This is our family's favorite recipe. My dad enjoys these in his lunch!"

¼ cup butter or oil
½ cup applesauce
1 cup brown sugar
1 cup sugar
2 eggs
1 teaspoon vanilla

1 teaspoon baking soda
1½ cups wheat flour
1½ cups white flour
1 teaspoon salt
1 cup chocolate chips

Combine butter, applesauce, sugars, eggs and vanilla. Mix at least 5 minutes in a mixer; until light and fluffy. Add flour, baking soda and salt. Mix just until moistened. Fold in chocolate chips. Bake 10-12 minutes at 350°. Use greased pans.

Printed in Volume 5, Issue 4 of KBR

Molasses Crinkle Cookies
Submitted by Alison Sauder, PA

"These are our favorite winter cookies, with our favorite spice...cinnamon! It also includes two other spices: cloves and ginger."

¾ cup shortening
1 cup brown sugar
1 egg, beaten
¼ cup molasses
2 ¼ cups flour
¼ teaspoon salt
2 teaspoons soda
½ teaspoon cloves
1 teaspoon cinnamon
1 teaspoon ginger
White sugar, for rolling

Cream shortening and sugar. Add egg and molasses. Beat. Add flour, salt, soda and spices and mix well. Shape into balls the size of walnuts. Roll in white sugar. Bake at 350° for 8-10 minutes.

Printed in Volume 8, Issue 1 of KBR

Dark Chocolate
Hazelnut Biscotti
Submitted by Hannah Schoenfelder, MI

1 cup sugar
⅔ cup butter, softened
1 (12-ounce) package semi-sweet chocolate chips, melted
3 eggs
1 teaspoon vanilla
2 ¾ cups all-purpose flour
2 ½ teaspoons baking powder
¼ teaspoon salt
¾ cup finely chopped hazelnuts
or almonds

Coating:
1 (12-ounce) package
semi-sweet chocolate chips
2 tablespoons shortening

Heat oven to 350°. Combine sugar and butter in large mixer bowl. Beat at medium speed, scraping sides of bowl often, until well mixed (1-2 minutes). Add 2 cups of melted chocolate chips, eggs and vanilla; continue beating until well mixed (1-2 minutes). Reduce speed to low; add flour, baking powder and salt. Beat until well mixed (1-2 minutes). Stir in hazelnuts by hand. Divide dough in half and shape each half into 14-inch long roll. Place 5 inches apart on ungreased cookie sheet. Flatten each roll to 2-inch width. Bake for 25 minutes or until set. Cool on cookie sheet for 1 hour. Reduce oven temperature to 300°. Cut roll diagonally into ½-inch slices with serrated knife. Place on ungreased cookie sheets, cut side down. Bake for 10 minutes. Turn slices; continue baking for 12-15 minutes or until dry and crisp. Cool completely. Melt 2 cups chocolate chips and the shortening over low heat, stirring occasionally, until smooth (2-4 minutes). Dip cookies halfway into chocolate. Place on cooling rack over waxed paper until set. Yields about 4 ½ dozen.

Received for Volume 8, Issue 2 of KBR

Lemon Cream-Filled Cookies

Submitted by Martha Joy Bullington, AL

"These are wonderful cookies to make for a tea party and are a delicious treat!"

Cookies:

¾ cup butter, softened
½ cup confectioners' sugar
2 teaspoons lemon extract
1 ½ cups all-purpose flour
¼ cup cornstarch

Filling:

¼ cup butter, softened
1 cup confectioners' sugar
1 tablespoon heavy cream
Juice of 1 squeezed lemon (2 tablespoons)
Grated zest of 1 lemon (2-3 teaspoons)

Cookie Dough: In a medium-sized bowl cream butter with an electric mixer set at medium speed. Add sugar, and beat until smooth, scraping down sides of bowl as needed. Add lemon extract, and beat until light and fluffy. Then add flour and cornstarch; blend at low speed until thoroughly combined. Gather dough into 2 balls of equal size and flatten into disks. Wrap the disks tightly in plastic wrap or a plastic bag. Refrigerate for 1 hour.

Filling: In a small bowl beat butter with mixer until fluffy. Gradually add sugar while continuing to beat. Add cream, lemon juice, and lemon zest. Mix until thoroughly blended and set aside. To harden filling quickly, refrigerate for 15-20 minutes. At this point, preheat the oven to 325°. Using a floured rolling pin, roll the chilled cookie dough on a floured board to ¼-inch thickness. Cut circles with a 2-inch-diameter cookie cutter or drinking glass. Place circles of dough on ungreased cookie sheets, ½-inch apart. Continue rolling out and cutting dough scraps until all dough is used. Bake for 15-17 minutes, or until edges begin to brown. Immediately transfer cookies with a spatula to a cool, flat surface. When cookies are cool, spread a cookie with 1 teaspoon of lemon cream. Place another cookie on top of the filling to make a sandwich. Complete entire batch. Enjoy!

Received for Volume 8, Issue 2 of KBR

Brown Sugar Shortbread
Submitted by Maggie Bullington, AL

1 cup butter (no substitutes), softened
½ cup packed brown sugar
2 ¼ cups all-purpose flour

In a mixing bowl, cream butter and sugar together. Gradually stir in flour. Turn onto a lightly-floured surface and knead until smooth—about 3 minutes. Pat into ⅓-inch thick rectangle measuring 11x8-inches. Cut into 2x1-inch strips. Place one inch apart on ungreased baking sheets. Prick with a fork. Bake at 300° for 25 minutes or until bottom begins to brown. Cool for 5 minutes; remove to wire rack to cool completely. Yields 3 ½ dozen.

Received for Volume 8, Issue 2 of KBR

Black Pepper-Cardamom Sugar Cookies
Submitted by Monica Watt, TX

"Whoever said black pepper is not a dessert spice?! The combination of the two spices lends these cookies a delicate and beautiful flavor."

½ cup butter
¾ cup sugar
½ teaspoon ground cardamom
¼ teaspoon ground black pepper
1 egg or 2 egg yolks
½ teaspoon vanilla
1 tablespoon milk or cream
1 ¼ cups flour
¼ teaspoon salt
¼ teaspoon baking powder

Cream butter until light and fluffy; beat in sugar. Add cardamom, pepper, eggs, and vanilla. Beat thoroughly. Add milk. Sift together flour, salt, and baking powder. Stir into the butter mixture and blend well. Arrange by teaspoonfuls on a buttered cookie sheet, one inch apart. Bake 8 minutes. Makes 50-60 little tea cookies.

Chocolate Chip Cookies
Submitted by Rebekah Wall, SK

1 cup butter
¾ cup brown sugar
¼ cup sugar
2 eggs
1 teaspoon vanilla
1 package vanilla instant pudding
2 ¼ cups flour
1 teaspoon baking soda
6 ounces chocolate chips

Cream butter, sugars, and eggs. Add vanilla, pudding, flour, soda and chocolate chips. Mix well. Drop onto greased cookie sheets and bake at 375° for 15 minutes. Yields about 4 dozen.

Apple Hermits
Submitted by Emily Parish, MO

2 cups soft white wheat flour
1 teaspoon baking soda
1 teaspoon ground cinnamon
1 teaspoon ground cloves
½ teaspoon ground nutmeg
½ cup (1 stick) softened butter
1 ½ cups sugar
1 egg, beaten
1 cup walnuts
1 cup chopped apples
1 cup raisins (optional)

Preheat oven to 350°. Line cookie sheets with parchment paper or foil. In a medium-sized bowl, sift together flour, baking soda, cinnamon, cloves, nutmeg, and salt. In a large mixing bowl, cream butter until light and fluffy. Mix in sugar and egg. Stir in flour mixture, and mix thoroughly (if it is too crumbly sprinkle a little water in it). Slowly add nuts, apples, and raisins. Roll into balls and place on cookie sheets. Bake for 12 to 14 minutes. Makes about 24 cookies.

↳ *Pies & Tarts*

Pumpkin Patch Pie
Submitted by Susannah Dorfsmith, CA

1 pie pumpkin (about 3 pounds)
⅔ cup sugar, divided
1 teaspoon cinnamon
⅛ teaspoon salt
1 ½ teaspoons pumpkin pie spice
3 beaten eggs
1 (5-ounce) can evaporated milk
½ cup milk
1 (9-inch) pie crust

Wash pumpkin; cut a 5-inch circle around top stem. Remove top and set aside; discard loose fibers and save seeds, if desired, for roasting. Combine ⅓ cup sugar, cinnamon and salt; sprinkle around inside of pumpkin. Replace the top. Place on a greased baking sheet and bake at 325° for about 1 ½ hours or until very tender. Cool. Scoop out pumpkin; puree in a blender until smooth. Place 2 cups pureed pumpkin in a bowl. Add pumpkin pie spice and remaining sugar. Stir in eggs, evaporated milk and milk until well blended. Pour filling into unbaked, 9-inch crust. Bake at 375° for 45-50 minutes or until knife inserted in center comes out clean. Cool completely and then serve with whipped topping, if desired. Yields 6-8 servings.

Printed in Volume 1, Issue 4 of KBR

Mile-High Raspberry Pie
Submitted by the Bullington Family, AL

Pie crust:
  ½ cup butter
  ¼ cup brown sugar
  1 cup flour
  ½ cup chopped nutmeats

Filling:
  1 (10-ounce) package frozen raspberries
  1 cup sugar
  3 egg whites
  1 cup whipping cream

Combine crust ingredients until blended; spread on a cookie sheet and bake at 400° for 12-15 minutes. Cool and spread crumbs in a 9-10-inch pie pan. (A baked pie shell or a cookie-crumb crust may also be used.) Whip cream. Beat thawed berries, sugar and egg whites in a large mixer bowl for 15 minutes at high speed. Mixture will be like meringue. Fold in cream. Pile mixture into prepared pie pan and freeze for 6-8 hours. Serve frozen wedges garnished with fresh berries if desired.

Zucchini Pie
Submitted by Anna Kirk, WA

"Tastes just like apple pie!"

Filling:
  6-8 cups seeded, peeled,
    sliced zucchini
  ⅔ cup lemon juice
  1 cup sugar
  1 ½ teaspoons cinnamon
  ¼ teaspoon nutmeg

Pie crust:
  4 cups whole wheat flour
  ½ cup sugar
  ½ teaspoon salt
  1 ½ cups butter

To prepare pastry, combine dry ingredients and cut in butter until crumbly. Press about ½ of the mixture into a 13x9-inch pan and bake for 10 minutes. Set aside. For filling, cook sliced zucchini in lemon juice until tender. Add sugar and 1 teaspoon of the cinnamon and simmer 1 minute. Stir in ½ cup of remaining pastry mixture. Simmer until it is thickened, while stirring constantly. Cool. Pour zucchini mixture over crust. Mix remaining ½ teaspoon cinnamon and ¼ teaspoon nutmeg with remaining pastry mixture. Sprinkle over pie and bake at 350° for 35-40 minutes or until lightly browned.

Printed in Volume 1, Issue 4 of KBR

Lemon Meringue Pie
Submitted by Mrs. Dana Bryant, KS

"I learned to make this when I was twelve years old. The first one I made by myself, I forgot to bake the pie shell!"

½ cup lemon juice

1 teaspoon grated lemon rind or ¼ teaspoon lemon extract

1 (15-ounce) can sweetened condensed milk

2 eggs, yolks separated

¼ teaspoon cream of tartar

4 tablespoons sugar

1 (9-inch) pie crust

Combine lemon juice and rind or extract. Gradually mix in milk. Add egg yolks and mix well. Pour into baked pie shell. In chilled bowl, beat egg whites. Adding cream of tartar, beat until stiff and then gradually add sugar. Spoon stiff egg whites onto lemon mixture, spreading carefully to edges of pie pan. Form peak on top by gently tapping spoon into whites and pulling up.

egg whites

"When beating egg whites, start with room temperature eggs and a completely clean beater and bowl. Any bits of dust or residue might hinder the beating process."

Bake at 325° only until peaks are brown. Watch carefully or it will burn. To make a really pretty pie, use 4-6 egg whites to make the meringue.

Printed in Volume 2, Issue 3 of KBR

Pumpkin Pecan Pie
Submitted by Emily Savine, NY

1 egg, slightly beaten
1 cup pureed pumpkin
⅓ cup granulated sugar
1 teaspoon pumpkin pie spice

Pecan layer:

⅔ cup corn syrup
2 eggs, lightly beaten
½ cup granulated sugar
3 tablespoons butter, melted
½ teaspoon vanilla extract
1 cup pecan halves
1 (9-inch) pie crust

For pumpkin layer: Combine egg, pumpkin, sugar and pie spice in medium-sized bowl. Spread over bottom of pie shell. For pecan layer: Combine corn syrup, eggs, sugar, butter, and vanilla in same bowl; stir in pecans. Slowly spoon the mixture over pumpkin layer. Bake at 350° for 50 minutes or until filling is set. Cool on wire rack.

Received for Volume 6, Issue 4 of KBR

Pumpkin Pie
Submitted by Sarah Niemela, MI

2 (8-inch) pie crusts
1 ½ cups brown sugar
1 teaspoon salt
4 teaspoons pumpkin pie spice
1 teaspoon maple flavoring

4 eggs, slightly beaten
1 (29-ounce) can pumpkin
2 cups hot milk
1 cup hot cream

Mix all ingredients together in order given. Put in two pastry-lined pie plates. Bake for 10 minutes at 425° and 40 more minutes at 350° or until a knife inserted near edge comes out clean.

Received for Volume 6, Issue 4 of KBR

Healthy Apple Pie
Submitted by Victoria Steiner, IL
"This is delicious served with homemade ice cream on top!"

1 (8-inch) pie shell, unbaked
1 cup cream
¾ cup sugar or ⅜ cup honey
⅓ cup flour (can use whole wheat)
½-¾ teaspoon cinnamon
¼ teaspoon salt
Apples, peeled and sliced, to fill up the pie

Topping:
½ cup flour
¼ cup butter
½ cup sucanat or brown sugar

Sprinkle 1 tablespoon flour and 1 tablespoon sugar on top of crust before adding apples and filling. This helps prevent the crust from becoming soggy. Place apples in crust. Mix pie ingredients and pour over apples. Combine topping ingredients and sprinkle on top of pie. Bake 10 minutes at 375°, and then 35 minutes at 350°. Enjoy!

Printed in Volume 7, Issue 2 of KBR

Black Raspberry Pie
Submitted by Bethany Zimmerman, PA

1 ½ cups raspberry juice
1 ⅓ cups water
1 cup sugar
4 tablespoons thermflo
1 (8-inch) pie crust, unbaked

Cook over heat until thickened. Pour into unbaked pie shell and top with pie dough or crumbs. Bake at 350° until golden.

Printed in Volume 7, Issue 2 of KBR

Chopped Apple Pie
Submitted by Beth Ann Cragun, IN
"The secret to this pie is the way you cut the apples; flavors mix better with smaller pieces."

3-5 firm baking apples (to fill crust)
⅔-1 cup sugar
¼ teaspoon salt
2 tablespoons flour
1 teaspoon cinnamon
1-1 ½ tablespoons butter
Your favorite 2-crust pie dough

Dice apples fairly small. Mix all dry ingredients. Mix with apples. Put in crust. Dot top with thin slices of butter. Make lattice top crust. Bake for 10 minutes at 450°. Turn oven down to 350° and bake for additional 35-45 minutes or until crust is browned. After pie is taken from the oven, sprinkle top with a little sugar.

Received for Volume 7, Issue 2 of KBR

French Silk Chocolate Pie
Submitted by Rachael Bryant, KS
"This is my mom's favorite pie recipe, and now I make it on holidays for our family!"

¾ cup sugar
½ cup softened butter
2 (1-ounce) packets pre-melted chocolate
1 teaspoon vanilla
2 eggs
Whipping cream
1 (8-inch) pie crust, pre-baked

Combine sugar, butter, chocolate and vanilla. Blend well. Add eggs one at a time, beating thoroughly for a total or 3-5 minutes. Pour into baked pastry shell. Serve with whipped cream and walnuts on top.

Received for Volume 7, Issue 2 of KBR

Grape Pie

Submitted by Beth Ann Cragun, IN

"This recipe came from my great-grandma. My grandma now makes it and shared the recipe with me."

> 3 cups Concord grapes, halved and seeded
> ⅔-1 cup sugar
> 2 tablespoons flour
> ¼ teaspoon salt
> 1 tablespoon lemon juice (optional)
> 1-1 ½ tablespoons butter
> Your favorite 2-crust pie dough

Mix sugar, flour and salt. Mix all ingredients except for butter and dough together. Pour into one pie crust. Dot top with thin slices of butter. Make lattice with the top crust. Bake at 450° for 10 minutes. Reduce heat to 350° and bake for additional 35-45 minutes. After pie is taken from oven, lightly sprinkle top with sugar.

Printed in Volume 7, Issue 2 of KBR

tip

pie decorations
"Cut dough into desired shapes, moisten back lightly, and lay on top of crust. Bake as usual."

Jell-o Pie

Submitted by Bethany Ward, TX

"We use orange flavored jello and this tastes like a 'dream sicle'!"

> 8 whole graham crackers, finely crushed
> 7 tablespoons melted butter
> 1 carton of whipped topping
> 1 box of jello, any flavor

Put graham cracker crumbs into a pie pan. Pour in the melted butter and stir around with your fingers, press to fit into the pan. Pour the jello powder directly into the carton of whipped topping. Stir until well mixed. Spread on top of your crust, cover with plastic wrap and freeze until hard.

Received for Volume 7, Issue 2 of KBR

Peanut Butter Pie
Submitted by Beth Ann Cragun, IN

2 chocolate Oreo pie crusts or graham cracker crusts

Filling:
> 1 cup melted butter or margarine
> 1 cup packed brown sugar
> 1 (18-ounce) jar creamy peanut butter
> 16 ounces whipped topping

Topping:
> 1 cup milk chocolate chips
> 2 tablespoons butter or margarine
> 2 tablespoons milk
> 1 tablespoon white corn syrup

Combine filling ingredients with mixer and pour into crusts. Put in freezer for 1 hour. Put topping ingredients in saucepan over medium heat. Stir until melted and well mixed. Pour and spread over chilled pie. Keep refrigerated until ready to eat. May also make ahead and freeze.

Received for Volume 7, Issue 2 of KBR

Lime Pie
Submitted by Amanda Silvey, AR

"Very easy. Great for the holidays."

> 1 (8-ounce) package cream cheese
> 1 can sweetened condensed milk
> 1 (8-ounce) container whipped topping
> ⅓ cup lemon juice
> 1 small box lime jello
> 2 (8-inch) graham cracker crusts

Mix cream cheese, milk and whipped topping. Add lemon juice and jello; mix. Put into crusts. Refrigerate. Makes 2 pies.

Printed in Volume 7, Issue 1 of KBR

Raspberry Custard Pie

Submitted by Maurya Petrick, TN

1 (9-inch) pie crust

Filling:
3 eggs
¾ cup honey
⅓ cup evaporated milk
½ cup flour
3 cups raspberries
2 teaspoons vanilla
Dash of salt

Topping:
½ cup flour
¼ cup brown sugar
¼ cup cold butter

Preheat oven to 400°. Combine all filling ingredients and mix well; set aside. Mix flour and sugar together. Cut the cold butter into the flour/sugar mixture. Put filling into a prepared pie shell of your choice. Sprinkle topping over the filling. Bake for 10 minutes. Reduce heat to 350°. Bake an additional 45-50 minutes. Eat hot or cooled with a scoop of ice cream!

blind baking crusts

"When a recipe calls for a pre-baked shell, simply pre-pare your crust, chill it well, dock it, and blind bake it.

"Docking allows air to escape from under the crust during baking to prevent air pockets forming, and simply entails pricking the bottom of the crust with a fork a few times.

"To blind bake a crust, cut a circle of parchment paper big enough to fit down into your chilled crust and then stick up a little around the edges. Add the paper to your crust and then fill the bottom of your paper-lined crust with dried beans of any sort. These beans will act as weights to hold your crust to shape during baking. You may need to remove these beans during the last few minutes of baking to finish cooking the crust."

Lemonade Pie

Submitted by Lauren Dornbirer, OH

"This is one of my favorite desserts—so tasty and simple! I prefer it frozen."

1 (6-ounce) can frozen lemonade, thawed
1 (8-ounce) tub of Coolwhip or whipped cream
1 (14-ounce) can sweetened condensed milk
1 (9-inch) graham cracker crust

Mix the first three ingredients and spoon into the crust. Cover and chill for six hours or overnight. Enjoy!

Vanilla Cream Pie

Submitted by Maggie Bullington, AL

½ cup sugar
3 tablespoons flour
1 tablespoon cornstarch
¼ teaspoon salt
1 ½ cups milk
3 egg yolks, slightly beaten
1 tablespoon butter
1 teaspoon vanilla
1 (8-inch) pie crust, pre-baked

Combine sugar, flour, cornstarch and salt in top of double boiler. Gradually blend in milk, then add egg yolks and butter. Place over rapidly boiling water so pan is touching water. Cook, stirring constantly, until thick and smooth—about 7 minutes. Remove from heat. Add vanilla and stir until smooth and blended. Pour hot filling into pie shell and chill several hours before serving. Yields 6-8 servings.

Berry Special Pie

Submitted by Elizabeth Bryan, FL

½ cup semisweet chocolate chips
1 ½ teaspoons butter
1 (8-inch) pie crust, pre-baked
2 cups fresh raspberries or 1 cup each of strawberries and raspberries
1 ½ cups heavy whipping cream
1 tablespoon sugar

In a small, heavy saucepan, melt chocolate chips and butter; stir until smooth. Spread over the bottom of pie shell. Top with berries. Beat cream on medium speed until soft peaks form; beat in sugar and continue beating until stiff peaks form. Refrigerate until serving. Yields 6-8 servings.

Printed in Volume 7, Issue 2 of KBR

Peanut Butter Pie

Submitted by Beth Ann Cragun, IN

2 chocolate Oreo pie crusts or graham cracker crusts

Filling:
    1 cup melted butter
    1 cup packed brown sugar
    1 (18-ounce) jar creamy peanut butter
    16 ounces whipped topping

Topping:
    1 cup milk chocolate chips
    2 tablespoons butter
    2 tablespoons milk
    1 tablespoon white corn syrup

Combine filling ingredients with mixer and pour into crusts. Put in freezer for 1 hour. Put topping ingredients in saucepan over medium heat. Stir until melted and well mixed. Pour and spread over chilled pie. Keep refrigerated until ready to eat. You can also make ahead and freeze.

Received for Volume 7, Issue 2 of KBR

Pudding Pie

Submitted by Bethany Ward, TX

8 whole graham crackers, finely crushed
7 tablespoons melted butter
1 package pudding, any flavor
1 ½ cups milk
1 carton whipped topping

Put graham cracker crumbs directly into your pie pan. Pour the butter over the crumbs and stir with your fingers. Press to fill the pan. In a bowl, mix the milk and pudding powder. Mix in half the carton of whipped topping into your pudding and then spread on top of your pie crust. Cover with plastic wrap and freeze until hard.

tip

the art of pie crusts

"*When making pie crusts, be sure to start out with all cold ingredients. Cut butter or lard into small pieces and then place in the refrigerator until needed. Measure your dry ingredients into a bowl, combine and cool in the fridge. Always use icy water in your crusts.*"

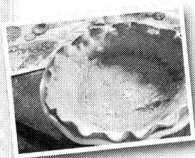

Pie Crust Mix

Submitted by Beth Ann Cragun, IN

"*This saves a lot of time if you make pies often.*"

3-pound can shortening
5-pound bag flour
Salt

Put a layer of flour, then of shortening in a large container. Lightly sprinkle salt over it. Continue layering until all of the flour and shortening are used. Cut together with pastry blender until crumbly. Will store several months if kept at room temperature in an airtight container. To make pie crust, get out amount needed (approximately one heaping cup per pie) and add ice water slowly until it is the right consistency to roll out.

Double Crust Pie Pastry
Submitted by Brittany Schlichter, TX

4 cups flour
1 ¾ cups shortening
2 teaspoons salt

½ cup water
1 egg
1 tablespoon vinegar

Use fork to mix flour, shortening and salt. In separate dish, beat remaining ingredients. Combine the two mixtures, stirring with fork until all ingredients are moistened. Mold the dough into a ball. Chill at least 15 minutes before rolling into desired shape.

Berry Tarts
Submitted by Elizabeth Adams, IA

"These are such a delectable, simple summertime tea treat! I altered a fruit pizza recipe to make small tarts for a young ladies' Bible study gathering."

Sugar cookie dough (page 159)
½ cup sugar
1 (8-ounce) package cream cheese
1 teaspoon vanilla
Blueberries, raspberries, blackberries or slices of strawberries
Glaze:
⅜ cup water
2 tablespoons lemon juice
½ cup orange juice
1 ½ tablespoons cornstarch or arrow-root powder
½ cup sugar

Roll out your favorite sugar cookie dough on a floured surface. Cut into circles about 5 inches in diameter, slightly pressing down to make a small edge (like a tart). Bake as directed in cookie recipe. Once fully cooled, mix together sugar, cream cheese, and vanilla. Spread mixture on shells with spatula or knife. Press fruit into each tart. Put glaze ingredients in a saucepan and cook over low heat until glaze is formed. Drizzle each tart with bit of glaze. Enjoy with a cup of tea!

Printed in Volume 8, Issue 2 of KBR

Pecan Tarts

Submitted by Jessica Steiner, OH

1 (3-ounce) package cream cheese, softened
½ cup butter or margarine, softened
1 cup flour
¼ teaspoon salt

Filling:

1 egg
¾ cup packed dark brown sugar
1 tablespoon butter or margarine, melted
1 teaspoon vanilla extract
⅔ cup chopped pecans

In a mixing bowl, beat cream cheese and butter; blend in flour and salt. Chill for 1 hour. Shape into 1-inch balls; press into the bottom and up the sides of greased mini muffin cups. For filling, beat the egg in a mixing bowl. Add brown sugar, butter and vanilla; mix well. Stir in pecans. Spoon into shells. Bake at 325° for 25-30 minutes. Cool in pan on a wire rack. Yields about 20 tarts.

Printed in Volume 8, Issue 2 of KBR

Cranberry Tassies

Submitted by Maggie Bullington, AL

½ cup butter, softened
3 ounces cream cheese, softened
1 cup all-purpose flour
1 egg
¾ cup packed brown sugar
1 tablespoon butter, melted
1 teaspoon orange zest, grated
½ cup cranberries, chopped
½ cup pecans, chopped

Cream ½ cup butter and cream cheese; stir in flour and blend thoroughly. Cover and chill for 1 hour. In a separate bowl, mix together egg, sugar, melted butter and orange zest. Fold in cranberries and pecans. Remove chilled dough from fridge and roll into 24 one-inch balls. Place each in a mini muffin cup, pressing dough along the bottom and up the sides. Spoon cranberry mixture evenly into the center of each cup and bake at 325° for 30 minutes or until cranberry filling is set. Allow to cool before serving. Enjoy!

Received for Volume 8, Issue 4 of KBR

Candy

Sugar Plum Mints
Submitted by Jessica Steiner, OH

½ cup butter
¼ cup whipping cream, heated
Approximately 5 ½ cups confectioner's sugar
Flavoring, as desired

Cream butter. Add sugar gradually and blend thoroughly together. Add heated cream and flavoring. Press small amounts into molds. Remove at once to wax paper. You can also use food coloring to make different colors.

Printed in Volume 8, Issue 2 of KBR

Mint Patties
Submitted by Sarah Bryant, KS

"My mom began making these for my dad shortly after they married and they were immediately his favorite! Each year we make these and share them with our neighbors."

1 cup sweetened condensed milk
10 drops peppermint extract
4 cups powdered sugar
3 bags chocolate chips or chunks
1 tablespoon shortening

Stir milk and extract in blender. Add little bits of sugar at a time until the mixture is not too stiff or sticky. Roll into 1-inch balls and flatten unto wax paper-covered cookie sheets. Place in freezer until cold. Melt chocolate and shortening on low and dip mints into chocolate. Place back on wax paper and freeze. Store in freezer. Makes approximately 70 mints.

Printed in Volume 2, Issue 1 of KBR

Holiday Fudge
Submitted by Megan Rippel, WI

"This is a really good fudge recipe and it always turns out right! Just make sure you cut up the marshmallows and chocolates before you start. If you like nuts, you can add some after adding the chocolate."

4 cups sugar
1 teaspoon vanilla
1 cup butter
1 cup milk
25 large marshmallows, cut into pieces
2 ounces unsweetened chocolate squares, cut into pieces

Mix sugar, vanilla, butter and milk together in a large pan. Bring to a rolling boil for 2 minutes. Turn off heat. Add marshmallows and stir until they are melted. Add the chocolates and stir until they are all melted. Pour the fudge into a greased 13x9-inch pan and let it set up in the refrigerator.

Printed in Volume 2, Issue 1 of KBR

Cakes & Frostings

Raspberry-Almond Crumb Cake
Submitted by the Bullington Family, AL

"We normally triple this recipe and bake it in a 15x10-inch pan for a crowd. You can also use frozen raspberries; feel free to cut out the almonds if you wish."

1 cup flour
⅓ cup sugar
⅛ teaspoon salt
¼ cup chilled butter, cut up
½ teaspoon baking powder
¼ teaspoon baking soda
⅓ cup sour cream
2 tablespoons milk
1 teaspoon vanilla

½ teaspoon almond extract
1 egg
3 ounces cream cheese, softened
2 tablespoons sugar
1 egg white
¼ cup raspberry jam
⅓ cup fresh raspberries
2 tablespoons sliced almonds

Preheat oven to 350°. Combine flour, sugar and salt. Cut in butter. Reserve ½ cup of this mixture for topping. Combine remaining mixture, baking powder and baking soda. Add sour cream, milk, flavorings and egg. Beat at medium speed. Spoon into a greased 8-inch round pan. Combine cream cheese, 2 tablespoons sugar and egg white. Beat. Spread over batter and then dot with the jam. Top with raspberries. Combine reserved topping with almonds; sprinkle over raspberries. Bake at 350° for 30 minutes.

Pumpkin Roll
Submitted by Beth Ann Cragun, IN

3 eggs
1 cup sugar
1 teaspoon lemon juice
⅔ cup pumpkin
¾ cup self-rising flour
1 teaspoon cinnamon
1 teaspoon baking soda
½ teaspoon allspice

Beat eggs on high for 5 minutes. Then beat in sugar and lemon juice with eggs. Fold in pumpkin. Sift together flour, cinnamon, baking soda and all-spice. Fold into pumpkin mixture. Spread in greased and floured 15x10-inch pan. Bake at 375° for 15 minutes. Cool for 5 minutes. Loosen sides and turn out on damp cloth. Sprinkle cake with powdered sugar then roll up in cloth until completely cooled. Unroll and spread icing (recipe below) over cake. If desired, sprinkle with chopped walnuts. Roll back up and slice in ½-inch slices.

Cream Cheese Icing:
6-8 ounces cream cheese
1 cup powdered sugar
½ cup margarine
½ teaspoon vanilla

Mix well and spread over cake.

Hershey Cake
Submitted by Abigail Gibbs, IN

1 chocolate cake, baked and cooled
1 large package whipped topping
1 (8-ounce) package cream cheese
½ cup powdered sugar
6-7 Hershey chocolate bars

Put Hershey bars in the freezer for 1 hour. Then put five of them in a Ziploc bag and mash them up. Mix whipped topping, cream cheese, powdered sugar and the crushed Hershey bars. Ice the cake with this mixture and decorate the top by shaving the remaining chocolate bars with a vegetable peeler and sprinkling the shavings over the top of the cake.

Cinnamon-Laced Sour Cream Pound Cake
Submitted by Maggie Bullington, AL

"We have good success when we cut down the sugar in recipes such as this one."

½ cup chopped pecans
2 tablespoons sugar
1 teaspoon ground cinnamon
1 cup butter, softened
2 cups sugar
2 eggs

2 cups sifted cake flour
1 teaspoon baking powder
⅛ teaspoon salt
1 teaspoon vanilla extract
1 cup sour cream

Combine pecans, 2 tablespoons sugar and cinnamon, stirring well. Set aside. Cream butter; gradually add 2 cups sugar, beating well at medium speed of mixer. Add eggs, one at a time, beating after each addition. Combine flour, baking powder and salt; add to creamed mixture, mixing just until blended. Stir in vanilla. Gently fold sour cream into batter. Pour half of batter into a greased and floured 10-inch bundt pan. Sprinkle half of the pecan mixture over batter. Repeat procedure. Bake at 350° for 55 to 60 minutes or until a wooden pick inserted in center comes out clean. Cool in pan 10 minutes; remove from pan, and let cool completely on a wire rack.

Coffee Crumb Cake

Submitted by Rebekah Wall, SK

2 cups flour
2 cups brown sugar
½ cup margarine
1 cup hot coffee

1 teaspoon vanilla
1 egg
1 teaspoon baking soda
¼ teaspoon salt

Mix flour, brown sugar, and margarine until crumbly. Reserve 1 cup. To remaining crumbs add rest of ingredients. Pour batter into greased 9x9-inch pan. Cover with crumbs. Bake at 350° for 30-40 minutes.

Gold Cake

Submitted by Maggie Bullington, AL

"This makes a good birthday cake. Pair with your favorite frosting or icing and decorate as elaborately as desired!"

½ cup butter, softened
1 tablespoon grated lemon rind (optional)
1 ¾ cups sugar
6 egg yolks
2 ½ cups sifted cake flour
1 tablespoon baking powder
½ teaspoon salt
1 cup, plus 3 tablespoons milk

Cream butter; add lemon rind, if desired. Gradually add sugar, beating well at medium speed of an electric mixer. Add egg yolks, one at a time, beating well after each addition. Combine flour, baking powder and salt. Add to creamed mixture alternately with the milk, beginning and ending with flour mixture. Mix after each addition. Pour batter into 2 greased and floured 9-inch round cake pans. Make at 350° for 25-30 minutes or until a wooden pick inserted in center come out clean. Cool in pans 10 minutes. Remove from pans and let cool completely on wire racks. Frost and decorate as desired. Yields one two-layer, 9-inch golden cake.

Perfect Chocolate Cake
Submitted by Caitlin Anderson , CA

"A very moist and soft cake."

1 cup cocoa
2 cups boiling water
1 cup butter
2 ½ cup sugar
4 eggs
2 teaspoons vanilla
2 ¾ cups flour
2 teaspoons baking soda
½ teaspoon salt
½ teaspoon baking powder

Caramel Frosting:
½ cup butter, melted
1 cup brown sugar
¼ cup milk
3 ¼ cups powdered sugar

Stir cocoa and water until smooth. Cool. Beat butter, sugar, eggs, and vanilla at high speed for about 5 minutes. Sift together dry ingredients and add alternately with cocoa mixture. Pour in 13x9-inch pan and bake at 350° for 40 minutes. Cool. For the frosting, mix melted butter and brown sugar together and boil for one minute, or until slightly thick. Add milk and sugar, adding more sugar until you reach desired spreading consistency. Spread on cake.

tip

greasing pans
"When baking a cake, always use butter or oil to grease the pan, and then coat with flour. Thus, the cake will come out more smoothly when baked."

Family Favorite Cheesecake
Submitted by Christy & Abigail Mothershed, WV

2 ½ cups graham cracker crumbs (about 40 squares)
⅓ cup sugar
½ teaspoon ground cinnamon
½ cup butter, melted

Filling:

3 packages (8 ounces each) cream cheese, softened
1 ½ cups sugar
1 teaspoon vanilla extract
4 eggs, separated

Topping:
 ½ cup sour cream
 2 tablespoons sugar
 ½ teaspoon vanilla extract
 ½ cup whipping cream, whipped

In a small bowl, combine the cracker crumbs, sugar and cinnamon; stir in the butter. Press onto the bottom and 2 inches up the sides of a greased 9-inch springform pan. Bake at 350° for 5 minutes. Cool on a wire rack. Reduce heat to 325°. In a mixing bowl, beat cream cheese, sugar and vanilla until smooth. Add egg yolks; beat on low just until combined. In a small mixing bowl, beat egg whites until soft peaks form; fold into cream cheese mixture. Pour over crust. Bake for one hour or until center is almost set. Cool on wire rack for 10 minutes. Carefully run a knife around edge of pan to loosen; cool one hour longer. Refrigerate until completely cooled. Combine the sour cream, sugar and vanilla; fold in whipped cream. Spread over cheesecake. Refrigerate overnight. Remove sides of pan. Yields 12 servings.

Wacky Cake
Submitted by Alison Sauder, PA

"This is a great easy recipe for beginners, but be sure to not make the mistake I did. The first time I made this cake, I read the recipe, gathered the ingredients and started mixing them together. Either carelessness or over-confidence found me putting 6 tablespoons of vanilla into the batter! Being a new baker, I never thought anything of it until I came to the cocoa, and realized it required 6 tablespoons of that, too. As I remember, it was edible, but very solid—and I got a good dose of humble 'cake'!"

3 cups flour	2 teaspoon vinegar
2 cups sugar	2 teaspoon baking soda
6 tablespoons cocoa	2 teaspoon vanilla
2 cups water	½ teaspoon salt
1 cup oil	

Mix all ingredients together. Bake cake at 350° for 45 minutes or cupcakes at 375° for 20 minutes.

Cranberry Coffee Cake
Submitted by Esther Lang, WI
& Jenny Berlin, TN
"This cake may also be made with red raspberries or blueberries."

½ cup wheat flour
½ cup white flour
½ teaspoon salt
½ teaspoon cream of tartar
½ teaspoon baking soda
⅓ cup white sugar
¼ cup oil
½ cup milk
1-1 ½ cups fresh cranberries, or frozen, thawed and drained

Topping:
⅓ cup wheat flour
⅓ cup sugar
⅓ cup walnuts or pecans
1 teaspoon cinnamon
1 tablespoon butter

Mix together all ingredients for the cake except cranberries. Pour into greased 8-inch pan. Sprinkle cranberries over cake batter.

To make topping: Mix flour, sugar and cinnamon; cut in the butter and add nuts. Sprinkle over cake. Bake at 375° for 30 minutes or until done. Enjoy hot or cold, for breakfast or dessert!

Received for Volume 8, Issue 4 of KBR

Whipped Cream Topping
Submitted by Lydia Vanderford, CO
1 quart whipping cream
1 tablespoon of powdered sugar
1 tablespoon of cornstarch

Whip together. For chocolate variation, add 1-2 cups of powdered chocolate chips.

Chocolate Decorator Frosting
Submitted by Esther Lang, WI

¼ cup Crisco
¼ cup soft butter
½ teaspoon vanilla
1 ¾ cups powdered sugar
⅓ cup cocoa powder
2 ¼ tablespoons milk

Beat until smooth. Two recipes frosts and decorates a 13x9-inch cake. For white frosting, use 2 cups powdered sugar and omit cocoa.

Other Desserts

Apple Crisp
Submitted by Stephanie Muto, MA

Apples, peeled, cored, and sliced
½ cup brown sugar
½ teaspoon cinnamon
1 egg
½ teaspoon salt
1 cup sugar
1 cup flour
½ cup brown sugar
½ teaspoon cinnamon
½ cup butter, melted

Slice enough apples to fill a 13x9-inch baking pan about ¾ full. Sprinkle brown sugar and cinnamon over apples. In a small bowl, combine egg, salt, sugar and flour. Mixture should be crumbly. Sprinkle over apples. Mix together another mixture of brown sugar and cinnamon and pour on top. Drizzle melted butter over the top; bake at 350° until crisp is bubbly and top lightly browned—about 40 minutes. Enjoy!

Cold Strawberry Soup
Submitted by Hannah Schoenfelder, MN

15 ounces frozen strawberries, thawed with juice
15 ounces sour cream
1 ounce vanilla extract
3 ounces powdered sugar
2 ounces half and half

Mix strawberries and sour cream. Beat slowly until well mixed. Add vanilla and sugar, mixing until smooth in consistency. Add half and half last, mixing only until well blended. Chill and serve. Shake well before serving.

Printed in Volume 8, Issue 2 of KBR

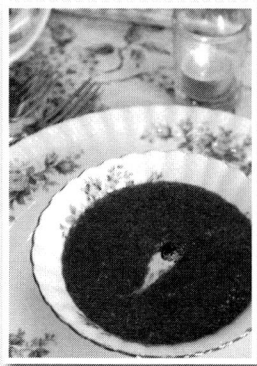

Strawberry Salad
Submitted by Megan Langham, WA

"This recipe is delicious! It's a long-standing Christmas tradition at our house."

2 cups boiling water
2 (3-ounce) packages strawberry gelatin
1 package frozen strawberries
1 can crushed pineapple
2 large bananas, sliced
1 container sour cream

Dissolve gelatin in boiling water. Add strawberries; break apart with a fork as they melt. Do not mash berries. Add pineapple and bananas. Pour ½ of gelatin mixture into a long baking dish and chill until firm. Spread sour cream over chilled gelatin and add remaining gelatin over the sour cream. Chill again. Cut into squares; serve chilled. Serves 8.

Printed in Volume 2, Issue 1 of KBR

Delicious Creamy Ice Cream
Submitted by Megan Dove, TX

Milk or cream
3 tablespoons arrowroot powder
1 cup maple syrup or ¾ cup honey
½ teaspoon pure vanilla extract (optional)

Pour about ⅓ of a 4-quart ice cream maker container with milk or cream. Add arrowroot powder, maple syrup, and vanilla. Mix well. Fill the container with milk or cream to the fill line. Freeze by ice cream maker instructions.

Rachael's Famous Ice Cream
Submitted by Rachael Bryant, KS

2 eggs
1 cup sucanat or honey
1 can sweetened condensed milk
¼ teaspoon salt
1 ½ teaspoons vanilla flavoring
Small amount of milk, plus approximately 7 cups milk

Mix in blender; put in ice cream churn canister. Add enough milk to fill your canister. Churn until firm, normally around 30 minutes. If the ingredients are very cold, the ice cream will not take as long to churn. Once churned, let sit 30+ minutes to ripen.

Fruit Variation (add before churning):
    2-3 tablespoons vanilla flavoring
    1 ½-2 cups chopped fruit

Mint Chocolate Chip Variation (add before serving):
    Peppermint flavoring, to taste
    1 cup chocolate chips

How sweet are thy words unto my taste! yea, sweeter than honey to my mouth!

PSALM
119:103

healthy *treats*

in the
kitchen
with brittany

🌿 Can you share a special-occasion menu?
One of my favorite meals would be meatballs and spaghetti. My dad was always the "meatball maker" with a recipe that he grew up with, until my mom found one that we all really enjoyed; it has a great taste. We usually place the meatballs in or serve with sauce, spaghetti, and sausage.

Family Favorite Meatballs

1 pound extra lean ground beef
½ teaspoon sea salt
1 small onion, diced
½ teaspoon garlic salt
1½ teaspoons Italian seasoning
¾ teaspoon dried oregano
½ teaspoon crushed red pepper flakes
1 ½ tablespoons Worcestershire sauce
⅓ cup skim milk
¼ cup grated Parmesan cheese
½ cup seasoned bread crumbs

Preheat oven to 400°. Place beef into mixing bowl, and season with salt, onion, garlic salt, Italian seasoning, oregano, red pepper flakes and Worcestershire sauce; mix well. Add the milk, Parmesan cheese, and bread crumbs. Mix until evenly blended, then form into 1½-inch meatballs and place onto a baking sheet. Bake until no longer pink in the center—about 20 to 25 minutes.

Do you incorporate healthy ingredients in your meals?

I use whole wheat instead of white flour, sucanat instead of white sugar, or coconut oil instead of butter. This has helped my family to eat better by using healthier ingredients.

What are your favorite sources for recipes?

My favorite source for recipes is a website called *Allrecipes. com*. We have gotten many of our family's treasured recipes from there, including wheat bread, cinnamon buns, and chocolate chip cookies. I also like a cookbook that my family has had for a long time titled, *Better Homes and Gardens New Cookbook*.

Do you have any special kitchen tips that have helped you to prepare meals?

One helpful hint I have learned is to read the recipe through first. This will help not only when deciding which recipe to make, but also aid you in knowing what to do and when to do it. For example, my sister and I used to make and sell fudge. With ingredients on the stove that needed to be stirred constantly, you only had a short amount of time to measure ingredients without allowing the heated mixture to burn. After experience we learned to set aside the ingredients that needed to be put in the pot before we needed to add them. Preparation may be crucial to your results!

What ways can you as a daughter bless your family and others through the kitchen?

One way that I have found to be a blessing both to my family and others is by baking cookies, providing a meal, or giving a loaf of bread to neighbors. This is not only God-honoring, but also provides a good reputation for my parents and entire family. Before delivering these things, we sometimes place a card or tag with Scripture verses on the plate, or bag containing the food. By doing this, you can share God's Word and the love of Christ with them!

Brittany lives with her family and her interests are cooking, baking, and music, through which she and her family minister at nursing homes.

healthy treats

The first recipes in this section are refined white sugar-free. Some refined sugar alternatives include honey, sucanat, white and green stevia, agave nectar, maple syrup, molasses, sorghum, or Xylitol sweetener. These can often be found at bulk or health food stores. Some experimenting may be necessary to convert your favorite recipes to using natural sweetener, but it is well-worth the effort! In most conventional recipes, the amount of sugar can also be dropped dramatically.

The second part in this section includes recipes for gluten-free sweets. Gluten intolerances are becoming more common, and finding gluten-free recipes may be a struggle. Also included in this gluten-free collection is a recipe for Gluten-Free Flour Blend (page 212). By making your own gluten-free flour blend, you can more easily make your favorite recipes gluten-free.

Healthy eating begins with a personal choice to eat nutritionally. We are the temple of God; we are bought with a price, therefore we are not our own (I Corinthians 6:20). May the Lord give us the strength to eat wisely and take care of the bodies over which He has given us stewardship!

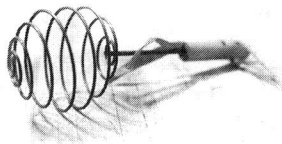

Refined Sugar-Free Section

Sugar-free Cookies & Bars

Healthy Oatmeal-Raisin Cookies
Submitted by Mrs. Dana Bryant, KS

1 cup butter, softened
1 ½ cups sucanat
2 farm-fresh eggs
1 teaspoon vanilla
1 ½ cups wheat flour
1 teaspoon baking soda
1 teaspoon cinnamon
½ teaspoon salt
3 cups oats, quick or old-fashioned, uncooked
1 cup raisins

Preheat oven to 350°. Beat butter and sugar until creamy. Add eggs and vanilla, beat well. Combine flour, salt, baking soda and cinnamon and add to butter mixture. Mix well. Stir in oats and raisins. Mix well. Drop by tablespoonfuls onto ungreased cookie sheets and bake 12 minutes or until brown. Makes about 4 dozen.

Printed in Volume 1, Issue 2 of KBR

Nutty Snack Bar
Submitted by Sharlyn Halteman, PA

1 cup nut butter of your choice
¼-½ cup sweetener of your choice
1 cup crispy almonds, chopped
1 cup crispy sunflower seeds
1 cup chocolate chips or dried fruit

Mix everything together and press into baking dish. You can leave this recipe raw and place it in the refrigerator as is, or allow the flavors to meld and chips to melt by baking it for approximately 20 minutes at 350°.

Printed in Volume 4, Issue 3 of KBR

Choco-Oat-Chip Cookies
Submitted by Emily Bow, NY

1 ¾ cups wheat flour
1 teaspoon baking soda
½ teaspoon salt
1 cup sucanat
2 tablespoons stevia
2 cups chocolate chips

1 cup butter, softened
2 eggs
2 tablespoons milk
2 teaspoons vanilla
2 ½ cups oats

Beat sugar, stevia and butter in a large bowl until blended. Beat in eggs, milk and vanilla. Combine flour, baking soda and salt, then beat into wet ingredients. Stir in oats and chips. Drop by tablespoons onto ungreased baking sheets. Bake at 350° for 8-10 minutes. Can also be pressed into a greased pan for bars.

tip

natural sweetener
"Sucanat is a natural sweetener made from dehydrated sugar cane juice. It is available from health stores and co-ops. You can substitute sucanat for sugar in a recipe. Be aware that it adds a slightly darker color to baked goods."

Mud Balls
Submitted by Angela Watt, TX

½ cup oats
½ cup powdered milk
¼ cup nuts
¼ cup butter
½ cup honey
¼ cup carob powder
1 teaspoon vanilla
½ cup peanut butter

Mix oats, powdered mik, and nuts; set aside. In a saucepan, melt butter. Add honey and carob, blending well. Bring to a boil, stirring constantly. Boil for 1 minute then remove from heat. Beat in vanilla and peanut butter. Pour over oat mixture. Roll into 1-inch balls and freeze.

"The Works" Cookie

Submitted by Jeana Price, PA

½ cup butter, softened
⅔ cup honey
1 egg
1 cup whole wheat pastry flour or regular wheat flour
1 teaspoon cinnamon
½ teaspoon baking soda
½ teaspoon salt
¼ teaspoon nutmeg
2 cups quick oats
1 cup raisins
1 cup chocolate or carob chips
1 cup walnuts
1 cup unsweetened coconut

Whisk together butter and honey; blend in egg. Mix together flour, cinnamon, baking soda, salt, and nutmeg in a separate bowl. Blend into butter mixture. Fold in oats, raisins, chips, walnuts, and coconut. Drop by tablespoons onto lightly greased cookie sheet close together (these do not spread). If dough does not hold together well, press each dropped cookie together with fingers. Bake at 350° for 8-10 minutes. Yields 35-40 cookies.

Received for Volume 5, Issue 4 of KBR

Monster Cookies

Submitted by Rebekah Schmit, PA

3 eggs
1 cup honey
1 teaspoon vanilla
1 tablespoon blackstrap molasses
2 teaspoons baking soda

1 cup shortening
1 cup peanut butter
5 ½ cups oatmeal
1 cup raisins

Mix in order given. Bake at 350° for 8 minutes, or until lightly browned. Makes 1 ½ dozen. You can substitute chocolate chips for raisins. Also, ¼ cup flour helps this hold together better.

Printed in Volume 5, Issue 4 of KBR

Sugarless Date Cookies
Submitted by Maggie Bullington, AL

½ cup butter, softened
1 egg
2 teaspoons vanilla
1 cup flour
1 teaspoon baking powder
¼ teaspoon salt
1 cup finely chopped pitted dates (about 25 dates)
1 cup walnuts/pecans, chopped finely
1 cup flaked coconut

Combine butter, egg, and vanilla; set aside. Combine flour, baking powder, and salt. Add this to butter mixture. Stir in dates, nuts, and coconut. Drop dough onto lightly greased cookie sheet, 2-inches apart. Bake at 375° for 11-13 minutes or until golden. Cool on racks.

Received for Volume 5, Issue 4 of KBR

Carob Oatmeal Cookies
Submitted by Annie Zimmerman, WI

1½ cups honey
½ cup butter
½ cup carob powder or cocoa
½ cup milk
6 cups quick oats
1 cup shredded coconut
2 teaspoons vanilla
1 cup peanut butter

Combine first four ingredients in a saucepan. Boil rapidly for 2 minutes. Remove from heat and add the remaining ingredients. Spoon onto waxed paper. Shape into 1½-inch balls.

Received for Volume 5, Issue 4 of KBR

Natural Tollhouse Cookies
Submitted by Alaina O'Neill, IL

1 cup butter
½ cup honey
2 eggs
1 teaspoon vanilla
1 teaspoon baking soda
1 teaspoon salt
2 cups whole wheat flour
2 cups carob chips
½ cup nuts
½ cup coconut
½ cup oats

Cream together butter and honey. Beat in eggs and vanilla. Sift together soda, salt, and flour, and add to butter mixture. Fold in rest of ingredients. Drop by tablespoons onto greased cookie sheets. Bake at 350° for 12-15 minutes.

Received for Volume 5, Issue 4 of KBR

Butterscotch Cookies
Submitted by Theresa Lober, MO

2 cups wheat flour, or rice flour
1 teaspoon salt
¼ cup butter
½ cup honey
2 teaspoons vanilla
2 eggs
1 cup coconut
1 cup chopped nuts

Beat together butter, honey, vanilla and eggs. Stir in flour, salt, coconut and nuts. Refrigerate for several hours or overnight. Roll into 1-inch balls and arrange on oiled baking sheet. Press flat with bottom of a glass. Bake at 350° for 10-12 minutes.

Received for Volume 5, Issue 4 of KBR

Chocolate Chip Pumpkin Cookies
Submitted by Rachael Bryant, KS

"A neighbor made these cookies for us when my brother Jonathan was born in Korea. They are a family favorite and we have fond memories of sharing them with others!"

4 cups whole wheat flour
2 cups uncooked oats
2 teaspoons baking soda

2 teaspoons cinnamon
1 teaspoon salt
1 ½ cups butter
1 cup sucanat
1 egg
1 teaspoon vanilla
16 ounces pumpkin puree
1 cup chocolate chips or raisins

tip

cake flour
"Since cake flour is lighter than regular flour, when you are substituting for 'sifted cake flour,' measure unbleached flour in the amount of cake flour called for, taking about 1 level tablespoon of flour from each cup. Sift and use as usual. This makes a lighter quality in the baked goods."

Combine dry ingredients. Set aside. Cream butter, slowly adding sucanat. Add egg and vanilla. Alternately add dry ingredients and pumpkin, mixing well. Stir in chocolate chips. Drop by tablespoons on a lightly greased cookie sheet. Bake at 350° for 15 minutes. Makes approximately 8 dozen.

Received for Volume 6, Issue 4 of KBR

Yummy Oatmeal Raisin Cookies
Submitted by Victoria Steiner, IL

2 cups whole wheat flour
½ teaspoon baking soda
1 teaspoon baking powder
1 teaspoon salt
1 teaspoon cinnamon
1 ½ cup raisins
2 cups oatmeal
1 ½ cups sucanat

¾ cup softened butter
2 eggs
2 teaspoons vanilla

In a bowl mix together flour, baking soda, baking powder, salt, and cinnamon. In second bow, mix together raisins and oatmeal. In third bowl, beat together sucanat, butter, eggs, and vanilla. After mixing all bowls, add the flour mixture to the butter mixture. Then add the oatmeal and raisins. Mix well with a big spoon, then drop onto cookie sheets. Flatten slightly. Bake at 375° for 10 minutes or until lightly browned.

Honey-Made, Egg-Free Brownies
Submitted by Maggie Bullington, AL

"This is the recipe that we recently made to use honey and omit the eggs. Arrowroot powder is a great egg substitute in several baked goods. These are almost cake-like. Yummy."

1 cup white flour
¾ cup wheat flour
½ cup cocoa powder
1 teaspoon salt
3 tablespoons arrowroot powder
½ cup honey
1 cup coconut oil
1 teaspoon vanilla
About ¾ of 14-ounce can coconut milk
1 teaspoon baking soda

Topping:
¼-½ cup butter, melted
1 cup dried, shredded coconut
2 tablespoons honey (to taste)
¼ cup milk or the remainder of the can of coconut milk

Grease a 13x9-inch pan. Mix all the above ingredients, except the coconut milk and baking soda, with electric beaters on medium speed. Combine coconut milk and baking soda; add to batter. Bake at 350° for about 20-22 minutes. Combine topping and spread over the hot cake. Return to oven and broil until browned.

Healthy Chewy Maple Cookies
Submitted by Maggie Bullington, AL

"Taking a delicious original recipe from some dear friends, I was able to cut out a cup of brown sugar and an egg. For the cup of coconut flakes, I used some sweetened coconut; if you are using unsweetened coconut, you may consider adding just a touch more maple syrup or two tablespoons of honey to make up the extra sweetness."

½ cup butter, softened
½ cup maple syrup
1 ½ tablespoons arrowroot powder, or 1 egg
1 cup white wheat flour
½ cup unbleached white flour
2 teaspoons baking powder
½ teaspoon salt
1 cup coconut flakes

Mix ingredients together. Grease baking sheets and drop dough on in tablespoonfuls. You may need to flatten the rounds out slightly. Bake at 375° for about 7-8 minutes or until done.

Honey Chocolate Chip Cookies
Submitted by Megan Dove, TX

½ cup honey
1 egg
1 ½ cups flour
½ teaspoon baking soda
½ cup nuts (optional)
½ cup butter, softened
½ teaspoon vanilla
¼ teaspoon baking powder
½ teaspoon salt
1 cup chocolate chips

Cream honey and butter. Add egg and vanilla. Sift flour, soda, baking powder, and salt. Mix all together. Add nuts and chocolate chips. Do not overmix; it will cause your cookies to flatten. If your dough is too thin, refrigerate 10-20 minutes. Drop onto buttered cookie sheet. Bake at 350° for 12 minutes.

Orange & Cranberry Scones
Submitted by Shiloh Strang, OR

4 cups spelt
½ cup sucanat
4 teaspoons baking powder
1 teaspoon baking soda
Dash of salt
½ cup melted butter
1 ½ cup buttermilk
⅔ cup whole milk yogurt
Handful of dried cranberries
Grated orange peel, to taste

Topping:
2 tablespoons evaporated cane juice crystals
Orange zest

Preheat the oven to 375°. Mix together the dry ingredients; add wet ingredients to the mixture. Add in the cranberries and orange zest and mix together well. Divide the dough in half and place on a cookie sheet lined with parchment paper. Pat each dough ball flat and score with a knife into eight scones. Stir together the "topping" and sprinkle over the scones. Bake for 20 minutes. Cut scones and serve warm, or cool and store for a future breakfast!

Peanut Butter Balls
Submitted by Elizabeth Adams, IA

1 ⅓ cups peanut butter
⅔ cup honey
1 ½ cups organic dry milk
½ cup wheat germ
Coconut flakes (optional)

Mix ingredients by hand in a large bowl or in a mixer or large bowl. Roll into balls that are about 1-inch in diameter. Refrigerate or freeze. Storing in snack bags is great for a quick, healthy snack!

Sugar-Free Pies

Sugar-Free Apple Pie
Submitted by Mrs. Dana Bryant, KS

"Often, apple desserts do not need any extra sugar, since they are naturally sweet. You can use this same recipe for a cheery pie, substituting the apples with pitted cherries."

1 (6-ounce) can frozen apple juice concentrate
1 teaspoon ground cinnamon
1 tablespoon cornstarch
¼ teaspoon nutmeg
6 cups apples, peeled and sliced
2 (8-inch) pie crusts, unbaked
Melted butter

Preheat oven to 325°. Place apple juice in saucepan and bring to boil. Combine cornstarch and spices in small bowl. Add a small amount of apple juice. Stir until well blended. Stir in remaining apple juice. Pour over apples, coating all slices. Pour into unbaked pie shell and top with another crust. Brush with melted butter and sprinkle lightly with cinnamon. Bake for one hour.

Printed in Volume 5, Issue 1 of KBR

tip

easy substitutions
Brown Sugar – For 1 cup brown sugar, use 1 cup white sugar and 1 tablespoon molasses.
Baking Powder – For 1 teaspoon baking powder, use ½ teaspoon cream of tartar and ¼ teaspoon baking soda.
Tomato Sauce – For a 16-ounce can of tomato sauce, use 6 ounces tomato paste, 1 ¼ cups water, 1 teaspoon parsley, ¼ teaspoon salt and ⅛ teaspoon garlic powder.
—Esther Lang

Sugar-Free
Cinnamon Apple Pie
Submitted by Brittany Schlichter, TX

Homemade pastry for a double crust pie (page 181)
4-8 Granny Smith apples, peeled, cored and cut into eighths
2-3 teaspoons cinnamon
1 cup light or blue nectar agave
2 teaspoons vanilla
3 tablespoons flour

Make pie crust. While it chills, mix together pie filling ingredients. Roll out top and bottom crusts, pour filling inside the bottom crust and put on top crust. Pinch together edges, pull off excess and use cookie cutters to make dough decorations for the top of the pie. Slit top crust and bake pie at 375° for 40-50 minutes. Enjoy!

Chocolate Banana Pie
Submitted by Mrs. Dana Bryant, KS

"We love this cool treat in the summer months for a healthy and easy dessert."

Crust:
    1 cup almonds
    2 tablespoons butter or coconut oil

Pie Filling:
    5 ripe bananas
    1 cup milk
    ½ cup cocoa powder
    1 teaspoons vanilla

Place almonds in a food processor with butter; blend until finely ground. Add butter and blend. Press evenly into the bottom of a greased 8-inch springform pan or pie pan. Mix pie filling ingredients in food processor and blend until smooth. Pour over pie crust and freeze until firm. Before serving, soften at room temperature and cut with sharp knife.

Sugar-free Cakes & Icings

Sugar-Free Chocolate Snack Cake
Submitted by Tiffany & Brittany Schlichter, TX

1 ½ cups flour
½ cup honey
¼ cup baking cocoa
1 teaspoon baking soda
½ teaspoon salt
⅓ cup vegetable oil
1 teaspoon white vinegar
½ teaspoon vanilla
1 cup cold water

Heat oven to 350°. Grease a round 9-inch pan with shortening, then flour it lightly. Mix flour, cocoa, soda and salt in medium-sized bowl. Separately mix oil, vinegar, vanilla and honey. Vigorously stir oil mixture and water into flour mixture about 1 minute or until well blended. Immediately pour into pan. Bake 25-35 minutes or until toothpick inserted comes out clean. Serve with whipped topping.

Chocolate Mousse Frosting
Submitted by Sarah Bryant, KS

"When we were looking for a sugar-free icing recipe for our favorite Chocolate Bean Cake recipe (page 218), we came up with this idea. This mousse is delicious, and since it is not sweet, one could almost eat it alone for a treat! You can add a bit of sweetener of choice, if desired, such as stevia or sucanat."

2 cups thick cream
2 tablespoons cocoa powder (to taste)
½ teaspoon vanilla extract

Whip cream in mixer until very thick, like frosting. Gently whip in cocoa and vanilla. Frost your cake with this "icing." You can use an icing tip to make fancy decorating designs.

Chocolate Avocado Pudding
Submitted by Sarah Bryant, KS

"This is a wonderful way to eat avocados, which are a great source of omega 3 essential fatty acids. We prefer to use sucanat in this recipe instead of maple syrup (add 2 table-spoons of water if you use a dry sweetener). You can use this as a chocolate icing recipe, adding a bit more sugar and cocoa to thicken it for spreading on a cake."

2 medium-sized avocados, peeled
⅓ cup maple syrup
1 teaspoon vanilla extract
⅓ cup cocoa powder
⅓ cup water, milk, or coconut oil
Pinch of salt

Blend all ingredients together in a food processor. Add water if needed to reach desired consistency. Enjoy after dinner, served with farm fresh cream, homegrown strawberries and blueberries!

Chocolate Ganache
Submitted by Maggie Bullington, AL

"This is great for use as a frosting for cakes."

¾ cup honey
¾ cup cocoa powder
⅓ cup coconut oil, melted
⅛ teaspoon salt
1 teaspoon vanilla
1 (8-ounce) package cream cheese

Blend in a food processor or blender until smooth. Scrape down the bowl. Add cream cheese that has been cut into cubes. Blend until smooth. Check taste and add more flavoring as needed. Spread on your cooled dessert.

Gluten-Free Section
Also try the gluten-free bread recipe for Brown & White Bread (page 128)

Gluten-Free Flour Blend
Submitted by Emily and Natalie Larsen, MD
4 cups brown rice flour
1 ⅓ cups potato starch
⅔ cups tapioca flour/starch

Mix together thoroughly and use as a gluten-free substitution for flour in your recipes.

Printed in Volume 7, Issue 3 of KBR

ℒ Gluten-free Cookies & Bars

Gluten-Free Sugar Cookies
Submitted by Sarah Niemela, MI
"These taste just like their non-gluten-free counterpart. We got this from our friend Amy."
3 cups white rice flour
1 teaspoon baking soda
1 teaspoon cream of tartar
1 tablespoon xanthan gum
¼ teaspoon salt
1 cup cold butter
1 cup sugar
2 cold eggs
1 teaspoon almond extract
Powdered sugar to use when rolling dough

Combine flour, baking soda, cream of tartar, xanthan gum and salt. Mix well. Cut in butter to pea size. In small bowl, cream sugar, eggs and almond extract. Add wet ingredients to dry ingredients. Work together with your hands and shape into a ball. Refrigerate 1 hour. Roll dough out onto wax paper that is taped onto your table and is "floured" with powdered sugar. Roll dough ¼-inch thick. Cut into shapes. Bake 12 minutes at 350°. Cool on wire rack or on paper.

Received for Volume 7, Issue 3 of KBR

Flourless Peanut Butter Chocolate Chip Cookies
Submitted by Maggie Bullington, AL
"If you like peanut butter and chocolate together, you are almost sure to like these!"

1 cup packed brown sugar	1 teaspoon baking soda
1 cup chunky peanut butter	½ teaspoon vanilla extract
1 large egg	1 cup chocolate chips

Stir first five ingredients in a medium-sized bowl, using a wooden spoon. Stir in chocolate chips. Drop dough by rounded tablespoonfuls onto a parchment paper-lined baking sheet. Bake at 350° for 12 minutes or until puffed and golden. Cookies will be soft in the center. Cool on baking sheet 5 minutes. Remove and cool on a wire rack.

Received for Volume 7, Issue 3 of KBR

Gluten-Free Snickerdoodles
Submitted by Emily & Natalie Larsen, MD

½ cup butter, softened
½ cup shortening, or organic palm oil
1 ½ cups sugar
2 eggs
2 ¾ cups gluten-free flour mix (see Gluten-Free Flour Blend on page 212)
2 teaspoons xanthan gum
2 teaspoons cream of tartar
1 teaspoon baking soda
¼ teaspoon salt
2 tablespoons sugar
2 teaspoons cinnamon

Heat oven to 400°. Mix butter, shortening, sugar and eggs thoroughly. Mix dry ingredients separate and then add to wet. Refrigerate 30-60 minutes. Mix 2 tablespoons sugar and cinnamon in a small bowl. Shape dough by rounded teaspoonfuls into balls. Roll in sugar mixture. Place 2 inches apart on an ungreased baking sheet or parchment paper. (Do not use a dark colored cookie sheet; they will burn quickly.) Bake 8-10 minutes and immediately remove from baking sheet. Makes about 6 dozen.

Received for Volume 7, Issue 3 of KBR

No-Egg Cocoa Fudge Cookies
Submitted by Lauren Kline, IA

"My family loves these cookies and I always end up making double batches!"

1 cup gluten-free flour
¼ teaspoon baking soda
⅛ teaspoon salt
5 tablespoons butter
7 tablespoons unsweetened cocoa
⅔ cup white sugar
⅓ cup brown sugar
⅓ cup plain low fat yogurt
1 teaspoon vanilla extract or powder

Preheat oven to 350°. Combine flour, soda and salt; set aside. Melt butter in a large saucepan over medium heat. Remove from heat; stir in cocoa and sugars. Add yogurt and vanilla, stirring to combine. Add flour mixture, stirring until moist. Drop by tablespoons 2 inches apart on baking sheets coated with cooking spray. Bake at 350° for 10 minutes. Cool on pans 2-3 minutes, then remove and place on cooling rack.

Printed in Volume 7, Issue 3 of KBR

Chocolate Chip Shortbread Treats
Submitted by Maggie Bullington, AL

1 cup unsweetened dried coconut flakes
1 cup raw walnuts
¼ teaspoon salt
6 pitted Medjool dates
Chocolate chips or raisins (optional)

Place the coconut, walnuts and salt in a food processor. Process until finely ground. Add dates and process until the mixture begins to stick together. Don't over process. Transfer this mixture to a bowl and add chocolate chips or raisins. Roll into 1-inch balls and serve.

Gluten-Free Ginger Cookies
Submitted by Sarah Niemela, MI
"We found this recipe from a recipe exchange that meets monthly in our area."

4 cups gluten-free flour (page 212)
1 teaspoon xanthan gum
1 tablespoon baking soda
2 ½ teaspoons ground ginger
1 teaspoon ground cinnamon
½ teaspoon ground cloves
¾ cup butter
2 cups sugar
2 eggs
½ cup molasses
1 teaspoon vinegar

Preheat oven to 325°. Grease cookie sheets. Whisk together dry ingredients; set aside. Blend liquid ingredients; add dry to liquid. The dough should be thick enough to form soft balls; if not, add more flour until dough is desired consistency. Put walnut-sized balls on cookie sheets. Bake 12-13 minutes. Makes about 8-10 dozen cookies, depending on how big you make them. For a special treat, dip in melted white chips after they are cool. Enjoy!

Printed in Volume 7, Issue 3 of KBR

Shiloh's Gluten-Free Macaroons
Submitted by Eden Strang, OR

½ teaspoon vanilla
2 egg whites
⅔ cup sugar
1 ⅓ cup flaked coconut
Chocolate chips (optional)

Grease cookie sheet or lay a sheet of parchment paper on cookie sheet. Beat together vanilla and egg whites until soft peaks form. Add sugar by tablespoons. Beat with sugar until stiff peaks form. Fold in coconut and chocolate chips. Spoon onto cookie sheet and bake at 325° for 20 minutes or until slightly brown around the edges. Enjoy.

Printed in Volume 7, Issue 3 of KBR

Peanut Butter Bars
Submitted by Mrs. Kathleen Bullington, AL

"These really do make into a brownie-like bar, though it may be hard to believe by looking at the ingredients!"

1 cup peanut butter
¼-½ cup honey
1 egg
½ teaspoon baking soda

Thoroughly mix all ingredients. Pour into a generously greased 8x8-inch baking pan and bake at 350° for about 25 minutes, or until an inserted knife comes out clean. Do not overbake!

Gluten-free Cakes

Awesome Chocolate Cake
Submitted by Elizabeth Miller, NY

"We grind our flour from grains, but you can also buy the flours from a health food store or co-op."

1 ¼ cups white rice flour
½ cup tapioca flour or cornstarch
1 teaspoon salt
1 teaspoon baking soda
3 teaspoons baking powder
1 teaspoon xanthum or guar gum
4 eggs
1 ¼ cups sugar
⅔ cup mayonnaise
1 cup milk
⅔ cup cocoa powder
2 teaspoons vanilla extract

In small bowl, mix together first six ingredients. In a liquid measuring cup, whisk cocoa into milk until smooth. In the mix bowl beat eggs, sugar, and mayonnaise until fluffy. Add a small amount of dry mixture to mixer bowl, then a little of the cocoa/milk mixture. Continue alternating until all is incorporated into mixer bowl. Lastly, add the vanilla. Pour into greased 13x9-inch pan, a greased bundt pan, or two greased 8-inch cake pans. Bake at 350° for 25 minutes or until toothpick comes out clean. Cool on racks in pans. Delicious plain, or you can frost them to be fancy.

Received for Volume 7, Issue 3 of KBR

Gluten-Free Angel Food Cake
Submitted by Maggie Bullington, AL

"This is very delicious and has a great texture! We serve it with a simple strawberry sauce."

1 ½ cups egg whites (about 10 whites)
¾ cup, plus ½ cup, sugar, divided
¼ cup cornstarch
¼ cup white rice flour
¼ cup tapioca flour
¼ cup potato starch
1 ½ teaspoons cream of tartar
¾ teaspoon salt
¾ teaspoon vanilla extract
Assorted fresh fruit (optional)

Place egg whites in a large bowl; let stand at room temperature for 30 minutes. Sift ¾ cup sugar, cornstarch, flours and potato starch together twice; set aside. Add cream of tartar, salt and vanilla to egg whites; beat on medium speed until soft peaks form. Gradually add remaining sugar, about 2 tablespoons at a time, beating on high until stiff peaks form. Gradually fold in flour mixture, about ½ cup at a time. Gently spoon into an ungreased 10-inch tube pan. Cut through the batter with a knife to remove air pockets. Bake on the lowest oven rack at 350° for 45-50 minutes or until lightly browned and entire top appears dry. Immediately invert pan; cool completely—about one hour. Run a knife around side and center tube of pan. Remove cake to a serving plate. Top with fresh fruit, if desired.

Cranberry Nut Cake
Submitted by Mrs. Kathleen Bullington, AL

½ cup coconut flour
1 teaspoon salt
1 teaspoon baking soda
5 eggs
½ cup oil
½ cup honey
1 tablespoon vanilla extract
1 cup frozen cranberries, chopped slightly
½ cup walnuts, chopped (optional)

Mix and spread in a greased 13x9-inch baking pan. Bake at 325° for about 15-18 minutes (test with a toothpick inserted in the center).

Gluten-Free Flourless Chocolate Cake
Submitted by Sarah Bryant, KS

"The first time we tried this recipe, we were surprised by how wonderful it is! This has become our family's favorite cake recipe, and knowing it is so healthy makes it all the more enjoyable."

1 (15-ounce) can black beans, drained and rinsed
    or 1½ cups cooked and rinsed black beans
5 eggs
1 tablespoon vanilla extract
½ teaspoon salt
6 tablespoons butter, softened
⅔ cup sucanat
6 tablespoons cocoa powder
1 teaspoon baking powder

½ teaspoon baking soda
1 tablespoon water

Preheat oven to 350°. Grease a 9-inch cake pan and dust with cocoa powder. Place the beans, three eggs, vanilla, sugar and salt into a blender or food processor; process until beans are completely smooth. Beat butter and sucanat until light. Add two remaining eggs, beating well after each. Add bean batter to egg mixture and mix. Stir in cocoa powder and water and beat for one minute. Pour batter into prepared pan. Bake for 30-40 minutes, until the top is firm to the touch. Do not overbake. Cool for 10 minutes and then invert onto a plate. Frost with Chocolate Mousse Frosting (page 210) when cool, and top with a pinch of cocoa powder or fresh strawberries.

Other Gluten-free Desserts

Auntie Kaggy's Apple Crisp
Submitted by Eden Strang, OR

6 cups apples, or enough to cover the bottom of pan
1 cup sugar or sucanat
¾ cup spelt flour
¾ cup oats
½ cup butter (add more if needed)
1 teaspoon cinnamon
1 teaspoon nutmeg

Mix sugar, spelt, oats, butter, cinnamon and nutmeg in a bowl and set aside. Cut apples and place in a greased 13x9-inch pan. Sprinkle topping oven apples until well covered. Bake at 375° for 30 minutes. Enjoy!

Received for Volume 7, Issue 3 of KBR

measuring honey *tip*

"When measuring honey or molasses, rub a little oil into your measuring glass before pouring the liquid in. This helps your honey slide out easily."

*Better is a
dinner of herbs
where love is,
than a stalled ox
and hatred
therewith.*

—PROVERBS 15:17

dips & snacks

in the
kitchen
with elizabeth

🌿 **What is a favorite snack to make for your family?**

Making healthy and delicious treats is so fun to do for my three younger brothers! One of our favorite recipes is Peanut Butter Balls (page 207). Others include popcorn, fresh fruit, nuts, and homemade juice popsicles. Recently I found a recipe for a snack we now all love: Pretzel Bites. Just a warning: they may disappear quickly!

Homemade Pretzel Bites

1⅛ cups water (70–80°)
3 cups whole wheat or white flour
3 tablespoons rapadura or brown sugar
1 ½ teaspoons active dry yeast
2 quarts water
½ cup baking soda
Coarse salt
Melted butter

Put the first four ingredients into a mixer. Knead for about 5 minutes. Let dough rise for an hour. Boil the water with the baking soda. Form the dough into small "bite-able" balls and drop the formed balls into the water. Count to ten and remove the small clumps of dough. Place on baking sheet and bake at 475° until slightly golden—about 7-10 minutes. Brush with butter and sprinkle with salt. Enjoy!

🌿 Have you learned any special kitchen tips?

There are so many little tips and ideas I have learned from those who are so much more experienced than myself. Here are a few ideas: When bananas and other fruits begin to turn brown, you can slice them and put them in the freezer—add them to smoothies to add sweetness. Freezing leftover broth and bits of leftover veggies can be used later to make a delicious soup. If you have some bread that has become dry, you can grind or crush it in a blender for homemade, healthy bread crumbs to use in recipes. Cooking extra hamburger or chicken, cutting it up, and putting it in baggies for the freezer can be helpful to easily add to meals.

🌿 Who taught you how to cook? Do you remember anything you loved to make when you were a little girl?

I learn new things each day as I prepare meals alongside my mom, which is another blessing about being home-educated! My mom would be the first to say she is not an expert in the kitchen and is always learning, but for as long as I can remember, she's "cheered me on" to try making new recipes, for which I am thankful. My grandmothers have also taught me about cooking. I remember working through my list of the baking section for a Keepers at Home study and making an assortment of goodies with my grandmother and mom. My aunt is also a gifted cook and when I watch her cook, I am inspired! She doesn't measure ingredients, but is similar to a chemist as she experiments and creates. A special memory I have is making homemade cinnamon bread with Daddy when I was young, and enjoying it warm from the oven!

🌿 What is your idea of a perfect picnic?

One memory that comes to mind is a picnic I surprised my brothers with in the early summer. With a bright day, the blue sky painted with clouds, a jar of flowers picked from the yard, a soft blue blanket unfolded on the green grass, the food and special blue dishes and cups atop a picnic basket—it was really memorable! On the picnic menu was watermelon, corn on the cob, carrots and spinach, garlic bread, organic pizza and chocolate milk.

🌿 What is your favorite type of table-top centerpiece?

My favorite would be bouquets of freshly-picked flowers, especially lilacs, tulips and lilies of the valley, arranged in glass jars or vases and accented with a ribbon. So simple, but so gorgeous! You can come up with a creative centerpieces with items around your home, such as scrapbook paper, pictures, Scriptures, pretty napkins, and fabric. In the fall, we sometimes make a centerpiece of pinecones and dried clusters of leaves.

🌿 In what ways can we bless our family and others through our kitchens?

Cooking and baking opens up doors for hospitality and sharing the love of Christ to those around us. Bringing meals to families with a new little one or who are having sickness, baking bread and giving it to neighbors, baking treats for a gathering, cooking a little extra to give to your grandparents or those around you, making homemade snacks for siblings—those are just a few ways to serve others through cooking. You can ask the Lord to provide opportunities to serve in this way. I know that I have been blessed by other sisters-in-Christ's thoughtfulness in this area.

Home cooking also provides an opportunity for creating healthy meals that are nourishing for our families. The Lord is so gracious to give us life; we are reminded in I Corinthians 3:19-20 to glorify the Lord with it: *"What? know ye not that your body is the temple of the Holy Ghost which is in you, which ye have of God, and ye are not your own? For ye are bought with a price: therefore glorify God in your body, and in your spirit, which are God's."* What an honor it is to serve Christ...for without Him we are nothing.

Elizabeth is a home-educated young lady who
is thankful for her Savior, Jesus Christ, and
it is her prayer that she would honor Him
in all she does and says.

in the
kitchen
with keturah

What is your favorite herb to use?
Rosemary is my favorite herb, because it goes so well with chicken. We like to grow it ourselves.

Who taught you how to cook?
My siblings and I have always been involved in food production and preparation with my mother, so I have been taught to cook from a young age. Cutter cookies were always fun when I was little.

Do you have any special kitchen tips that you have found helpful as you make your family's meals?
We have a book called *Substituting Ingredients* that I find very helpful. Because we live quite a distance from a grocery store, we cannot just run and buy a missing ingredient; being innovative is a necessity, as well as a lot of fun!

How do you enjoy blessing your family with cooking?
I like to bake a special cake to fit each member of my family as a surprise on their birthdays. It is fun to be creative in thinking of treats to bless that individual with to show them appreciation.

Keturah lives on a farm and enjoys serving her family and helping with her family's business. She enjoys studying God's Word and desires to live each day wholly for Him.

✒ Dips & Spreads

Shrimp Spread
Submitted by Susanna Dorfsmith, CO

12 ounces softened cream cheese
1 cup chopped onion
1 (6 ounce) can small shrimp, rinsed and drained
Paprika
Stuffed olives
Assorted crackers

In a small bowl, beat cream cheese until smooth. Stir in the onion and shrimp. Spread onto a platter and sprinkle with paprika. Dot with olives. Serve with crackers. Yields 10-12 servings.

Printed in Volume 2, Issue 2 of KBR

Sun-Dried Tomato Dip
Submitted by Maggie Bullington, AL

"To prepare your own tomatoes, you may slice and dehydrate your own in the tomato growing season. To store, either freeze or pack in olive oil. These make a great snack on crackers and cream cheese!"

½ cup oil-packed sun-dried tomatoes, drained and chopped
8 ounces cream cheese
½ cup sour cream
¼ cup mayonnaise
1 clove garlic or ½ teaspoon garlic powder
Hot pepper sauce to taste
¾ teaspoon salt
¾ teaspoon pepper
¼ cup fresh basil or 1 teaspoon dried basil

Mix together. Serve with crackers or veggies.

Printed in Volume 6, Issue 2 of KBR

Easy Veggie Dip
Submitted by Esther Lang, WI

¼ cup mayonnaise
¼ cup plain yogurt
⅛ teaspoon dill
1/16 teaspoon paprika
1/16 teaspoon pepper
¼ teaspoon salt
¼ teaspoon lemon juice
1 teaspoon sugar
1/16 teaspoon dry mustard

Mix well. Serve with carrot sticks or zucchini slices.

Printed in Volume 6, Issue 2 of KBR

Italian Bean Dip
Submitted by Maggie Bullington, AL

3 garlic cloves
2 sprigs fresh rosemary, washed and dried
⅓ cup olive oil
1 (15-ounce) can organic garbanzo beans
Ground cayenne pepper, to taste
Salt, to taste

Peel each garlic clove and smash them, one at a time, under the flat side of a knife or a cutting board. Strip the leaves off of the rosemary stems; discard stems. Warm the garlic and oil together in a small pan or skillet over medium-high heat, stirring until the garlic is golden—about 3 minutes. Remove from the heat and add the rosemary to the hot oil. Cool slightly. Rinse and drain the beans. Put all the beans and all the garlic-rosemary oil into a food processor. Season with salt and cayenne pepper as desired and then puree until smooth. Serve with crackers, vegetable slices, or tortilla chips. Delicious!

Gluten-Free Hot Artichoke Dip
Submitted by Natalie Larsen, MD

1 (14-ounce) can artichoke hearts, drained and chopped
1 cup mayonnaise
1 cup Parmesan cheese
2 garlic cloves
¾ teaspoon salt
Nut Thin crackers for gluten-free option

Preheat your oven to 350°. Place the drained and chopped artichoke hearts into an ovenproof bowl and add the mayonnaise, Parmesan cheese, garlic and salt. Mix well and bake until hot and bubbly.

Printed in Volume 7, Issue 1 of KBR

Delicious Hummus Dip
Submitted by Mrs. Dana Bryant, KS

"This is a delicious dip which we often serve with pita bread slices."

2 cups dry chickpeas, cooked for 20 minutes in water, drained
2 cups water
1 ½ cups olive oil
2 garlic cloves
2 tablespoons cumin
1 tablespoon salt
½ teaspoon pepper
¼ teaspoon cayenne pepper

Blend all ingredients except chickpeas in blender for 10 seconds. Add cooked and drained chickpeas slowly and blend until smooth. This recipe makes enough for two meals and freezes well for a quick and healthy lunch.

Cheese and Herb Dip
Submitted by Jeana Price, PA

1 cup mayonnaise
½ cup chopped parsley
¼ cup grated Parmesan cheese

2 tablespoons lemon juice
1 clove of garlic
1 teaspoon dried basil leaves

Mix together and serve.

Printed in Volume 6, Issue 2 of KBR

Cheesy Dip
Submitted by Rachel Abernathy, MO

8 ounces cream cheese or cottage cheese
½ cup milk or water
½ teaspoon salt
8 ounces Cheddar cheese

Put cream cheese or cottage cheese, milk or water and salt in blender. Blend until smooth. Cut Cheddar cheese into chunks. Add chunks a small amount at a time. Blend until smooth. Add more milk/water or Cheddar cheese to make thinner or thicker. Serve immediately or chill for an hour to thicken. Serve with vegetables, fruit or chips. Makes about 2 cups.

Easy Cracker Spread
Submitted by Esther Lang, WI

8 ounces cream cheese, softened
3 tablespoons plain yogurt
3 tablespoons mayonnaise
1 teaspoon dry onion
½ teaspoon parsley
½ teaspoon chives

¼ teaspoon dill weed
⅛, plus 1/16 teaspoon
    garlic powder
1/16 teaspoon paprika
1/16 teaspoon pepper
1/16 teaspoon salt

Mix well. Serve with crackers or spread on wheat bagels and warm in the oven until slightly toasted. More yogurt and mayonnaise may be used for a softer spread—less for a firmer spread.

Great Guacamole
Submitted by Maurya Petrick, TN

2 avocados, mashed
¼ cup salsa
¼ cup sour cream
¼ cup finely chopped cilantro
Juice of one lemon
2 tablespoon finely chopped jalapeno
Salt and pepper, to taste

Mix ingredients together well, and serve in fajitas, or just by itself as dip.

ℒ Sweeter Snacks

Protein Balls
Submitted by Megan Langham, WI
"Delicious and filling."

1 ½ cups peanut butter
½ cup honey
¾ cup powdered milk
Coconut, for rolling
Wheat germ, for rolling

Mix all ingredients together in a small mixing bowl with a wooden spoon. When the mixture becomes stiff, mix it with your hands. If desired, you can add raisins, carob or chocolate chips, nuts, or sesame seeds—the possibilities are endless. Roll into 1-inch balls and roll in coconut or wheat germ.

Printed in Volume 2, Issue 4 of KBR

Apples 'n Yogurt
Submitted by Sarah Bryant, KS

¾ cup vanilla yogurt
1 apple, cubed
Berries or nuts of choice, if desired
Mix in a bowl and enjoy.

Printed in Volume 2, Issue 2 of KBR

Finger Jello
Submitted by Sharlyn Halteman, PA

3 tablespoons gelatin
½ cup grape juice concentrate
1 cup boiling grape juice concentrate

Soften gelatin in grape juice concentrate. Stir into boiling grape juice concentrate. Pour into 13x9-inch pan and chill to set. Cut into squares or shapes with cookie cutters.

Printed in Volume 4, Issue 3 of KBR

Health Nut Balls
Submitted by Brittany Schlichter, TX

¼ cup whole flax seeds   1 ½ cups raisins
1 cup almonds, chopped   Dash salt
½ cup pecans, chopped   Cocoa powder

Pulse all ingredients except for the cocoa powder in a food processor until a ball forms. Press into balls and roll in cocoa powder. Chill.

Snack Balls
Submitted by the Stoltzfus Ladies, TN

"This recipe was invented by Becky when she was five years old."

1 cup peanut butter
1 cup honey
2 cups powdered milk
1 cup puffed wheat or rice cereal

Mix ingredients in a bowl. Add more powered milk if dough is too sticky. Form into letters or balls. Great with tea, cocoa, or cappuccino. For a variation, you can add any of the following or whatever else you may have on hand: oatmeal, chocolate chips, chopped nuts, sunflower seeds, coconut, raisins, other dried fruit pieces, vanilla or maple flavoring. Enjoy!

Received for Volume 8, Issue 2 of KBR

Salty & Savory Snacks

Caramel Popcorn

Submitted by Rachael Bryant, KS

"Caramel popcorn is perfect served with hot chocolate after sledding on a winter afternoon! It also makes nice gifts. Package the cooled caramel popcorn in cellophane gift bags and place into a sturdy, yet decorative, plastic bowl—a ready-made snack."

½ cup melted butter
3 quarts popped popcorn
½ cup honey or sorghum
½ teaspoon salt
½ teaspoon baking soda

Heat butter and honey. Pour over popped popcorn and mix well. Spread popcorn on a baking sheet in a thin layer and bake in a preheated 350° oven for 10 minutes, or until crisp. It will burn very easily.

Printed in Volume 7, Issue 1 of KBR

Pizza Popcorn

Submitted by Maggie Bullington, AL

"We tried this simple recipe while Daddy and the boys were gone camping at an archery shoot, and we enjoyed the whole batch! I think they'll love it when we introduce it to them. This is an easy recipe when everyone wants a snack and is a switch from something sweet."

2 ½ quarts popped popcorn
⅓ cup butter, cubed
¼ cup Parmesan cheese
½ teaspoon garlic salt
½ teaspoon dried oregano
½ teaspoon dried basil
¼ teaspoon salt
¼ teaspoon onion powder (or more garlic powder)

Place corn into an ungreased 13x9-inch baking pan. Melt butter; add other ingredients. Pour over popcorn and mix well. Bake, uncovered, at 350° for 15 minutes. Delicious!

Chickaritos
Submitted by Megan Rippel, WI

"This is a delicious finger food recipe that I received from my friend, Heidi. It has become a favorite of ours!"

3 cups finely chopped cooked chicken
1 (4-ounce) can diced green chilies
½ cup finely chopped green onions
1½ cups shredded Cheddar cheese
1 teaspoon hot pepper sauce
1 teaspoon garlic salt
¼ teaspoon pepper
¼ teaspoon ground cumin
1 (17 ¼-ounce) box frozen puff pastry sheets, thawed
    or pie pastry for a double-crust 10-inch pie
½ cup Parmesan cheese
Salsa and guacamole for dipping

In a medium-sized bowl, combine chicken, chilies, onions, cheese, hot pepper sauce, garlic salt, pepper, and cumin. Mix well and set aside. Remove one sheet of puff pastry and roll out on a lightly floured counter (the puff pastry should be about 9x12-inches). Cut into approximately 15 little rectangles (about 3x4-inches each). Place about 1 tablespoon of filling across the center. Wet one long edge of the puff pastry and roll pastry around filling. Crimp ends with a fork. Roll in Parmesan cheese. Place seam side down on a lightly greased cookie sheet. Bake at 425° for 20-25 minutes. Serve warm with salsa and guacamole.

Printed in Volume 4, Issue 3 of KBR

tip

healthy snack
"Lightly coat dried pumpkin seeds with olive oil. Spread on a baking sheet and sprinkle with salt. Bake at 400° for about 10 minutes, turning often, until brown and crisp."

Ranch Pretzels
Submitted by Megan Kunkel, MI

1 bag pretzel nuggets
½ cup butter
1 package dry ranch dressing
1 tablespoon dill

Melt butter and pour over pretzels in pan. Mix to coat pretzels. Mix dill and dry ranch dressing together and sprinkle evenly over pretzels. Stir it and bake 1 hour at 250°, stirring every 15 minutes.

Printed in Volume 2, Issue 2 of KBR

Nanny's Sausage Kolaches
Submitted by Tiffany Schlichter, TX

"My grandmother enjoys making these for us when we go on a road trip—the only problem is that we usually devour all of them before we have gone too far!"

5 cups flour
¾ cup sugar
1 ½ teaspoons salt
2 packages or 4 ½ teaspoons rapid rise yeast
1 (13-ounce) can evaporated milk
½ cup oil
4 egg yolks, beaten
1 pound smoked beef sausages

Combine all dry ingredients, including yeast, in a large bowl. Heat evaporated milk and oil together to 125-130°. Add to dry ingredients. Add egg yolks and stir well. Batter will resemble a thick pancake batter. Sprinkle with flour and let double in size in a warm place—this should take approximately 30-40 minutes. Drop large tablespoonfuls onto foil-lined cookie sheet. Push a sausage into each ball and pinch closed. Let rise to double size again. Bake at 375° until done—about 20 minutes.

NOTES & RECIPES

Blessed
are they which are
called unto the
Marriage Supper
of the
Lamb.

Revelation 19:9

home *made*

in the
kitchen
with martha joy

🌿 How can a daughter bless her family by planning and serving menus?

We often do not realize how much our mother does, since she not only has to make meals and clean up afterward, but also has to do laundry, clean the house, and much more. By cooking a meal, even just once a week, and helping with kitchen cleanup, we can really help her, allowing her more time to do other things.

🌿 What is your most frequently used recipe that you use as a replacement for "store-bought" products?

We like making our own condiments, mayonnaise, salad dressing, ketchup, and our own hot sauce. Our favorite mayonnaise recipe is found on page 62.

🌿 On a hot summer afternoon, what kind of cooling beverage do you like to make for your family to enjoy?

We enjoy water, kefir and fruit tea. Also, one cool beverage that I enjoy making is strawberry lemonade. It is delicious!

Strawberry Lemonade

6 cups water	¾ cups honey or sugar
1 cup lemon juice	1 cup frozen strawberries

Stir together the first three ingredients in a pitcher. Put a small amount of mixture in a blender, and add strawberries. Blend. Add back to pitcher. Stir, and serve cool.

How can a daughter help keep the freezer and pantry stocked so as to assist in the cooking process?

We grow a big garden and raise our own beef, so we have fruits, vegetables and meat to store. That saves a lot of time and trips to the grocery store. We also like buying big blocks of cheese, grating it and putting it in bags in the freezer. That makes a quick solution, when you need grated cheese for a recipe. We do the same with vegetables. We like making brownie mixes, which can be great for a quick dessert.

Do you have a place where you store away kitchen- and home-related tools to use in your future home?

I love storing away kitchen items for my future home! I have a hope chest which my great-grandmother made for my mommy; in it are many items, such as cooking utensils, cups, towels, and dishes, many of which came from family members. It will be fun one day to pull them out, and remember the story behind them!

How would you encourage younger sisters to help their older sisters serve their family in the kitchen?

Our older sisters diligently help our mothers in meal preparation and planning. It is a great encouragement to them if we, as younger sisters, help with their dish washing for the day or help prepare a meal.

How do you deal with kitchen cleanup?

We like to switch helpers, so that each of us gets a day off. For instance, one day, my sister and I will do the dishes, the next Mommy and I, and the next Mommy and my sister. The person who has the day off of doing dishes, will sweep the kitchen floor. This is an easy way to get kitchen cleanup done—"Many hands make light work!"

Martha Joy strives to seek the Lord and serve her family at home. She also enjoys raising animals, playing fiddle, and more.

✑ Sauces, Seasonings & Mixes

Pizza Sauce
Submitted by Esther Lang, WI
"This recipe was invented by my dad."

¼ teaspoon garlic
1 teaspoon dry minced onion
¼ teaspoon green bell pepper flakes (optional)
½ teaspoon parsley
1 teaspoon basil
2 teaspoons oregano
2 teaspoons sugar
16-ounce can tomato sauce

Mix together and spread on top of homemade pizza crusts (page 133).

Salsa
Submitted by the Schlichter Ladies, TX

1 (28-ounce) can whole tomatoes, with juice
2 (10-ounce) cans "Rotel" (diced tomatoes and green chilies)
¼ cup chopped onion
1 whole jalapeno, quartered and sliced thin
2 large handfuls cilantro, chopped
1 tablespoon lime juice
¼ teaspoon salt
Garlic powder

Combine all ingredients in a food processor and pulse 15 times. Serve with tortilla chips.

Fresh Tomato Salsa
Submitted by Laura Newcomer, ME

4 cups chopped fresh tomatoes
¼ cup finely chopped onion
1-4 jalapeño peppers, seeded and finely chopped
1 tablespoon olive or vegetable oil
1 tablespoon vinegar
1 teaspoon ground cumin
1 teaspoon salt
1 garlic clove, minced

Combine all ingredients, mix well. Let stand for one hour. Serve at room temperature. Cover and store in refrigerator for up to one week.

Best Ever BBQ Sauce
Submitted by Jenny Berlin, TN

"We love to use the BBQ sauce in hamburgers, meatballs, chicken, meatloaf, and many other dishes!"

1 cup ketchup
½ cup brown sugar
⅓ cup sugar
¼ cup honey
¼ cup molasses

2 teaspoons prepared mustard
1½ teaspoons Worcestershire sauce
¼ teaspoon salt
¼ teaspoon Liquid Smoke
⅛ teaspoon pepper

In a medium-sized sauce pan, bring all ingredients to a boil, than cool. Store in the refrigerator until ready to use. Yields 1 ½ cups.

Nacho Sauce
Submitted by Lydia Vanderford, CO

"Tangy cheese sauce with a spicy kick. Omit the hot sauce and jalapeños for a mild flavor."

4 ounces cream cheese
8 ounces sharp Cheddar cheese, cubed or grated
1 and ¾ cups milk
¼ cup milk
Hot sauce
⅛ cup jalapeño peppers, diced
⅛ cup red bell pepper, diced
2 tablespoons flour or corn starch

Soften cream cheese in a covered sauce pan over low. Stir frequently. When cream cheese is a soft consistency, add Cheddar cubes. In separate bowl add flour to ¼ cup milk. Mix thoroughly with a fork and put it aside for later use. Add hot sauce to taste, diced red bell peppers, diced jalapeños and ½ cup milk. Stir and melt mixture. Increase temperature to medium. When mixture is homogenous, add remaining milk (less the flour and milk mixture). Mix thoroughly. Add flour-water mixture to cheese sauce. Stir constantly and bring to a boil. Let boil for 1 minute while stirring. Turn off burner and remove from heat. Makes 32 ounces of nacho cheese sauce.

Onion Soup Mix
Submitted by Maurya Petrick, TN

¾ cup dried minced onion
½ teaspoon dill weed
¼ cup beef bouillon powder
1 teaspoons sugar
4 teaspoons onion powder

Mix well and store in an airtight container or bag. Use instead of a packet of Lipton's Onion Soup Mix. If you make a large batch of this and store it, use ¼ cup for each soup mix packet.

Taco Seasoning
Submitted by Emily Rebhan, WI

2 tablespoons chili powder
5 teaspoons paprika
4 ½ teaspoons ground cumin
3 teaspoons onion powder

3 teaspoons salt
2 ½ teaspoons garlic powder
⅛ teaspoon cayenne pepper

Combine ingredients. Store in an air-tight container in a cool, dry place for up to 6 months.

Printed in Volume 2, Issue 3 of KBR

Taco Spice Mix
Submitted by Esther Lang, WI

4 tablespoons chili powder
4 tablespoons cumin
4 tablespoons oregano
4 tablespoons garlic powder

4 tablespoons dried onion
2 tablespoons cayenne pepper
2 tablespoons salt
2 teaspoons ground cloves

Store in a 16-ounce jar. Shake well before using. For taco meat, use 2 tablespoons of this mix, plus ¼ cup water, for each pound of ground meat that you use. For dip, stir 2 tablespoons of mix into 1 cup of sour cream or yogurt.

Bisquick Mix
Submitted by Laura Newcomer, ME

8 cups flour
½ cup baking powder
3 tablespoons salt
1 ½ cups shortening

Sift together dry ingredients. Cut in shortening to make very fine crumbs. Store in tight container. Keeps indefinitely in freezer.

Cream Soup

Submitted by Amanda Hahner, WA

"This is equal to one can of cream soup."

3 tablespoons butter
3 tablespoons flour
1 cup milk
Salt and pepper to taste

Melt butter in saucepan. Mix flour, and milk. Whisk into melted butter, and heat until thickened. Season with salt and pepper.

For cream of mushroom soup: Add canned or sautéed mushrooms.

For cream of chicken soup: Substitute equal amount of chicken broth for milk.

For cream of celery: Add chopped celery.

Cream Soup Mix

Submitted by Laura Newcomer, ME

"You can use this recipe instead of store bought cans of cream soup for recipes."

2 cups dry milk powder
¾ cup cornstarch
2 tablespoons dried onion
1 tablespoon dried parsley
¼ teaspoon pepper (optional)
¼ cup chicken bouillon (optional)
1 teaspoon garlic or onion salt (optional)

Mix well and store in an airtight container. To use, combine ⅓ cup mix and 1-1 ¼ cups water. Cook and stir constantly until thickened.

Cocoa Mix

Submitted by the Stoltzfus Ladies, PA

"This is much better than any store bought kind, as we and our tea-party friends have found out. You can add cinnamon or extra cocoa powder if desired."

1 cup powdered milk
1 cup creamer
¾ cup sugar
½ cup cocoa

Mix well and store in an airtight container. Use ¼ cup dry mix to 1 cup hot water.

Received for Volume 8, Issue 2 of KBR

Instant Cappuccino Mix

Submitted by the Stoltzfus Ladies, PA

"This is our favorite hot winter drink. We usually make 6 times the recipe since it always disappears quickly. For those who love spice, add a teaspoon or two of cinnamon to the dry mix. Use ¼ cup of mix to 1 cup of hot water."

¾ cup creamer
¾ cup powdered sugar
¼ cup instant coffee
⅔ cup dry milk
½ cup Nestle Quik (or Cocoa Mix recipe above)
¼ teaspoon salt

Layer all ingredients in an air tight container and shake until thoroughly combined. Store in a cool, dry place.

Printed in Volume 8, Issue 2 of KBR

≈ Homemade Foods

Fresh Homemade Butter
Photos and recipe submitted by Sarah Bryant, KS

"The first time I made butter, I used warm water to rinse the butter, and by the time I realized what I was doing, it had all melted down the drain. You can purchase fresh milk from a local dairy, or if you milk your own cow, all the better! The cream should rise to the top of the milk within an hour after it was last stirred. Jersey or Guernsey cow's milk is the richest and therefore makes the richest, yellowest butter."

Cream from one gallon of raw cow's milk

Skim the cream off the top of a gallon of fresh cow's milk. Pour into a blender or butter churn. Blend until it separates (photo 1—you will know it is ready when the buttermilk separates and the butter globules have risen and clumped in the middle). Depending on the type of blender you use, it will take from 30 seconds to 8 minutes to separate. In a strainer layered with cheesecloth, pour the buttermilk and butter from the blender (photo 2), catching the buttermilk in a cup under the strainer. If you like your butter salted, now is the time to add about 1 teaspoon of salt. Rinse the butter in cold water, stirring with a spatula, until the draining water is clear. When all the buttermilk is washed out, squeeze the butter with the cheesecloth until all the liquid is drained out. Remove from cheesecloth and mold (photo 3). Put in the refrigerator as soon as possible. One gallon's worth of cream makes approximately ½ pound of butter, depending on the time of year and thickness of cream.

Printed in Volume 3, Issue 2 of KBR

Priscilla's Pickles
Submitted by Esther Lang, WI

"This is a recipe for pickles from our neighbor, Priscilla."

7 cups sliced cucumbers
1 cup sliced onions
2 cups sugar
1 cup vinegar
1 tablespoon salt
1 teaspoon celery seed

Mix together cucumbers and onions. Separately mix together remaining ingredients; heat until sugar is dissolved (do not boil). Pour over onions and cucumbers. Let stand one hour, stirring occasionally. Store in refrigerator or freezer.

Pumpkin Butter
Submitted by Emily Savine

"For a decorative touch, cut a 5 ½-inch square of material of your choice. Unscrew lid and place square of material on top. Screw lid back on."

3 ⅔ cups pureed pumpkin
¾ cup apple juice
3 ½ teaspoons pumpkin pie spice
1 ½ cups sugar
2 tablespoons brown sugar

In a crock pot, combine ingredients. Set on high and let cook for about 6 hours, stirring about every hour. If you use store-canned pumpkin, cook for about 4 hours. While still hot, pour into sterilized jars, leaving ¼-inch head space. Place upside down for at least an hour to seal. Makes about four 8-ounce jars.

Printed in Volume 6, Issue 4 of KBR

Apple Butter
Submitted by Samantha Parker, VA

12 cups apples, chopped, unpeeled (using 3 different varieties makes it especially flavorful)
¾ cup apple cider
1 cup sugar
1 teaspoon cinnamon
½ teaspoon cloves

Combine apples and cider in 3-quart slow cooker. Cover and cook on low for 8 hours or until apples are soft. Puree in food sieve or food mill. Return mixture to slow cooker and add sugar and spices. Cook on low for 1-2 hours. If thicker apple butter is desired, uncover and cook on high until desired consistency. The apple butter will keep for several weeks in refrigerator or may be frozen in freezer containers. If you wish to can apple butter, pour hot apple butter into clean, hot jars leaving ¼-inch head space. Wipe the rim clean and place the lids on. Process 10 minutes in boiling water at 180°. Makes 3 pints. Enjoy!

Printed in Volume 6, Issue 3 of KBR

tip

beautiful gifts
"Canned goods can make wonderful, homey gifts for holidays or as a 'thank you' when someone invites you to their home for a meal. The lid can easily be decorated with greenery or ribbon to match the jar's contents. This makes a lovely and practical gift!"

Dilly Beans
Submitted by Maggie Bullington, AL

"A favorite way to preserve green beans! You may double or triple the recipe."

2 pounds green beans
¼ cup canning salt
2 ½ cups vinegar
2 ½ cups water
1 teaspoon cayenne pepper, divided
4 cloves garlic, divided
4 heads dill, divided

Trim ends off green beans. Combine salt, vinegar and water in a large saucepan. Bring to a boil. Pack beans lengthwise into hot jars, leaving ¼-inch headspace. Add ¼ teaspoon cayenne pepper, 1 clove of garlic and 1 dill head to each pint. Add ½ teaspoon cayenne pepper, 2 cloves garlic and 2 heads of dill to each quart. Ladle hot liquid over beans, leaving ¼-inch headspace. Remove air bubbles. Adjust two-piece caps. Process pints and quarts 10 minutes in a boiling-water canner. Yields about 4 pints or 2 quarts.

Received for Volume 6, Issue 3 of KBR

Homemade Mayonnaise
Submitted by Sarah Bryant, KS

"Homemade mayonnaise tastes great and is so simple to make."

2 fresh eggs
2 cups safflower or light olive oil

Beat eggs well in blender. Slowly pour in oil while blending. If you add oil too fast, it will not thicken. Beat until thick. Use immediately.

Printed in Volume 3, Issue 4 of KBR

Homemade Ketchup
Submitted by Maggie Bullington, AL

1 stick of cinnamon, broken
1 teaspoon mustard seed
1 teaspoon celery seed
¼ teaspoon cayenne pepper
1 cup vinegar
8 pounds fresh tomatoes or 1 (#10) can crushed tomatoes or sauce
1 cup chopped onion or the equivalent in dried, minced onion
½ cup honey
2-3 teaspoons salt

Place cinnamon stick, mustard seed and celery seed in a spice bag (or small muslin bag); add to vinegar. Bring vinegar and spices to a boil; remove from heat and let stand.

If using fresh tomatoes: Peel, core and quarter tomatoes. Combine tomatoes, onion and cayenne pepper. Simmer until soft. Press through a sieve or food mill. Add honey to tomato pulp. Bring to a boil; simmer until reduced by half.

If using canned tomatoes: Place contents of can into a pot and add honey. Proceed to next step.

Remove spice bag from vinegar. Add vinegar and salt to tomato mixture. Simmer until desired consistency is reached—about 30 minutes. Cool. Ladle into can-or-freeze jars or freezer boxes, leaving ½-inch headspace. Seal, label and freeze.

"Maple" Syrup for Pancakes
Submitted by Esther Lang, WI

2 cups white sugar
1 ½ teaspoons molasses
¼ cup corn syrup
1 cup water

Bring to a boil, remove from heat and add 1 teaspoon maple flavoring. This makes 16-ounces.

Homemade Jerky

Submitted by Maggie Bullington, AL

"With this recipe around, you don't need store-bought jerky for camping trips or snacking anymore! Delicious when made using beef or venison, homemade jerky makes a great snack. We make this often during deer-hunting season."

½ cup vegetable oil
1 cup Bragg's Liquid Aminos or soy sauce
3 tablespoons brown sugar
3 mashed garlic cloves
1 tablespoon grated fresh gingerroot
2 tablespoons cooking sherry or vinegar
About 10-15 pounds of thinly sliced beef

Combine all seasonings and mix together thoroughly. Marinate meat in this for about 12-24 hours in the refrigerator. Drain excess seasonings off each piece of meat and dehydrate until desired doneness. Store in refrigerator or freezer.

Homemade Tortillas

Submitted by Rachael Bryant, KS

"We usually make four recipes for a meal and love tortillas served best with eggs and fried potatoes."

2 cups flour (can use portion of whole wheat)
½ teaspoon salt
¼ cup safflower or light olive oil
⅔ cup warm water

Place dry ingredients in large bowl. Add oil and water and mix well. If the dough is too sticky, add more flour. Roll into golf-ball sized balls. Heat tortilla press; flatten and cook each ball.

Homemade Yogurt
Submitted by Mrs. Kathleen Bullington, AL

"Start with yogurt from a previous batch or with plain, organic, store-bought yogurt. This will be your 'culture.'"

⅓ cup yogurt
About 3 ⅓ cups milk

Put yogurt in a quart jar. Slowly heat milk in a saucepan to room temperature. Hot milk will kill the culture. Pour the warmed milk into the jar with the yogurt and stir to combine. Place a heating pad in a large stockpot and cover it with plastic wrap or a towel. Place the jar on top of this. Plug the heating pad in on low and keep covered for 24 hours. At the end of this time, you should have yogurt! Store in refrigerator.

Pigs in a Blanket
Submitted by the Bryant Family

"Our family loves to make these treats for our annual family vacation each winter. They freeze easily and can be quickly heated at a gas stop."

Pizza crust dough recipe (page 133)
6 nitrate-free hotdogs

Make homemade pizza dough recipe. Roll dough out thinly into a 12-inch circle, and then cut like a pizza. Cut hotdogs in thirds (about 2-inch lengths). Wrap each hotdog in the dough, starting from the widest point of the dough triangles, rolling toward the narrow point. Pinch dough together and bake at 350° on a flat pan until light brown—about 10 minutes.

✒ *Beverages*

Soft Custard
Submitted by Naomi Watt, TX

"I love the warm spiciness of nutmeg! Our family makes this a gallon or two at a time."

4 cups milk
½ cup sugar
Dash salt
4 eggs, beaten
½ teaspoon vanilla
Ground nutmeg (freshly ground is best)

Scald milk. Add sugar and salt. Gradually whisk in the eggs. Cook over medium heat, stirring constantly, until mixture thickens enough to coat spoon. Do not let it curdle. Remove from heat. Stir in vanilla. Pour into 4 mugs. Sprinkle nutmeg over the top.

Grape Juice
Submitted by Maggie Bullington, AL

"This is simple and delicious. We have used grape juice like this for years."

Grapes, washed, with stems removed
Warm honey
Boiling water

Using jars which have been slightly warmed in warm water, fill clean quart canning jars about half full with the grapes. Pour ⅓ cup of the honey over the grapes in each jar. Fill to 1-inch from the top with boiling water. Wipe rims and fit with warmed lids and canning rings. Process for 8 minutes at 5 pounds of pressure in a canner (use parental assistance when pressure-cooking).

Hot Cider
Submitted by Esther Lang, WI

"Spiced cider like this is the perfect thing on a cool evening, and also delicious icy-cold in summer months. The orange juice is a delicious addition."

2 quarts cider or apple juice
2 cups orange juice

½ cup honey
2 sticks cinnamon

Simmer in crock pot and serve warm.

Printed in Volume 8, Issue 1 of KBR

Sweet Nectar Lemonade
Submitted by Megan Dove, TX

2 quarts lukewarm water
2 cups lemon juice
1 ½ or 2 cups honey (depending on how sweet you like it)

Mix lemon juice and honey in bowl. Allow mixture to rest for 1 hour. Stir. Add to a large pitcher; stir water in gently. Serve over ice. Makes 2 ¼ quarts.

Holiday Eggnog
Submitted by Megan Dove, TX

1 ¼ cups whole milk, preferably raw
2 egg yolks, raw
2 teaspoon vanilla
2-3 ice cubes
Dash of salt
½ teaspoon cinnamon
¼ teaspoon nutmeg
3 tablespoons sweetener (honey or maple syrup)

Combine all ingredients in a blender. Top with an extra dash of nutmeg.

Spiced Chai Tea
Submitted by Monica Watt, TX

"I love nothing better than to cuddle up with a hot mug of Spiced Chai on cold, wet afternoons. The black pepper adds a nice warming zing of its own! Traditionally, chai is a beverage containing 5 key ingredients: black tea, milk, honey, cardamom and black pepper."

1 quart of water
8 tea bags of Black Peko tea
    or 1 teaspoon loose leaf tea per 1 cup, plus 1 teaspoon for the pot
½ teaspoon black pepper corns, coarsely crushed
1 ½ teaspoons ground cardamom
1-2 cinnamon sticks
1 quart of milk
½ cup honey, more or less, if desired
1-2 teaspoons vanilla (optional)

Bring water to boil; reduce heat. Add tea, pepper, cardamom, and cinnamon. Simmer for 5 minutes. Remove from heat and cover to steep. In a separate pan, heat milk to scalding, stirring frequently. Add honey and vanilla. Strain the tea and spices and add to the milk. Stir well. Remove from heat; serve immediately. Can top with whipped cream sprinkled with nutmeg. Spiced chai tea can be stored in the fridge and served hot or cold. Makes ½ gallon.

Delicious Mocha Shake
Submitted by Sarah Mast, KY

4 cups vanilla ice cream
⅓ cup milk
1 teaspoon instant coffee granules
¼ cup hot water
¼ cup chocolate syrup
1 tablespoon vanilla
1 teaspoon cinnamon

Dissolve instant coffee granules in hot water. Blend all ingredients together and serve as a refreshing cooler.

✢ Other Recipes

Play-Dough Recipe
Submitted by Megan Rippel, WI

"I've tried many play-dough recipes over the years, looking for the perfect one. I found that the uncooked ones resulted in a grainy texture from the salt, while some of the cooked ones were greasy from too much oil. After many test batches, I finally found the perfect recipe. I was particularly intrigued when I saw that it called for vanilla. I tried it without the vanilla and, sure enough, I noticed a big difference between the two batches' textures. The batch without the vanilla was okay, but the batch with the vanilla had a nice, pliable texture. Imitation vanilla works well because of its clear color, but you can also use real vanilla, if you do not mind the color it adds. At last, I had found a wonderful play-dough recipe!

"Working with homemade play-dough is an enjoyable activity that will provide your siblings with hours of play. Set your brother or sister up at a table and have different items with neat sizes and textures available that he or she can use the make imprints in the dough. You'll be amazed at how many of these items you have around the house! Some items include paper clips, a fork, old keys, bubble wrap, a comb, buttons and interesting varieties of dry pasta. Cookie cutters can also be fun to use!"

1 cup flour
¼ cup salt
1 teaspoon cream of tartar
1 cup water
1 tablespoon oil
1 tablespoon vanilla extract

Combine flour, salt, and cream of tartar in saucepan. Add water and oil; whisk until smooth. Cook over medium heat until the play-dough is nearly set. Remove from heat and let sit until cool enough to handle. Remove from pan and knead in vanilla. Store in a sealed bag or air-tight container.

Printed in Volume 2, Issue 4 of KBR

Health & Hair Care Alternatives

No-Scale Lip Balm
Submitted by Sarah Bryant, KS

3 teaspoons beeswax
5 teaspoons olive, almond or avocado oil
6-7 drops essential oil

Melt wax and oil in a double boiler. Add essential oil for scent, pour into tubes or tins, and let cool.

Printed in Volume 1, Issue 4 of KBR

tip

natural colorant
"You can easily add a subtle tint to your lip balm by using beet powder, pumpkin powder, or other colored dried food powders. Stir into melted balm just before pouring into tubes."

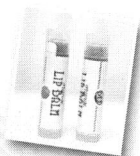

Bubble Bath
Submitted by Anna Kirk, WA

Bar of soap
Dried milk
Food coloring, if desired

Grate the soap with the smallest holes on your grater, add dried milk (the amount of which you will have to decide upon yourself), and a few drops of food coloring to tint. This makes a powdery substance with some small flecks of soap. For a nicer look, grate different colors of soap together. You may want to thoroughly blend about half the soap flakes and all the milk in your blender. Add the other half of the soap and stir to mix.

Printed in Volume 1, Issue 4 of KBR

Lotion Bar

Submitted by Sarah Bryant, KS

"Lotion bars are hand lotions in a solid form. When you rub them on your skin, the warmth of your hand releases the oils and nourishes your skin."

3 ounces each of beeswax, cocoa butter and almond oil
2 ounces shea butter
Essential oil for scent (optional)

Melt together. Add essential oil after all main ingredients are melted. Pour into molds. Cool at least 2 hours, preferably in the refrigerator. Store in sealed bag. Rub this on your hands when they are chapped in the winter.

Printed in Volume 1, Issue 4 of KBR

Hand or Foot Lotion Bar

Submitted by Sarah Bryant, KS

"These make great gifts for the holidays!"

1 part beeswax   1 part coconut oil
1 part shea butter   Peppermint essential oil (optional)

Melt ingredients in either a double boiler or in a microwave on half power. Stir. Add scent, if desired. Pour into molds or tins.

Facial Cleanser

Submitted by Sarah Bryant, KS

"This is an oil-based cleansing paste that can be used for all skin types."

3 ounces almond oil   2 ounces spring water
4 ounces ground almonds   6 drops essential oil of choice
2 ounces apple cider vinegar

Place all ingredients in blender and mix for two minutes until a sooth paste. Store in jar. Use to remove dead skin cells on your face by gently rubbing on daily and rinsing with water.

Homemade Lotion
Submitted by Rachel Abernathy, MO

"This is a recipe my Dad adapted from an online source. With this homemade lotion, you can control what goes into the mixture and customize for your specific needs. It works so much better than store-bought lotion, and can be made in larger batches and stored in the refrigerator for later use.

"This recipe is a lotion base, so you can add your favorite herbal tincture after you combine the mixtures. If you make your own herbal fusion, be sure to filter through a coffee filter. My dad uses an herbal fusion of 1 teaspoon of dried comfrey and 1 teaspoon dried aloe as a shaving lotion. You can also substitute shea butter for the jojoba oil if you need an extra moisturizing lotion for chapped hands. Lotion will keep for about 3 months."

1 ¼ cups water
¼ cup emulsifying wax (not beeswax)
¼ cup cold-pressed vegetable oil (sunflower, olive, jojoba, safflower)
1 tablespoon jojoba oil
1 drop grapefruit seed extract (natural preservative/antibacterial agent)
6 tablespoons MSM crystals (optional; healing agent)
Herb tinctures for fragrance or healing properties (optional)
1 pint canning jar

Combine water, MSM crystals and grapefruit seed extract in a pan and heat to 120°. In a separate thick-bodied pan, combine the emulsifying wax, vegetable oil and jojoba oil. Heat on medium to low heat to 155°. Be very careful not to mix the oil or water mixture while heating, chemically it will not thicken later on. Make sure to wipe off your thermometer with a towel before checking each temperature. Once both mixtures are at their correct temperatures, pour the water mixture into a jar. Pint canning jars work well. Immediately pour the wax mixture into water mixture and stir well. Continue to occasionally stir as the mixture cools, as it sometimes separates.

Natural Freshening Toothpaste
Submitted by Mrs. Dana Bryant, KS

1 tablespoon ground/dried orange peel
2 teaspoons ground dried sage
2 teaspoons baking soda
1 teaspoon salt
5 drops lemon oil
1 drop peppermint oil

Mix very well and store in a small jar. Dip slightly wet toothbrush in mixture and brush teeth.

Baby Wipes
Submitted by Mrs. Cheryl Schlichter, TX

"We found this recipe to be very economical when we had three babies in diapers!"

2 cups hot water
1 roll (cut in half) Bounty select-a-size paper towels
2 teaspoons baby soap
2 teaspoons baby oil
5 drops lavender oil (optional)
5 drops tea tree oil (optional)

Mix all ingredients, except the towels, with a whisk in a large plastic container with a lid. Set towels in, cover and let sit for 15 minutes or until soaked through. When the cardboard tubing in the center of the towels is wet, pull it out.

Editor's Note: *"This recipe can be used as hand sanitizer wipes, adding disinfectant essential oils such as tea tree, eucalyptus, and lemon essential oil."*

Baking Soda Cleansing "Shampoo"
Submitted by Sarah Bryant, KS

"*Often we train our hair and skin to produce more oil than necessary by washing it too often, stripping it of its natural oils. The following shampoo recipe has been more successful for my hair than commercial organic shampoo, causing it to be softer and healthier. Using this baking soda method may take several weeks or even months for your hair to adjust to, but perseverance is the key. Once your hair is adapted to this more mild cleanser, it will not need to be washed as frequently as with commercial shampoos. This recipe can be rotated every few weeks with a mild shampoo (recipe below works very well), if needed. Also, if you have hard water, you might consider washing your hair with distilled water. This baking soda method is especially good for curly hair, which tends to be very delicate and dry.*"

    1 quart water
    ¼-½ cup baking soda

Bring water to a good boil; pour water in large jar and add baking soda. Wait for the fizz to go down and the water to cool, then store in an old shampoo bottle. Apply liberally to scalp in shower (¼ to ½ cup, depending on how much it takes to dampen scalp hair), shaking first if necessary. Massage, then rinse well. I make this recipe in large batches and store the extra in the refrigerator.

Herbal Shampoo for Oily Hair
Submitted by Sarah Bryant, KS

"*This is a mild, gentle shampoo that effectively cleans the hair and reduces natural production of scalp oil. We love it!*"

    2 cups distilled water
    1 tablespoon each of dried lemon balm, lemongrass, peppermint leaf,
    and yarrow
    2 teaspoon chopped lemon peel
    20 drops lemon, rosemary, tea tree, ylang ylang, or sage essential oil
    ½ cup organic shampoo base

Bring water to boil. Remove from heat and add herbs and lemon peel; let steep covered for 30 minutes. Strain and add essential oils. Whisk in shampoo base and store in containers. Keeps in refrigerator for up to four weeks. We store small amounts in the shower for 1-2 weeks.

Apple Cider Vinegar Hair Rinse
Submitted by Sarah Bryant, KS

"For those who use the baking soda method (previous page), this is used as conditioner."

¾ cup water
¼ cup apple cider vinegar
2 tablespoons aloe vera gel
1 tablespoon honey

8 drops peppermint oil
8 drops tea tree oil

Combine all and shake well. After cleansing hair, squirt all over scalp and hair. Allow it to sit for a few minutes, then rinse well.

Aloe Vera Conditioner
Submitted by Sarah Bryant, KS

"Aloe vera nourishes the scalp. After washing my hair, I style it loosely with aloe vera gel; once it has dried, my hair has much more volume. I only lightly brush it and keep it off the scalp as much as possible, which helps my hair from getting oily as fast."

Handful of aloe vera gel

After cleansing hair, rub the aloe through hair and style. Let dry, then gently brush as normal.

All-Natural Citrus Hair Spray
Submitted by Sarah Bryant, KS

1 orange, peel removed and chopped in pieces
1 lemon, peel removed and chopped in pieces
2 cups water

In a small saucepan, boil ingredients until reduced by half. Strain and store to a bottle with a spray pump. Use as you would hairspray, lightly spraying on hair. Preferably, this is kept refrigerated, but I only make in small batches and add a few drops of essential oil (rosemary or peppermint) to add a pleasant smell. Keeps up to three weeks unrefrigerated.

Go Smell Go Deodorant
Submitted by Mrs. Shelly Weinhold, MO

"This is the most effective deodorant recipe we have ever tried; it works very well."

½ cup baking soda
10 drops each of tea tee and peppermint essential oil

Mix together well and store in an old spice shaker with holes in the top. Rub under arms.

Toxin-free Home Cleaners

Room Freshener
Submitted by Sarah Bryant, KS

White distilled vinegar
30 drops essential oil of choice

Shake together in a spray bottle. Mist in a room and leave the room. This is helpful for rooms that are musty or have an undesired scent.

Laundry Detergent
Submitted by Laura Newcomer, ME

⅓ bar Fels Naptha Soap
Water
½ cup washing soda (not the same as baking soda)
½ cup borax powder
2 gallon buckets

Grate soap; place in saucepan. Add 6 cups of water and heat until soap melts; add the powders. Stir until dissolved. Remove from heat. Pour 4 cups hot water into bucket. Add soap mixture and stir. Add 22 more cups water and stir well. Pour into jugs. Let sit 24 hours. Use ½ cup per load for front-loading washers and 1 cup for top-loading washers. This is a low-sudsing soap.

Homemade Stain Remover
Submitted by Sarah Bryant, KS

¼ cup clear liquid dishwashing detergent
¼ cup glycerine
1 ½ cups water

Pour ingredients into a squirt bottle. On stained clothing or fabric, squirt lightly; scrub and allow to soak if needed, to loosen the stain. Rinse well. This removes most stains, especially if you use it immediately after the spill.

Sparkling Window Cleaner
Submitted by Sarah Bryant, KS

"Each spring and fall, I like to clean our house windows. This cleaner works great, and does not have harsh chemicals, if you use the vinegar or lemon juice. This is a less expensive alternative to commercial solutions, with less toxins for our bodies to process."

2 tablespoons ammonia, or 3 tablespoons vinegar or lemon juice
½ cup rubbing alcohol
¼ teaspoon dishwashing detergent

Add all ingredients to a small spray bottle, then fill the bottle with water and shake well. Lightly squirt on dirty window and wipe with dry soft cloth. Wash one side of the window with horizontal strokes and the other side with vertical strokes, in order to see any streaks left behind. A squeegee is handy for drying the window. Do not wash the window in sunlight, because that will cause the cleaner to dry too quickly. You can use an old toothbrush or cotton swab to clean corners.

NOTES & RECIPES

The judgements of the
LORD
are true and righteous
altogether. More to be
desired are they than
gold, yea, than much
fine gold: sweeter also
than honey and the
honeycomb.

Psalm 19:9-10

substitutions *for cooking*

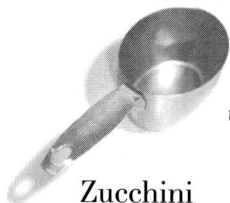

"There are many foods that can be substituted in cooking; following are some creative ideas to get you started."

Zucchini

If you are having a great zucchini crop this summer, you can include them in your pickles as you would cucumbers. Just prepare the zucchini as you would the cucumbers and process as normal. From our experience, the end product only differs in texture. Make sure to label your zucchini jars well because they are easily mixed with normal cucumber pickles.

You can also use zucchini as a cucumber replacement in homemade relish.

Also, finely-shredded zucchini can be added to tomato sauces. Not only do you add an extra vegetable to your meal, but you also use more of that plentiful zucchini. Frozen shredded zucchini stuffed in the back of your freezer is not exempt either! This addition stretches tomato sauce, while adding a little extra texture.

Squash for Pumpkin

The called-for pumpkin in your pie recipe may be substituted with squash. Bake winter squash as normal, and then scrape the flesh into a food processor or blender. Process until smooth. Substitute an equal amount of blended squash for the pumpkin, or use a mixture of both squash and pumpkin. This substitute works especially well with rich, sweet squash such as a seasoned butternut.

Milk

Sometimes, a very simple milk substitute can be in order: water. This works well in breakfast breads like muffins, biscuits, waffles, pancakes, and other quick breads. Water also works in some cake and cookie recipes. Gravy can be made without milk or cream; just use water instead.

In addition, if you can tolerate nuts, research on how to make your own nut or seed milk. Almond, rice, and hemp milks are on the market as well. Research and experiment!

Cheese may be omitted when simply sprinkled on top of dishes like spaghetti or stuffed peppers. For those who can tolerate it, alternative cheeses are on the market, such as rice and almond cheeses.

Butter may be substituted with shortening or lard in all types of recipes, and sometimes with equal amounts of liquid cooking oil. Examples include pastries, garlic bread, Texas toast, cakes, cookies, breads, biscuits, sautéed vegetables, and more recipes. Be warned that the flavor may change with your substitute. In light recipes, like plain sugar cookies, lard might not be a very good option. Experimenting is critical when substituting fats; each recipe is a little different. Sometimes, butter and/or shortening are meant to give a specific texture to a recipe.

As a side note, if you are sensitive to dairy, try eating cultured milk products and see if you tolerate them better than plain milk or butter. The enzymes and good bacteria can aid in digestion, sometimes lessening sensitivities.

Sugar-Free Apple Pie

One can make a delicious apple pie without any additional sweetener. The fruit alone can be sweet enough for a satisfying desert. In addition, try making many apple products with unpeeled apples; the skin is so nutritious and flavorful.

Chocolate Bar

Melt one tablespoon of shortening or oil in a thick-bottomed pan and add three tablespoons of unsweetened cocoa powder. Stir until smooth, and then add the mixture to your recipe as you would a melted one ounce square of unsweetened chocolate.

Oats

Not everyone can tolerate all grains, and oats are no exception. According to our experience with spelt and barley flakes, one can substitute equal amounts of alternative flakes for the oats. With spelt and barley, flavor is not impaired.

I hope these tips will help you become a better cook with the means to customize for your family's needs. Your situation is different than anyone else, and both experience and experimenting are critical for success.

May God bless you as you strive to glorify Christ through your food, family, and faith!

—*Rachel Abernathy*

cooking *tips*

Sautéing

When a recipe calls for sautéing the ingredients in oil or butter, let the pan heat thoroughly before starting the cooking process. After heated, add the oil or butter and allow this to heat. Lastly add your ingredients to be sautéed. During the cooking time, if the food begins to burn or stick to the cooking pan, add more butter/oil in moderation.

In most recipes, butter and oil are interchangeable when sautéing. So many different vegetables make a delicious side dish when sautéed. Some of our favorites are brussels sprouts and cabbage, asparagus, mushrooms, carrot slices, and whole green beans.

Baking Time

Sometimes ovens vary greatly, so when making a new recipe, check it for doneness before the recommended baking time. For example, if you are making cookies and the recipe says to bake them for 8-10 minutes, check them after 7 or 8 minutes. By watching your baked goods closely like this, you will be less likely to over-bake your finished product.

Eye-Watering Onions

Onions produce strong fumes when they are cut; these tips might be helpful in avoiding this. Cutting an onion in half, or even smaller pieces, and storing it in the refrigerator in a sealed plastic bag seems to help some of the strength to go away. If you use fresh onion frequently, then you can just keep a bag like this in your fridge at all times. Another trick is to cut a fresh onion in half and hold it under cold running water for a while and then cut it quickly.

Kitchen Decorations

Flowers on your kitchen windowsill can really cheer up the kitchen while you work. We've had fun maintaining orchids on the sill and their amazing beauty is so exciting to observe!

Curtains are a fun touch, especially when you can sew them yourself. Patterns are available and there are many different styles and fabrics to choose from. Depending on the size of the window and its placement in the room, consider a simple valance or a long, flowing affair with tiebacks.

Play with color as you match your curtains, dish towels and pot holders. Try crocheting or knitting some of your own dish cloths.

For a country-style kitchen, consider displaying colored canning jars filled with beans or other bulk goods. This adds charm and is also useful. For a fancier look, display your china or glassware in a china cabinet or along a high shelf.

Turntable

Putting a turntable on your kitchen table with necessary items such as salt and pepper, vinegar, or toothpicks can be a great idea. This keeps everything handy so everyone can have easy access.

Spoon/Fork Holders

Our family has two small pottery containers which sits on our turntable. In one, you'll find clean spoons, and in the other clean forks. It makes it so easy to have the utensils you use often handy.

Healthy Camp Cooking

Camping with your family can be such a fun adventure, but when it comes to eating somewhat healthily on the trip...well, that can be a challenge! Here are some ideas that may help you fill your coolers for a weekend outdoors.

Instead of bringing along hotdogs, which normally contain nitrates and preservatives, try making a vegetable and meat stir fry. At home, brown ground meat until thoroughly done, and then freeze it. Package sliced onions, sliced sweet peppers and really any other kind of vegetable that you want to take along. When you get to camp, heat a little oil in a skillet over a gas-powdered camp stove (or open fire) and sauté your peppers and onions until they're done. Add the cooked beef and heat well. You can add any seasonings to this—home canned salsa tastes great with a little bit of garlic powder, chili powder, salt and pepper mixed in. Be creative, keeping your family's tastes in mind.

Happy cooking!

—*Maggie Bullington*

herbs *for cooking*

"Dried herbs can be expensive, so why not grow your own? Live plants can be purchased at garden centers and then planted in an attractive pot. Seeds can also be purchased and started in your backyard.

"To store fresh herbs, wrap stems in a damp paper, put in a plastic bag, and refrigerate.

"When it comes time to harvest the herbs for drying, pick unblemished leaves and wash them carefully. You don't have to have a fancy dehydrator to dry your own herbs. Just lay them out on a baking sheet and dry them in the oven at 150°. Pack the dry herbs in small glass bottles and label accordingly."

—Maggie Bullington

Basil
Substitute: Sweet Marjoram
Pairings: Fresh tomatoes, tomato soup, sandwiches, corn, green beans, pizza, pesto

Bay Leaves
Substitute: Thyme
Pairings: Simmered with soup or stew for long periods of time so that the flavor can develop

Chives
Substitute: Scallions (Green Onions)
Pairings: Baked potato, potato salad, mashed potatoes, pasta salad, cream cheese spread for bagels

Cilantro
Substitute: Parsley
Pairings: Salsa, guacamole, Mexican foods, garnishing soups

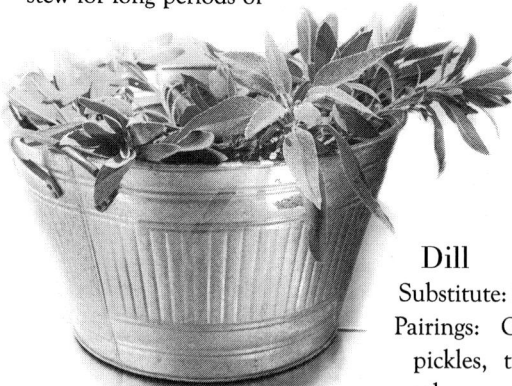

Dill
Substitute: Caraway
Pairings: Green beans, carrots, pickles, tuna salad, egg salad, salmon, sour cream based dips

Garlic

Substitute: Garlic Chives

Pairings: Beef roasts, guacamole, garlic bread

Lavender

Substitute: Rosemary

Pairings: Pork, chicken, berries, apples, desserts, tea

Lemongrass

Substitute: Lemon Zest, Lemon Verbena

Pairings: Asian cuisine, stir-fry, soups, coconut

Mint

Substitute: Spearmint, Peppermint, Chocolate Mint, Pineapple Mint

Pairings: Desserts (in particular, ice-cream and chocolate) carrots, peas, tea, lamb, fruit salad

Oregano

Substitute: Sweet Marjoram, Basil

Pairings: Pasta, pizza, tomatoes, chicken, beef

Parsley

Substitute: Cilantro

Pairings: Soup garnish, omelets, stuffing, salads, dressings

Rosemary

Substitute: Oregano

Pairings: Pork chops, chicken, lamb, stews

Sage

Substitute: Thyme

Pairings: Turkey, chicken, meatballs, stuffing

Sweet Marjoram

Substitute: Thyme or Oregano

Pairings: Stuffing, sprinkled on top of spaghetti

Tarragon

Substitute: Fennel or Anise

Pairings: Mushrooms, fish, chicken

Thyme

Substitute: Lemon Basil

Pairings: Vegetables, poultry, stews

Although they are not as flavorful, dried herbs can be substituted for fresh herbs. One tablespoon chopped fresh herbs equals 1 teaspoon crumbled dry herbs or ¼ teaspoon ground dry herbs.

—*Compiled by Megan Fisk*

"The grass withereth, the flower fadeth: but the *word of God* shall stand for ever."

Isaiah 40:8

index of recipes

SIDE DISHES

MAIN DISHES
Beef Main dishes

Chicken Main Dishes
No-Meat Main Dishes
Sandwiches

DIPS & SNACKS

"HOMEMADE"

photo credits

Rachel Abernathy · Pages 247, 249

Elizabeth Adams · Pages 13, 181

Amelia Breeden · Page 26

Maggie Bullington · Pages 15, 23, 28-29, 31, 34, 41, 45, 55, 58, 74, 127, 135, 139, 159, 167, 171, 175, 180, 216, 217, 228, 245, 255, 260

Martha Joy Bullington · Pages 21, 264

Nicole Gross · Page 256

Anna Parish · All Cover Images; Pages 65, 77, 117, 149, 154

Hannah Schoenfelder · Pages 22, 165, 181, 183 192, 195

Courtney Vetter · Page 131

All Other Images · Sarah Bryant (SarahLeePhoto.com)

All Original Calligraphy · Sarah Hulslander

NOTES & RECIPES

NOTES & RECIPES

NOTES & RECIPES

NOTES & RECIPES

NOTES & RECIPES

NOTES & RECIPES

NOTES & RECIPES

KBR MINISTRIES
ORDER FORM

The Maiden's Menu: Recipes for the King's Blooming Roses
____$14.00 each　　　　　　　SUBTOTAL:_____

The Family Daughter: Becoming Pillars of Strength by Sarah L. Bryant
____$12.00 each　　　　　　　SUBTOTAL:_____

One Thing I Desire: To Know Christ More by Sarah L. Bryant
____$11.00 each　　　　　　　SUBTOTAL:_____

"The King's Blooming Rose" Quarterly Magazine
____$8.00 for One-Year USA Subscription
____$12.00 for One-Year Canadian Subscription
____$14.00 for One-Year Foreign Country Subscription
　　　　　　　　　　　　　SUBTOTAL:_____

USA SHIPPING RATES
$0.01-15.00..........add $3.50
$15.01-35.00..........add $5.50
$35.01-75.00..........add $7.50
over $75.01.................$11.00

BOOK TOTAL:_____

Please double rates for foreign orders.

+SHIPPING:_____

When figuring your shipping price, do not include the price of magazine subscriptions; shipping has already been included in subscription rates.

=GRAND TOTAL:_____

Prices subject to change. Shop online for discounts.

SHIPPING INFORMATION:

Name:_____Age:_____
Address:_____
City:_____State:_____ Zip:_____
Phone:_____
Email:_____

Make checks or money orders payable to Sarah Bryant;
mail to address on page 4, or order online at
WWW.KINGSBLOOMINGROSE.COM

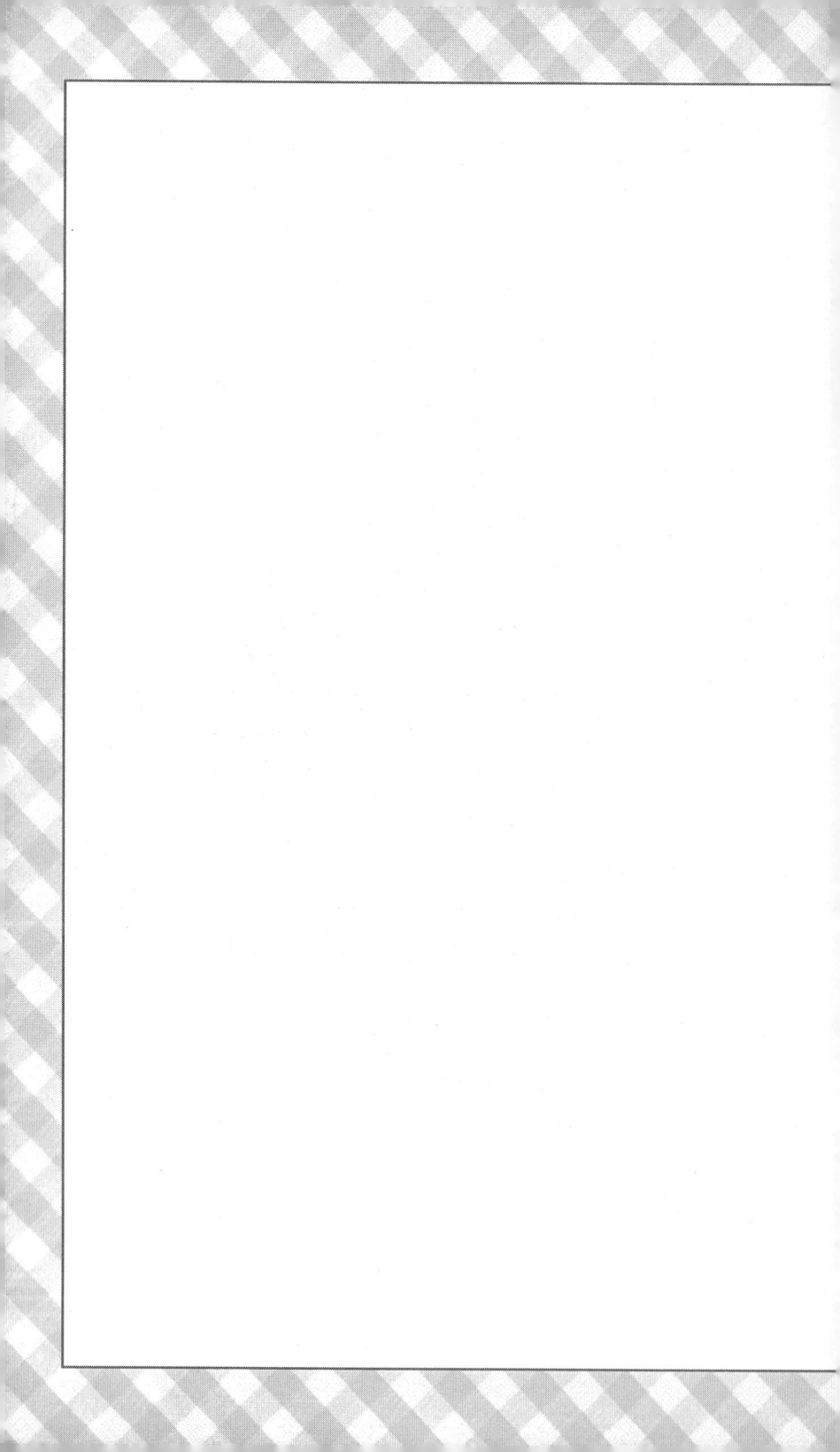

The eyes of all
wait upon
thee; and
thou givest
them their
meat in due
season.
Thou openest
thine hand,
and satisfiest
the desire of every
living thing. Psalm 145:14-16

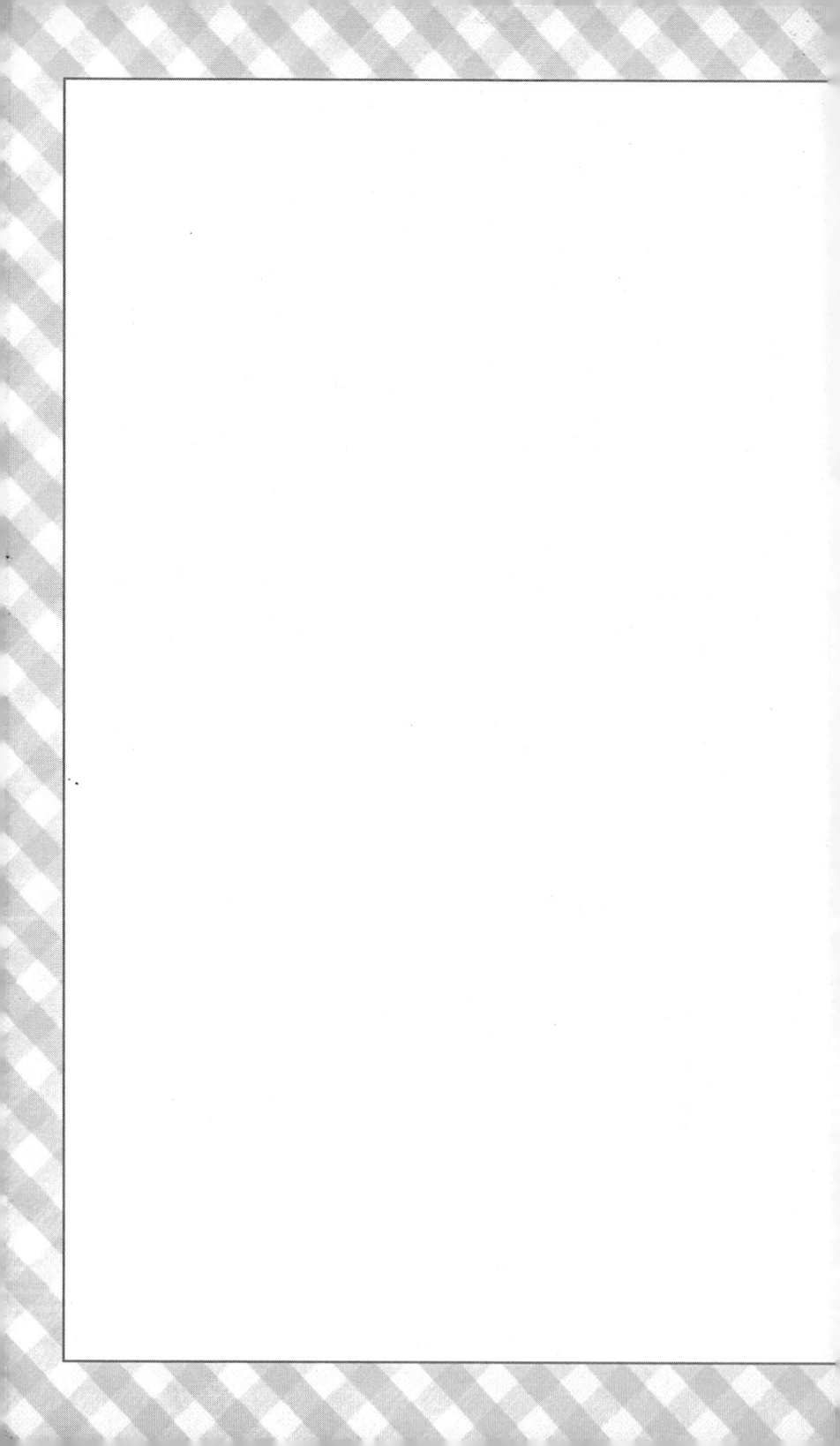